FACE OFF

EMILE

USA TODAY BESTSELLING AUTHOR ALICIA HUNTER PACE

Nashville Sounds, Book 1

Crimson Romance
New York London Toronto Sydney New Delhi

CRIMSON
ROMANCE

Crimson Romance
An Imprint of Simon & Schuster, Inc.
1230 Avenue of the Americas
New York, NY 10020

For information about special discounts for bulk purchases, please contact Simon & Schuster Special Sales at 1-866-506-1949 or business@ simonandschuster.com.

The Simon & Schuster Speakers Bureau can bring authors to your live event. For more information or to book an event contact the Simon & Schuster Speakers Bureau at 1-866-248-3049 or visit our website at www.simonspeakers.com.

ISBN 978-1-5072-0694-2
ISBN 978-1-5072-0563-1 (ebook)

DEDICATION

For Rick Hatten, who made us better people for the blessing of knowing him. Rest well, dear friend. We miss you, but carry you in our hearts. —SLJ and JPH

And to Ian, Brandon, and Kevin, my defenseman, forward, and goalie. You lived though this book with me and continue to enrich my life. Thank you for that and for answering my endless hockey questions. And thank you for making my days brighter when grief for the loss of a friend who died too soon came calling. —JPH

CHAPTER ONE

If it works on paper, it will work in implementation.

Amy Callahan lived by those words—had ever since she was eight years old when she drew a diagram of how she wanted to rearrange her bedroom furniture in a way that her mother had said would never work. She wouldn't have used the word *implementation* back then, but her plan had worked and the philosophy had taken shape. It hadn't failed her yet—twenty years, give or take a month or six.

"We're here." Cameron reached for her hand as he turned down Main Street of Beauford, Tennessee. It had been a long time since there had been any hand-holding. That was also a good sign.

She squeezed his hand and took in the sights of the charming storefronts where some of the best artisans in the country had set up shop.

With all the October trappings—pumpkins, mums, and scarecrows—it was even more charming than she'd thought. Maybe she'd draw the decorations in her bullet journal when she got home.

"It's just as I imagined!"

Cameron laughed, but his laugh wasn't framed in the hard edge that had become the norm lately. "But you didn't really imagine it did you, so much as you did your research?"

It was true. Amy thumbed through the pages she had recently added to her bullet journal. They featured this little artisan boutique town that she had been intending to visit since moving to Nashville a year ago to live with failed pro football player, but successful sports agent, Cameron Snow. She never mentioned the failed football player part to him, tried not to even think it. He didn't like it. In fact, these days it seemed he didn't like a lot of things, and she was beginning to wonder if she was one of them.

That's why she'd been especially pleased—and surprised—when earlier this week he had suggested that he take a day off so they could make the forty-three-minute drive to Beauford to explore the unique shops. (She knew the exact driving time because she'd Googled it and recorded it on her bullet journal Beauford General Information page.) Cameron never took a day off, seldom made advance plans that weren't business related, and hated shopping—so she'd taken this as a sign that he was sorry for his cantankerous mood of late.

And it certainly seemed she'd been right. He'd wakened her this morning with his mouth on the nape of her neck in that oh, so sensitive spot and his hand making circles on the small of her back. He'd done it a good long time until she was fully awake and ready for the best lovemaking they'd had in she couldn't remember when.

Cameron glanced at the book on her lap. She had looked up the websites of each shop she wanted to visit and made a bullet journal page for each one, complete with whimsical renderings of the storefronts, hours of operation, and possible purchases she might want to make. It had taken hours, but the process had been pure pleasure.

The journal was open to the pages for the Gossamer Web, the lace shop, and String, the knitting shop. Amy didn't knit but she might start. After all, she hoped that in the not too distant future she might have need of some baby booties and blankets.

Cameron slid his finger along the lace border she had painstakingly drawn along the edges of the Gossamer Web page. "You know, some people would say you could just print out pages from the Internet and highlight what's important. They might say anyone who has time for this doesn't have enough to do. Not that I think that," he hurried to add. "I'm glad you have time for your little hobby."

That stung a bit, regardless of his disclaimer. Truth was, she *didn't* have a lot to do, though that hadn't always been true. Until eighteen months ago, she'd had a small, but growing and extremely successful, professional organizing business that she had built out of nothing except her uncanny talent for making sense of the worst kind of disorder.

Based in Atlanta, she'd started out helping Buckhead housewives bring order to their linen closets and holiday decorations, but as she honed her skills, word of her flawless reputation spread. Her client list grew until she found herself flying to Italy to organize kitchens for world-class chefs and to Paris to design closet systems for elite supermodels. She'd dug the mother of a two-time Oscar winner out of hoarder chaos—and kept her mouth shut about it.

Then came the offer. She and Cameron had been dating about six months when Order This, the New York-based, professional organizing company, had offered to buy her out for a cool five million. All she had to do was sign a five-year non-compete agreement.

Cameron had urged her to do it, pointing out that at her age—twenty-six—five years was nothing. Why shouldn't she secure her future and take some time off? Then in five years, if she wanted to start another business, she could. He'd even offered to handle her investments, just as he handled the investments of his clients, but without a fee.

In the end, it seemed like a win-win situation. A few months later, Cameron had asked her to move to Nashville, hinting that he had marriage and children on his mind. So she'd done it, done it all—sold her business, moved in with Cameron, and started dreaming about white lace and promises.

Only that last part hadn't panned out—not yet. And she could understand. Cameron was a busy, busy man. Whereas most agents concentrated on one sport, Cameron had both football and hockey clients. Right now he was a one-man operation, but his long term plan was to own an agency that represented all sports, and he wanted to have as many connections as possible. Although Cameron desperately wanted some baseball and basketball clients, he hadn't been able to close the deal on that yet. With the agency goal in mind, he paid meticulous attention to all sports. Baseball season bled into football season. Football season collided with basketball season. Soccer and golf were always hanging around. Hockey started early, stayed late, and seemed to go on forever. His clients were from all over the country, and he was always flying somewhere to hold this hand or driving cross-country on a moment's notice to pander to that ego.

Meanwhile, Amy kept the home fires burning. He always came home to an immaculate, well-ordered household with a full pantry, a comfortable bed, and his Armani and Brooks Brothers suits freshly dry cleaned and organized by color in his walk-in closet. His sports magazines were arranged in chronological order with his favorites within first reach. Because he had no taste or time for it, Amy read the newspapers and popular culture magazines for items about his clients and followed their social media so she could alert him if they posted inappropriate things.

And all this was little enough for her do in exchange for his managing their finances and making her money grow. Despite the success of her company, business was not her strong suit. Though she'd had inquiries, she'd never branched out into business organizing. She just could not get excited about sifting through someone's backlogged email and computer directories, whereas turning a hopeless roomful of jumbled craft supplies into a beautiful, productive space that inspired creativity filled her with joy. And she loved Cameron. Of course, she did. Otherwise, she would not have moved in with him, especially considering the discord it had caused between her and her family.

Back in Campbell, Georgia, her grandmother had advised against it. "Why buy the cow when you can get the milk for free?" she'd said. Amy loved Mimi, but men didn't think like that anymore, if they ever had. No one did—not even her parents.

Yet they had been far from enchanted about the changes she'd made in her life. Her father was a fourth-generation peach farmer who still rode shotgun to the orchard in the pickup truck with *his* father. Amy's brother, Terrance, would be fifth generation. She had never been pressured to join the family business, though there would have been plenty for her to do. The family rule was "everybody works."

Her mother ran The Peach Stand, which had started as a fruit stand, but now sold not only peaches, but everything that could be made from them, too—cider, preserves, pies, salsa, syrup, and homemade ice cream. There were even little novelty items made from peach wood. Last year, they'd finally put up a website and started to ship items all over the country.

Her parents, grandparents, and older brother had been proud of Amy's business success. When she'd announced she was going to sell, her family had been less impressed with the money she was getting and more alarmed that she would be doing nothing. Not exactly in keeping with the family motto. When she'd pointed out that she couldn't work in her field for five years, her father had said, "There are other fields. We've never pressed you to join the family business, but there's work here if you want it. If not, do something."

But she hadn't. Not really. Cameron had encouraged her to take some time off. She thought she'd keep house and cook meals—at least until time to plan a wedding and have a baby—but that had come to nothing. Cameron had a housekeeper and a laundry service. Cooking was something she wasn't inclined to do for herself, and Cameron was seldom available for dinner. When he was, he wanted to go out. But she did have lots of menu ideas in her bullet journal if that ever changed.

"Where do you want to go first?" Cameron brought her back to Beauford, Tennessee.

Good question. She was most eager to go to Sparkle, Neyland Beauford's custom jewelry shop. Neyland's mass-produced sterling silver chatelaine necklaces were all the rage and had made her famous, but Sparkle was her original workshop. Amy hoped that visiting there with Cameron might spur him toward thinking about an engagement ring, but probably best not to start there. She didn't want it to appear like she'd wanted to come to Beauford for the sole purpose of going to Sparkle. Better to start somewhere else and just drift in there. So, where?

Spectrum, the stained glass studio? Once Upon a Page, the handmade paper store? She flipped to the page for Piece by Piece.

"How about the quilt shop?" She wouldn't mention that it was owned by NHL star Nickolai Glazov's wife. Cameron had tried and failed to lure the Nashville Sound's center away from his present agent, and it was a sore subject. Unfortunately, it came up all too often since they lived in Sound Town, the area of downtown Nashville called that because of the location of the Sound practice rink and the number of players and team-connected people who lived there.

If she told Cameron of Glazov's connection to Piece by Piece, it was bound to put him in a sour mood, but there was no reason for him to know. Still, she was planning to buy a quilt. It wouldn't fit in the modern, gray granite, and stainless steel condo where they lived now, but she didn't intend to live there forever. She hoped to buy and restore one of the nearby historic houses.

"Where is this quilt place?" Cameron asked.

Amy turned to the color-coded map she'd drawn. "Should be here somewhere. Oh! Just there. On the right. And there's a parking spot right in front. We can park there and walk to the other shops."

He pulled into the space and rubbed the spot between his eyes. "I have a headache. I think I need a cup of coffee." He looked up and gave her a weak little smile.

Disappointment washed over her. "If you aren't feeling well, maybe we should go home."

"Oh, no, no!" He cupped her cheek. "This is your day. I just need some caffeine. You go on into the quilt store. I'll be back in thirty minutes, and we'll get on with our day. I promise."

"I could go with you." It had been so long since they'd done anything together that she wanted to share the whole day.

"No need of that when you don't even drink coffee. I'll be back before you know it."

Actually, that wasn't a bad idea. She had read that Noel Glazov's quilts were made completely by hand and could cost as much as five thousand dollars, and Cameron wouldn't see the sense in that. Plus, there was a remote chance that the Glazov connection might come up.

Amy nodded and flipped a few pages forward in her journal. "There's a coffee shop two blocks down on the left. Java Heaven."

"I don't want fancy coffee. I think I'll just go out to the Cracker Barrel by the interstate."

"Whatever you like." Amy didn't point out that he could have gotten plain coffee at Java Heaven. Cameron wasn't one to take suggestions from anyone. Besides, what did it matter?

"Can I bring you anything? Iced tea? Coke?"

"No, but thank you for asking." It only occurred to her then that he had stopped asking after her needs a long time ago. Maybe that was over.

"Then I'll meet you back here." Cameron leaned over and gave her a quick kiss—the kind that stable couples exchanged when they parted, because they knew they'd be seeing each other again soon.

CHAPTER TWO

Emile Giroux exited Eat Cake, doing just that—eating cake. His sister Gabriella, who was an apprentice at the Beauford, Tennessee bakeshop, had made it. Apple cider cinnamon, she'd called it. Why such tasty cake had to be a limited edition flavor for October, he didn't understand. You could get apples any time. That's one of the things he would have asked Gabriella if he'd been allowed to hang around and talk to her while he ate his cake. But no. She'd thrown him out because she had an important birthday cake to make for some country music star. Brad somebody. Emile couldn't keep up with all that.

Eat Cake wasn't the first place Emile been thrown out of this morning. Hélène-Louise, the owner of the Gossamer Web, was the only person he knew within a hundred miles—including his sister—who could carry on a conversation with him in fluent French. But one of those lace-making apprentices needed help and she hadn't had time for him either—just like she'd never really had time for him when he was trying to date her. That ship had sailed, of course. She'd married Bennett Watkins, who she claimed was the love of her life.

How did you get a job like that? Being the love of someone's life. Maybe he'd ask Bennett next time he saw him, but probably not. Bennett didn't care much for him.

The frosting on his square of limited edition cake began to melt. Packi—Oliver Klepacki, the Nashville Sound head equipment manager—would say that Emile shouldn't be eating cake this close to the season opener next week. He was probably right. This would be his last sweet for a while.

He licked the melting frosting off his fingers. A native of Quebec, Emile would never get used to the heat in the Southern United States—especially in the fall. Of course, if the rumors he'd heard at training camp were true, he might not be around this time next year to wear shorts in October. Word on the ice was that the Nashville Sound owner, Pickens Davenport, was considering selling the team to someone who planned to move them to Massachusetts. Emile didn't hate the idea as much as some of his teammates did, but he didn't especially like it either. First, it would mean leaving Gabriella, because there was no way she'd consider leaving Eat Cake until her apprenticeship was complete, and maybe not then. And second, Massachusetts was Bruins country—always would be. Apart from those things, he didn't care where he played. His world was the net, and no one in the NHL defended it better.

But the net was a lonely place. Sometimes it seemed like that old song, "You and Me Against the World." Only in his case, the *you* was his stick—Bauer TotalOne NXG, P31 curve, cut to exactly twenty-seven and a quarter inches. That's what he was using right now.

Unlike some of his teammates, Emile wasn't afraid to change his stick. If something better came along, he'd give it a try.

He wiped his sticky fingers and tossed his napkin in a garbage can. That ought to hold him until lunch. He'd tried to guilt Gabriella into saying she'd take a break at noon and eat with him, but Gabriella hadn't been her usual cooperative self. He hadn't even tried with Hélène-Louise.

There was one more stop he always made when he was in Beauford. The Sound team captain Nickolai Glazov's wife, Noel, owned Piece by Piece, and he always went in to say hello. Often as not, Glaz was there, but even if he wasn't, Noel would be. Maybe she'd go to lunch with him.

But sure enough, when Emile opened the door, Glaz was putting the new baby in her little basket bed on wheels.

"O Captain! My Captain!" Emile said.

"O goaltender! My goaltender!" Glaz replied.

Noel gave Emile a little wave from across the way where she was showing quilts to a pretty woman with dark hair. He waved back but didn't interrupt her.

Emile went to look at the baby. "And how is my goddaughter, the beautiful Amelie?" He liked babies; he always had. Too bad she was asleep.

"You are not her godfather."

"I should be. I can shower Amelie with jewels, cars, and furs. I am going to have a tiny replica of my sweater made for her to wear to games."

"*I* can shower her with jewels, cars, and furs."

"But I *would*. You will not. You are too cheap."

Nickolai didn't deny it, just as Emile knew he wouldn't. He was proud that his favorite restaurant was Cracker Barrel and that he shopped at Dollar General.

"She will not be wearing the sweater of a crazy goaltender." But Nickolai smiled, amused. Emile was good at amusing people. "And stop calling her Amelie. We told you from the start we would not call her by a French name that sounds like yours. You know her name is Anna Lillian. Is bad luck to call the wrong name."

"Bah! You and your bad luck and superstitions. Silly." Anna Lillian yawned and put her fist in her mouth. So cute. Maybe he would pick her up. He could do it without waking her. Probably.

"I have no superstitions. Only a few rituals," Glaz said. "And don't even think about picking up Anna Lillian. She just went to sleep."

"I was not going to pick her up." And apparently he wasn't. "Ritual. Superstition. It is all the same. You wear the same suit for every road trip, and Noel must send you a text exactly one hour and seven minutes before puck drop. And you know what happens when anyone says the words *Stanley Cup*, unless we have just won it." Which the Sound had done twice in the last three years.

The big Russian's nostrils flared. "Don't say that!"

"See? *Non.* I am the one with no superstitions." Next to baseball, hockey players were known for being the most superstitious in the sports world, but win or lose, Emile would do it without superstitions or rituals. He just played.

"No superstitions? What do you call refusing to talk between periods and going out of your mind if anyone touches your head while you are wearing your helmet?"

"I call that concentrating on the game. And I don't like having my head touched. That's all."

"And taping your stick between every period? You may think no one knows you leave a bit of tape on if it was a good period and you spit on it and flush it down the toilet if it was a bad one. If there was a stat for the NHL player responsible for the most clogged toilets, you would win it."

It was true. He did do that, but not because he was superstitious. It was just a thing he did. He would never be superstitious, because his son-of-a-bitch stepfather had been—for all the good it had done him. Andre had never gotten beyond being a fourth-rate forward on a third-rate minor league team that barely paid the bills. But just the same, he'd changed his skate laces and eaten a peanut butter and jelly sandwich before every game of his life—at least that's what Emile's mother had said. Emile didn't remember.

Emile's biological father had died from a skate to the jugular when Emile was a baby, and his mother, Bridget, had married Andre when Emile was two. Andre immediately set about turning

Emile into a hockey player. By the time Emile was seven, he showed real promise, but Andre was washed up.

Maybe Emile should thank him for that, but he didn't. Hard to be grateful to a man who beat the hell out of you every time you missed a save. And that was the least of his sins.

"So, no superstitions, Mr. French Kiss? *Da.* If you say." Glaz smirked, and Emile wanted to hit him but fought the urge, like he always did. Glaz was his friend and only savages hit people.

Emile shrugged and called on the funny man inside him to take the reins. "Think what you like. *The Lifeguard* should have been my nickname." Though he did love being called French Kiss. A female sportscaster had called him that because she said he had such a beautiful, kissable mouth. He'd tracked her down and let her try it out, but it had come to nothing. It always did.

Glaz caught sight of something over Emile's shoulder and put up a hand. "No, Noel. Do not climb that ladder. I will take the quilt down." And he stepped away from Emile without a word.

Emile wouldn't have been much of a goaltender if he hadn't learned a long time ago how to seize an opportunity. The opposing team's forward makes a misstep, and you make that puck your own. In this case, Glaz was the forward and little Anna Lillian was the puck. He swooped in and picked her up—only he swooped with too much enthusiasm, and she began to cry.

There was going to hell to pay now. He put her on his shoulder and began to bounce her. "*Ne pleure pas, chérie.*"

"I told you not to pick her up!" Glaz shouted and Anna Lillian cried harder.

"*Silencieux,*" Emile said. "See what you did."

"What *I* did! And stop speaking French in front of my baby."

"Now, now," Noel said as she came toward him with her arms outstretched. "This isn't the first time she's been wakened, and it won't be last." She smiled at Emile as she took the baby.

"You have a sweet way about you, my lovely Noel. I know this beautiful *bébé* will be such as you."

"Leave my wife and child alone." Glaz was on the ladder removing a quilt from the dowel where it hung. "Make yourself useful and let me hand this down to you."

Emile winked at Noel, gave Anna Lillian a little pat, and took his sweet time about crossing the room.

"*Bonjour*," he said to the dark-haired woman. "You are buying the lovely Noel's quilt?"

"I am." Emile did not find all Southern accents easy on the ear, but hers was—more slow than flat, more like sharp molasses than overly sweet honey. Might be a little bourbon mixed in. "You are lucky to own such a thing. Noel is an artist."

"I *am* lucky. It's one of the most beautiful things I've ever seen." Her eyes were purple. He'd never seen purple eyes before. Was there a trick to making them appear that way, or was it real?

Emile looked at the quilt. It was a wild swirl of colors and shapes that he couldn't make sense of, but everyone said Noel's quilts were fine textile art, so it must be true. In an attempt to improve himself, he'd taken some art classes at the University of North Dakota but he didn't remember them saying anything about quilts.

"*Oui*. A real work of art."

"Mr. French Kiss?" Glaz said. "Do you think you could take this work of art from me so it does not get soiled from the floor?"

"If I can stop a puck, I can stop a quilt." He folded it and laid it on the table. "Come out to lunch with me, my captain. I will buy."

"*Nyet*." I am to watch Anna Lillian until time to practice."

"Go," Noel said. "Anna Lillian is asleep again. You can put her in the stroller and take her."

"I'll push!" Emile volunteered.

Glaz frowned, but he nodded. "Let me put away the ladder."

"Excellent," Emile said. "I will get the pushchair." He smiled at the purple-eyed woman and briefly wondered who would be under that quilt with her.

• • •

It was a good thing Cameron had gone for coffee. Never in her wildest dreams had Amy imagined there was any chance Nickolai Glazov would actually be in the shop. She watched him exit Piece by Piece with the one he'd called French Kiss pushing the baby. She hadn't paid attention to their whole conversation, but it seemed he was a hockey player and teammate. She had only been to one Sound game with Cameron, though he went all the time. She had been raised on football—SEC college and Atlanta Falcons. Aside from hearing Cameron rant and rave about Glazov, she knew nothing about hockey players or hockey. But there was something familiar about Mr. French Kiss, and it was easy to see how that one had gotten his nickname. He had the most beautiful mouth she'd ever seen. The thought of his mouth jarred her memory.

Wasn't he the one in that candy commercial? At the end he said, "*Au Chocolat*," smiled, and bit into a piece of chocolate with a filled center. Then came the capper. The camera zoomed in on that beautiful mouth as a tiny bit of syrupy filling ran from the corner of his mouth. It made every woman watching want to lick the TV screen.

She tossed her head to shake off the thought. She shouldn't be looking at other men's mouths—even exceptional ones with full lips that smiled easily. Maybe, apart from the dripping candy, that was the attraction—the easy smile. There hadn't been a lot of that in her life lately, not in the mirror and not across the dinner table.

"I am so pleased you like this quilt." Noel Glazov had refolded it and was wrapping it in tissue paper. "I have never made a crazy quilt before. I didn't think I ever would. But I made it when I was pregnant."

Amy was thankful Noel had distracted her from thinking about mouths. The quilt with its swirling patterns and wild colors was not what she had imagined buying, but she'd known it was hers the moment she'd seen it—even though it was priced at three thousand dollars.

"I thought I would want one made of squares like the one with the leaves there." Amy pointed to the quilt display. "But *this* is my quilt. How is a crazy quilt different?"

"There's no real plan to a crazy quilt. You just start sewing together fabric of all shapes, sizes, and patterns." Noel smiled warmly. "Not usually my way at all. I always like a plan of exactly what is going to happen."

"I understand that," Amy said. "I used to be a professional organizer." Were *used to be* the saddest words in the English language?

"Really?" Noel was now wrapping the quilt in brown paper. "We could sure use some of that around here."

Amy laughed. Everyone said that. It was like English teachers hearing, "I'll have to watch my grammar," or people saying to a minister, "I'll have to watch my language."

"Nonsense," Amy said. "The shop is lovely. How did you decide to make a crazy quilt?"

"Well, it was right after we found out I was pregnant." Noel tied the parcel with twine from an old-fashioned dispenser. "I was on a plane, on the way to see my husband's hockey game. I reached for my project bag and found that I had brought the wrong one—something I would probably not have done had I not had baby brain. What I'd brought was a bag of scraps. It's a wonder I had scissors and a needle. So I just started stitching, thinking maybe I'd make a pincushion from it. Then there was enough for a pillow. But I just kept going." She patted the box she had placed the bundle in. "And here it is. I call it Stir Crazy—which I was later on in my pregnancy."

"That's a lovely story. I'll bet you have stories for all your quilts."

Noel stopped and considered, then laughed. "I suppose I do. I live with them a long time. It took me almost as long to make Stir Crazy as it did to make Anna Lillian." She reached under the counter and pulled out a pamphlet. "This is how to care for it. And there's something else. After I named the quilt, I hid seventeen spoons in it. Different sizes, some embroidered, some appliquéd. I can give you a diagram that shows where they are, but I hope you'll try to find them first. You can call me anytime and I'll send you the diagram—either when you find them all or give up."

"So, spoons for Stir Crazy? I love it!" If she'd been charmed before, now she was enchanted.

"And"—Noel gave her a sly little grin—"I thought it might be a good quilt to spoon under."

A nice thought. There hadn't been much of that lately, but maybe better times were coming. Amy removed her credit card from her wallet and slid it across the counter.

Noel picked up the card. "I'll have you ready in just a jiffy."

"Take your time," Amy said.

Noel swiped the card and frowned. "Odd. Let me try again."

Amy didn't think much of it. Transactions sometimes failed the first time. But Noel did not brighten and say, "There it goes," as merchants always did when this happened. In fact, she seemed to be trying for a third time.

Finally, Noel looked up. "I'm sorry. Your card has been declined."

"That's impossible," Amy said. That's probably what everyone said, but it really *was* impossible. The limit on her card was ridiculous, and Cameron paid it off every month.

Noel handed her the card. "I'm sure it's just a glitch. Would you like to call them? Or use another card?"

She didn't have another card, except for her debit card, which she seldom used.

"I'll call the bank." She flipped the card over and punched in the number. She didn't even step away out of earshot. Why should she? She had plenty of money and nothing to be embarrassed about.

But after a long, tortuous wait listening to elevator music with a recorded voice interrupting at regular intervals to ask her to be patient, she finally hung up. Now, reason or not, she was embarrassed. She couldn't stay on hold forever. Cameron would be here soon. She'd work this out later. She fished her debit card out of her wallet.

"I don't know what's going on," Amy said, "but I'm tired of being on hold. I'll just use my debit card."

Noel smiled. "Certainly. Believe me, this kind of thing happens all the time."

"Maybe my fiancé got new cards and forgot to give me mine." Uncomfortable at calling Cameron her fiancé, Amy hid her left hand. She wouldn't have called him that if she had a better word, but *boyfriend* was so juvenile, and *partner* sounded like someone you had a business arrangement with—or maybe a cowboy, though wouldn't that be *pardner?* She tried to picture Cameron in chaps and a cowboy hat, but couldn't quite get there.

"I'm sorry, Amy," Noel said. "You debit card has been denied, too."

What!

Amy shook her head. "This has never happened to me before. I don't understand."

Noel looked as embarrassed as Amy felt. "You could call them."

No way was she going to stand here and make another call in front of this woman.

"It's the same bank. I'd just be on hold again." She closed her eyes for a moment. Maybe Cameron had moved all their banking business and not told her—not that she was going to admit to this successful businesswoman and wife of a millionaire hockey player that she didn't know anything about her own finances. Then she reminded herself that she—Amy—was a millionaire in her own right. Lots of people had other people handle their finances. Nikolai Glazov probably did. It was no different. Amy just didn't have to pay Cameron.

She lifted her chin and looked Noel in the eye. "I don't know what is going on, but my fiancé is supposed to meet me back here. He handles our finances, and I know there has been some big misunderstanding. He'll have the right cards."

Noel smiled, clearly relieved. "I'm sure that's it. Why don't you have a seat?" She indicated a cozy little sitting area around a fireplace where Amy imagined that people sat to sew. "Would you like a cup of coffee or a Coke?"

No way. Amy wanted out of here and now. The next time she set foot in this shop, she wanted to have the right card and collect her package. If Nickolai Glazov and his French friend were back by then, Cameron would just have to suck it up. Served him right for leaving her with no way to buy anything.

But she didn't say all that, of course. Instead, she smiled. "I think I'll watch for him outside and enjoy everyone's fall decorations. The weather's so nice."

Noel nodded. "See you soon, then. I'll just put this aside for safekeeping." She placed the box with Stir Crazy behind the counter.

CHAPTER THREE

Emile settled the check at The Café Down On The Corner as Glaz settled Anna Lillian into her pushchair.

"Have you heard from Swifty since yesterday?" Glaz asked, referring to the Sound's top defenseman and Emile's closest friend, Bryant Taylor. He'd earned his nickname back in his junior hockey days for his backward skating speed, though that little blond country music star, Taylor Swift, told a reporter it was for her.

"He's fine. A little rest. A little ibuprofen. He will be on the ice today. He might have lost that little altercation with the boards yesterday, but he never loses for long."

Glaz nodded and picked up the bag with the takeout they had gotten for Noel. "Good. Would not want to face the Blackhawks without him next week."

"I am in front of Eat Cake." Emile pointed down the block to where his Bugatti Chiron was parked. There were four teenage boys gathered around, taking pictures with it.

Glaz shook his head. "I am surprised anew every time I see that vehicle. I do not know what is crazier—that you paid three million dollars for a *mode of transportation* or that you painted it up like a circus train." In keeping with his notoriously thrifty ways, Glaz had driven a used Jeep until the baby was born. Then he'd replaced it with some kind of American-made SUV.

"Not a circus train. It matches my goalie mask." Emile was proud of that design. He'd thought it out very carefully, and everything had symbolic meaning—the metallic silver and purple were the Sound's colors. The giant wolf head and stars on the hood were for his name—Emile meant *excellent* and Giroux meant *wolf.* The Sound's logo—a musical note—and his sweater number—30—were interspersed with the stars that orbited around the wolf's head.

"Thor told me the manufacturer of that car threatened to sue you for defacing it. Is that true?"

Emile shrugged. "They wrote a letter. I gave it to Miles Gentry, and he made it go away."

Glaz nodded. "Agents are good that way. At first, I did not want to pay the fee, but Jean Luc has made me much more money." Glaz looked at the car. "Is crazy, what you did. That is for sure. But if you want to paint your car, is for you to say. No one else."

Emile stopped in front of his car. "So, a man has a right to be crazy."

Glaz laughed. "Keep making the saves, I will defend your right to be crazy."

"See you later at practice." Emile bent to give Anna Lillian a goodbye pat, but Glaz wheeled her away from his reach.

"If you must wake more babies today, go find someone else's."

Emile watched the boys taking pictures of his car for a moment after Glaz moved on, and then he stepped closer and waited for them to notice him. Noticing him never took long.

"Why aren't you young men in school?" he asked. Emile believed in education. He'd gone to college less than a year before going to play for the St. Louis Blues. He'd wanted Gabriella to finish college, but she'd been set on being a baker and didn't want to go at all. He could have sent her anywhere, but in the end they compromised, and she agreed to attend the community college near home for two years. After that, Miles had found the apprenticeship for her with the pastry chef in Beauford and negotiated a nice deal for Emile with the Sound so he could be near his sister. Pickens Davenport had paid dearly, but Emile had earned every cent. He gave the boys a stern look. "You should be in school."

The boys looked startled.

"Teachers' work day," one of them said. "We got out at noon."

"So you've been to school today?"

They all nodded. Emile believed them, so he smiled.

"Then, maybe I will take a picture of all of you together with my car."

"This is your car?" That came from the short redheaded one.

"Of course it is! That's Emile Giroux!" the skinny blond said. "I told you I heard about his car on ESPN."

So lots of picture taking and autograph giving ensued. Emile never charged for autographs. He didn't even care if they sold them. He admired enterprising people.

He considered going into Eat Cake to say goodbye to Gabriella but decided against it. She had that birthday cake that she was so excited about.

He slid behind the wheel and pulled the car out into traffic. Even considering the half hour it would take him to get back to Nashville, he still had couple of hours to kill before practice. Crazy practice schedule. Eight in the morning some days, noon, others. Sometimes late afternoon like today. Some of the guys didn't like it, but Emile didn't care. He didn't have much else to do. He passed Glaz, who had stopped on the street to talk to Miss Sticky from the knitting shop. He waved and drove past Piece by Piece.

It was three doors down in front of the shop called the Pottery Wheel that he noticed the purple-eyed woman from Piece by Piece sitting on a hay bale beside a scarecrow. There was something about the slump of her shoulders and the way she was looking at her hands folded in her lap. She looked distressed.

Had there not been a parking space right in front, he would probably not have stopped. Or maybe he would have. Emile tended to respond to stimuli rather than thinking things through. A goalie who thought things through was a doomed goalie.

When he parked, her head snapped up, her eyes seeking and hopeful. He gave her a little wave, but she didn't return it. The hope went out of her face as she looked up and down the street. Then she looked down again.

A mystery. Not for him to solve, but interesting. He should get back to Nashville. He could get to the rink early, maybe visit with Packi. He went to pull back out into traffic but then killed the motor and opened the door instead.

• • •

Where was Cameron? It had been more than two hours now since he'd dropped Amy off at Piece by Piece. At first, she'd been patient, but then after an hour, she'd been annoyed. That was when she'd tried to call him and found that her phone wasn't working. It wasn't dead exactly—she could see the time and date—but the phone wouldn't unlock.

After her experience in Piece by Piece, she'd felt too awkward and conspicuous to stand in front of the shop, so she'd walked across the street and stood to watch for him. After the same couple had passed her twice, she'd gotten the feeling that people were looking at her, so she'd moved locations every ten minutes or so, never getting too far from where Cameron expected her to be. She didn't dare go into a shop, in case she missed him.

Now she was worried, terrified. What if he was dead? That had to be it. Or dying. He would not have left her sitting here for two hours. She wished a policeman would walk by so she could ask for help. Or a man or woman of the cloth. Of course, she wouldn't know one without a clerical collar. Nuns should never have been allowed to stop wearing habits. She wasn't Catholic, but a nun would help her. She was sure of it.

These were hysterical thoughts. Amy knew that. But there was reason there, too. Maybe she should start walking until she found a church or a police station. That nice Noel would probably help her, but she'd rather find a nun. Though if she left here, Cameron would surely come back and wouldn't know where she was. He'd probably been trying to call her and tell her why he was delayed.

If he was still alive.

For what seemed like the millionth time, the sound of an approaching car made her heart leap. But it was only that French hockey player in a car that looked like it belonged to a radio station. Maybe he worked as a deejay part time.

And great. He was getting out. She'd wished for a nun and gotten a hockey player/deejay.

"Hello." And he wasn't just passing by. He stopped in front of her. "I was in the quilting shop before when you were there."

"Yes." She had nothing to do with her hands—no phone, no coffee, no cigarette. Never mind that she didn't smoke or drink coffee. Wait! Her bullet journal was in her purse. She pulled it out, along with the navy-blue LePen she liked to use when making new notations. She could start a new page: What to Do When You Are Left with No Phone, No Money, No Credit Card, and No Nun. Except she didn't have any bullet points to make, because she didn't know what to do.

"You are sitting with your friend the scarecrow?" He spread that gorgeous mouth into a smile she would have enjoyed if she'd been of a mind to enjoy anything.

Amy nodded. "Lovely weather." *Now, go away!*

"Can I help you in some way?"

Was it that obvious that she needed help?

"No, no. I am waiting for my … er … fiancé."

"Is he late?"

Did this man have a crystal ball in that ridiculous car?

"A bit," she admitted. "I'm sure he's tried to call, but my phone suddenly stopped working."

His brown eyes danced like magic. "So, I can help you." He reached into his pocket and pulled out his phone. "You would like to, maybe, use my phone to call him?"

The phone he held out to her looked like a lifeline—a lifeline with a custom phone case with a picture of this man spread-eagle on the ice in front of a hockey goal. Across the top it said "Emile Giroux, French Kiss" in silver metallic letters. Not that she cared. It was a phone and he was offering it to her.

"Yes." She took the phone. "If you don't mind. That's so kind."

"I hope you know the number." He stepped over and leaned a shoulder on the building. "Me? I am bad with numbers. I depend on my phone to tell them to me."

"I don't know phone numbers as I should." She opened her bullet journal. "Luckily, I have important numbers written down." When all else failed, you could trust pen and paper.

"So your phone isn't out of charge? But will not work. Funny." He frowned like he was trying to reason it out. He probably thought she hadn't paid her bill. And she hadn't. Cameron did that. She was pretty sure he had it set up to auto pay.

No matter. She punched in the number. Pretty soon, Cameron would answer and all this would be resolved.

Except he didn't.

"That can't be right." She hadn't meant to say that out loud.

"You did not reach him?"

"I got a message that the phone had been disconnected. I must have dialed wrong. Do you mind if I try again?"

"Please." He nodded, and his messy black curls bounced around his cheeks.

So, she tried again. And again, with the same result.

Out of desperation, she dialed his business number, though she knew he wouldn't answer. He screened those calls and only returned the ones that interested him. His clients all had his private number. She left a message. "Cameron, I'm still here waiting for you. My phone isn't working and well—there have been other complications." Out of habit, she almost said to call her, but how would he do that? She couldn't keep this man's phone. "Come and get me, please."

Knowing it was futile, she dialed his private number again. It was like the rejected credit card all over again. There was nothing to do but hand the phone back.

"No luck?"

"No." She looked at her hands. "I'm really worried that something has happened to him." She had to say it to someone.

He looked sympathetic. "We have not exchanged names. I am Emile Giroux."

She nodded. "I read it on your phone case. Amy Callahan. Thank you for the use of your phone."

She thought he would leave then, but he shoved the scarecrow off the hay bale and sat down beside her.

"What should we do now?"

"Pick up that scarecrow before the pottery people find out and get mad?" Where had that come from? Making jokes when Cameron was dead or kidnapped—it must be shock. "Anyway, this isn't your problem."

"No, but I am gallant. Like Lancelot."

"Didn't he have sex with his best friend's wife?"

"My best friend doesn't have a wife. And I wouldn't do that anyway. Why don't you tell me what happened."

"Nothing happened. We were going to spend the day in Beauford shopping. He dropped me at Piece by Piece and was going to the Cracker Barrel out by the interstate to get a cup of coffee. He was coming right back. He said he'd pick me up in a half hour. But he didn't come." She felt the tremble in her voice and hoped Emile didn't hear it. "Now, I'm afraid something's happened to him—a wreck or maybe he's been kidnapped …"

"Kidnapping a grown man seems unlikely. A wreck? I don't know. I can call Bradley Stanton. I am friendly with him from the time he dated my sister. She grew tired of him after two dates, but he still likes me."

"Who's that?"

"The sheriff. He would know if there has been a wreck."

"Then, yes. Please. If you don't mind."

"I have his private number."

He put the call through. "*Bonjour*, Bradley! This is Emile. Yes, yes. The Blackhawks will regret that they came to Nashville, Tennessee. If you would like tickets, you have but to ask. I do have a question. I am here with a friend, and it seems her fiancé has gone astray."

They were friends? No. And Cameron hadn't gone *astray*, not really. Of course, he wasn't her fiancé either. Was nothing true?

"She wondered if there had been any car accidents this morning. *Non*. Not that early. In the last two to three hours. No? Good." He met her eyes, shook his head, and said, "Amy, Bradley asked his name and what he was driving."

"Cameron Snow." Was it her imagination, or did Emile react with surprise when he heard Cameron's name? "We drove over from Nashville in my car. Audi sedan. Blue."

Emile repeated the information into the phone and continued, "He went to get coffee at the Cracker Barrel two hours ago and hasn't come back. Yes. I will tell her. Thank you." He hung up the phone. "No accidents, so that's good news. Bradley cannot officially do anything until Cameron has been missing twenty-four hours, but he said he would keep his eyes and ears open and check around, call the hospital. He'll call me if he hears anything. He said to tell you that in cases like this, it's usually nothing. Cameron probably decided he wanted some biscuits and gravy with his coffee and started surfing the net or answering emails. Lost track of time."

That was certainly possible. "Sounds like him." And he would have had his laptop and tablet. He never went anywhere without them.

"Bradley offered to go to the Cracker Barrel," Emile went on, "but I told him we could do that. Cameron is probably having a crisis with one of his clients."

That sounded like him, too. "You know Cameron?"

"No, not really. He is the agent of my teammate Jan Voleck. He gave me his card once, but I did not call. No offense. My agent is Miles Gentry. I … what is it? Ride out on the horse who dances with me?"

Despite her stress, Amy smiled. Now that she had pictured Cameron with his laptop open at one of those wooden tables, with a plate of pancakes, she felt better. Their phones being shut off was surely a glitch. That's it. He was on his laptop, emailing, trying to get their phones straightened out.

"I believe you are trying to say, 'Ride out on the horse I rode in on,' or 'Dance with the one who brought me.'"

Emile nodded. "Yes. That. Should I take you to Cracker Barrel? I have been there many times. It's Glaz's favorite eating establishment. I'm sure Cameron will be there."

Amy nodded. "I really would appreciate it."

Emile stood up, restored the scarecrow to its rightful place, and began to look around and behind the hay bales.

"What are you looking for?" Amy asked.

"You package—the quilt that you bought from Noel."

Damn. "I didn't get it after all."

"No? You seemed to like it so much."

She almost told him she'd changed her mind, but lying was against her nature, even to save pride. She had already trotted out the word *fiancé* too many times. Besides, he was clearly friends with the Glazovs and saw them often. If it came up, Noel would tell him.

She took a deep breath. "I don't know what went wrong. It has never happened to me. My credit card and debit card were denied. I was waiting on Cameron to come back so I could find out what happened and get another card. He takes care of our finances."

Emile's eyes widened, and he drew his lower lip into his mouth and bit it.

He was going to say something, something bad that she didn't want to hear and absolutely was not possible. She'd seen those late night cable TV shows with people who disappeared without a trace. But that hadn't happened. Cameron couldn't do that if he wanted to. He had famous clients. And he *hadn't* wanted to. They'd made love no more than four hours ago. He was at Cracker Barrel trying to rid their phones of whatever virus had shut them down. And that was that.

But when Emile spoke all he said was, "I would be happy to get the quilt. We can settle up later."

Amy put her hand. "No. Please. I'll take care of it once I find Cameron. I just need to go to Cracker Barrel if you are still willing to take me."

"But, of course, *chérie.*"

And he held open the door of that car that looked like a ride at the county fair.

CHAPTER FOUR

At the Cracker Barrel, Emile found exactly what he expected—nothing. Cameron Snow wasn't there and hadn't been there. All the wait staff knew Emile from his visits there with Glaz, and he talked to each of them, showing a picture that he'd found on Snow's website and saved to his phone. They had all been on duty the entire morning and were very sure they hadn't seen him. Barbara Ann from the Shell station was the only one who had come in for takeout coffee, and she had gotten a sausage biscuit, too.

It would have been better if Amy had stayed in the car, but there was no stopping her from going in. As Emile questioned person after person, Amy deflated a little more and grew a little more demoralized—and shocked.

But Emile wasn't shocked. He wasn't even surprised. He'd begun to put it all together. He hadn't come up with an answer, but this man was not dead, hurt, kidnapped, or detained. He was gone.

Maybe. Or maybe he'd never been here in the first place. Amy claimed he was her fiancé, but she wore no ring. Maybe she was delusional. His gut told him that wasn't true, but life had taught him that his gut wasn't very reliable.

He turned to Amy. "What would you like to do?" Because he might have shortcomings and plenty of them, but he damned sure wasn't going to leave a woman standing in Cracker Barrel in the middle of all those cast iron cooking pots and T-shirts with writing on them.

She shook her head. "I don't know what to do. Should I go back to Piece by Piece, so he can find me when he turns up? I know the police won't do anything yet."

"Maybe you could call his parents? Do they live here?" That would be great. Maybe they would come get her.

"No. They were killed in a boating accident the year Cameron played for Kansas City. That's why he had such a bad year."

"Brothers and sisters?"

"No. An only child. I don't know anyone to call."

What kind of man had no friends? Or maybe he did—parents and siblings, too, but Amy didn't know them because she didn't really know him.

Amy covered her face with her hands. "What I really wish is that I could go home."

An excellent idea. "Why can't you? I will take you there. Didn't you say you lived in Nashville?"

"Yes. In Sound Town. Star View Towers."

Well, that was interesting. "That's where I live."

"Really? I've never seen you."

"A big building. Lots of people. What floor?"

"Eight. Unit D. You?"

"The fourteenth floor," he answered.

"What unit?"

"All of it."

"Ah."

"Let me take you there. Perhaps Cameron went back there. Maybe he forgot something?"

She looked hopeful. "Do you really think so?"

Emile did not. Either Cameron didn't exist—at least in Amy's world—or he was in the wind.

He smiled and put a hand on Amy's arm. "Come. Let's get you home."

• • •

Home. Somehow, Amy thought if she could just get home, everything would be all right. Even if Cameron hadn't gone back there, maybe there would be a note or some kind of clue.

Maybe he'd had a client emergency and he'd had to return home to deal with it—or maybe even fly to the West Coast or New England. Probably California. His biggest client, Reynolds Fallon, played for the 49ers and Cameron had been spending a lot of time there lately. Maybe he'd left her a voice mail or email telling her he'd pick her up later, but her phone had gone wonky. He wouldn't know that.

Yes. If she could just get home, even if he wasn't there, she could check her email on her laptop or tablet. Next she'd get her cell phone straightened out. Then everything would make sense again.

Maybe. Or maybe she'd just drink a bottle of wine and pass out on the couch. *Sofa.* Cameron didn't like for her to say couch. He thought *sofa* sounded classier.

Emile pulled into the underground parking garage. Maybe she should ask him to drive by their reserved parking spots. But no. He was already pulling into his own spot—which was right by the lobby doors. She could still ask him. He'd do it, but why bother? The real answers were inside.

He helped her out of the car and held the lobby door for her.

"How did you get such a good parking place?" Amy asked. "Ours are all the way on the other side."

"Sometimes things just happen. Sometimes it's good." He shrugged. "Sometimes not so much."

That was the truth—especially that last part and especially today.

Amy preceded Emile into the lobby. She had been in many luxury condos, but she'd never wanted to live in one. She was more of a house-with-a-porch-and-yard person, a house like the one she'd grown up in. But Cameron loved all the amenities—the fitness center, Olympic-size pool, in-building restaurants and shops, and around the clock security and concierge service. Those things just gave Amy the feeling that she was staying in an overgrown hotel.

Speaking of the concierge—Lila was behind the desk today. The lobby was relatively quiet, and Lila looked their way immediately. Maybe she had a sixth sense, or maybe it was the noise they made on the marble floor. Probably the floor. That's why they'd picked it. No sneaking.

Lila looked surprised—probably because they were together. "Mr. Giroux. Ms. Callahan?" There was a definitely a question in Lila's voice and narrowing of her eyes when she said Amy's name. "Is everything in order?"

"Of course." *No, Lila, it's not. Can you find Mr. Snow for me? He says the concierge staff at Star View Towers never fails. So produce him, speedy quick. Please.*

"*Bonjour*, Lila," Emile said. "I like the pumpkins that you have used to decorate. And those yellow flowers. Nice."

She smiled. "Mums. Thank you, but I didn't do it. We contract that out."

"Ah, Lila! I thought you did everything here." Despite his running commentary, Amy had to give Emile credit. He never slowed his steps but continued to move them toward the elevator.

Amy beat Emile to the keypad and punched in her code—except it didn't work. She tried again. Nothing. Credit card. Debit card. Phone. Now elevator security code. Her heart began to pound, which was a comfort. At least her heart was still working.

"Let me," Emile said quietly as he punched in his own code. The elevator door opened immediately.

When the doors opened again on her floor, Amy turned to Emile. "I can't thank you enough, but I can take it from here."

He raised one eyebrow. "Can you?" He followed her out of the elevator. Amy had the feeling there was no stopping him, so she didn't even try.

Please, let Cameron be there. Please, let this all be some silly misunderstanding. She reached into her bag and brought out her key fob, but just she was about to unlock the door—with Emile right behind her—the door swung open.

Cameron! But no. It was a member of the Star View maintenance staff who stepped out. Shane. It said so on his shirt.

"What's going on?" Amy asked.

"Just going for another gallon of paint."

"Paint? I didn't ask for my condo to be painted."

"We always paint when people move out," Shane said.

"Move out? We haven't moved out!" Could she have taken a wrong turn and gone to the wrong place? Even after living here over a year? She checked the small brass plate on the door with the unit number. No. This was home. Wasn't it?

"Could have fooled me," Shane said.

"But there has been a mistake." Amy said the words just as Emile walked past her, opened the door, and entered.

Shane forgotten, Amy stepped inside—to emptiness, except for buckets of paint, drop cloths, and men on ladders.

Her mouth went dry and her head spun.

"My furniture is gone," she said to Emile. "I don't know what's going on."

"Can we help you, ma'am?" This man—Royce—was older than Shane.

She shook her head. "This is my home. I don't understand what's going on." Even in the unlikely event that Cameron had decided to have the place painted, they wouldn't have moved the furniture out. "Where is my furniture?"

Royce came down off the ladder. "I don't know anything about that. We got a work order last week to paint the whole condo oasis beige, like we always do when a place is going up for sale."

"But it's not for sale."

Royce shook his head. "Ma'am, I think you need to go speak to Mr. Fairly."

"But my things …" She was going to be sick. This was crazy. She moved toward the kitchen.

"Ma'am, I'm going to have to ask you to leave. If there's been a mistake, the office downstairs will straighten it out."

She couldn't leave. Why should she? This was where she lived.

"Royce, my friend." Up until now, Emile had been silent. He removed his wallet, but he didn't offer Royce money. Instead, he handed him a small laminated card. "Season tickets for two for all Sound home games. Be my guest."

Royce looked skeptical. "What are the strings?"

"None. The tickets are yours for the taking, though I hope you will let her look around. Ten minutes. No more. She won't take anything."

"Well," Royce looked longingly at the card, "I suppose it couldn't hurt. There's nothing to take."

And there wasn't. Not a tea kettle or her favorite mug. No laptop, tablet, toothbrush, or one single shoe or garment—hers or Cameron's. All the beautiful wrapping paper and ribbons she loved to collect—gone, and with them the special pens, stencils, stickers, and rubber stamps that she used to create her bullet journals. Someone had taken it all—including all her bullet journals, except the one in her purse.

But who? Who would do such a thing? Who would even want it?

She stood in the empty bedroom—the one she'd shared with Cameron, at least when he was home.

She felt Emile's hands on her shoulders before she heard him.

"Come along, *chérie*. Let's go down to the office."

And she let him lead her away.

CHAPTER FIVE

By the time Emile had Amy on the elevator headed down to the second floor, he was convinced that he had a certified psycho on his hands—and he was about to make her someone else's problem. That's what Star View Towers promised—your problems were theirs. Having a package delivered? It would be there waiting for you. Need your place cleaned? Absolutely, they would take care of it. Need your car washed? Don't even think about it.

Take a lunatic stalker off your hands with no fuss? Well that's what security guards were for.

When Amy had been rushing from room to room looking in cabinets and closets, Emile had taken advantage of the time to do a quick, but clandestine, Google search on Cameron Snow.

He'd been somewhat of a minor star tackle at Utah State and gone to the Kansas City Chiefs in the fifth round of the NFL draft, where he'd lasted one season and gotten little play time. Though Wikipedia hadn't said so, apparently that's when he'd set himself up as a sports agent, which would mean he hadn't been to law school like Miles.

Maybe Amy was a stalker, though Emile couldn't figure out why she would pick Snow to stalk. He didn't seem all that impressive, though stalkers were probably not the greatest at making logical decisions. If they were, they wouldn't stalk. She could have become enamored with him when he'd played football. She might even be a former girlfriend. Glaz had had to get a restraining order against

Tewanda, a former girlfriend, who'd never gotten the message that they weren't a couple anymore.

If Amy had dated—or even lived with—Snow at some point, that would explain why Lila knew who she was but had clearly found it odd that she was in the building. But even if Snow had a restraining order against her, a Star View Towers staff member would be unlikely to say anything since Amy had been with him. After all, *he* didn't have a restraining order against her. He'd had a few stalkers, but it had never come to that.

Maybe Snow had moved out to get away from her, though Emile had found changing his elevator code to be sufficient. But who knew? Maybe Snow had never lived here at all. For all Emile knew, the man might not even live in Nashville. That would mean Amy was completely delusional, since she hadn't balked at going to the condo office.

The elevator door opened, and she didn't even wait for him. Obviously, she knew the way. As luck would have it Adam Fairly, the head guy, was here today, so there wouldn't be any phoning around or, "I need to check with Mr. Fairly." Emile didn't have time for all of that. He had to go to practice.

To Emile's surprise, Amy walked right past the receptionist without a word and opened Fairly's door without knocking. Despite probably being mad as the hatter in charge of all the other hatters in Wonderland, Amy had shown good manners until now, but she was hanging by a thread. He hoped to be long gone before that thread broke—and he'd have no guilt, either. That's why he paid an association fee.

"Hello, Peggy. We need to see Adam." He smiled and nodded to the receptionist, but he didn't slow down. He didn't intend to miss a second of this. The woman looked confused, as confused as Lila had been.

Adam Fairly did not look confused, but confusion was not allowed in his occupation. It was his job to make sure the residents of Star View Towers remained happy at all times. Adam had once told Emile in confidence over a beer that the regular residents were harder to please than all the country music stars, Tennessee Titans, and Nashville Sound players combined. Emile found it odd that Adam was willing to say anything remotely negative about any of the residents in the building, but Emile liked for people to tell him things. Maybe Adam sensed that.

"Amy. Emile." Adam called all the residents except the elderly by their first names. Maybe he thought it made them seem more like a family—and he knew Amy's name. Doubt began to creep into Emile's gut. Maybe Amy wasn't so crazy. How many times had he changed his mind today? He didn't know what to think.

She didn't waste any time and she didn't sit down. "Adam, my condo is being painted and my things are gone."

He nodded. "Of course. That's a service we offer—to arrange for packing, moving, and readying the unit for the market. We take care of our residents from first day to last—if there must be a last."

"But we aren't moving," Amy whispered. "Where's Cameron?" She dropped into a chair as if she couldn't stand another minute. Maybe she couldn't.

Adam took his own chair and gave Emile a questioning look.

"I gave Amy a ride back from Beauford this morning when Cameron failed to pick her up." He settled himself in the chair beside Amy.

Adam closed his eyes and seemed to be searching for answers. Finally, he threaded his fingers together, placed his hands on the desk, and leaned forward.

"Amy, Cameron came to my office a month ago and told me y'all were moving. He made all the arrangements."

"Moving *where?*" Amy demanded.

"California. He said he was relocating for his job. And you mean to say, he told you none of this?"

Amy shook her head. "There has to be some kind of mix-up."

Adam tapped a few keys on his computer. "Here's the file. He checked in with me twice by phone after our initial meeting. He emailed three more directives after that. The movers were to arrive at ten this morning. He sold the Audi first and the Jaguar a few days later. That would have been two weeks ago. The new owners were to pick up the keys at eleven. And I see by Lila's notes that they have."

"What? He sold my car?" Amy exploded. "He would not do that."

So Amy wasn't crazy or a stalker. Time for a save.

"Adam," Emile said, "how is it that Cameron Snow could have done these things without Amy's knowledge?"

Adam shrugged. "The unit was in Cameron's name alone."

Emile turned to Amy. "This is true?"

She nodded. "Cameron already lived here when I came to live with him. We weren't married … It was something I never thought about."

"But you were going to be married?"

She looked at her hands. "I thought so. We weren't officially engaged, but I assumed. He always talked like we would. Or he used to." Her face had gone from snow white to bright red. Now she was embarrassed.

"But her things," Emile said. "And how could he sell her car?"

"Our directive was to have the contents of the condo packed. It never occurred to me that Amy didn't know what was going on, but even if I had known, I could not have legally told her. As for the car, I have no knowledge of that. We had no part of that transaction apart from surrendering the keys to the people with proper ID."

Emile reached out and put a hand on Amy's shoulder. She jerked away. He could understand that—not wanting to be touched. Who would after such a betrayal?

"We will call the police. He stole your car. Probably forged your name."

Amy didn't look up, but shook her head.

"Don't tell me you want to protect him? This man has stolen from you and abandoned you."

"I'm trying to process it all." When she finally looked at him, her face was filled with shame. "I have no legal grounds. Cameron thought I needed a new car. I found what I wanted online. He made all the arrangements. He handled my finances like he handles his clients', so you see, he had access."

"Well, not quite like his clients'. Else he'd be in jail." This might be worse than Emile imagined. It sounded like she had money of her own.

"I'm sorry," Adam said. "I am so sorry all this happened."

"It isn't your fault," Amy said.

"I was expressing regret," Adam said. "I wish there was something I could do."

"Here's the thing I don't understand," Amy said. "If he didn't want to be with me anymore, why didn't he just say so? Why go through all of this?"

Whoa, no. Hell, no. Giving a cute girl a ride was one thing. Discussing a relationship was another. Plus, Emile had about twenty minutes before he needed to head to the practice rink. It was only two blocks away, but he liked to be early. First, if possible.

He stood. "Is there somewhere I can take you? Your family? Are they in town?"

She shook her head. "They live in south Georgia." Emile was a little sketchy on American geography, but he was confident he didn't have time to make it to Georgia—south or not—in twenty minutes.

"Then a friend or a workmate?"

"I don't work. I sold my business a while back, and I can't work in my field for four more years." Then a look of surprise came over her face. "I guess I haven't really made any friends since I moved here." She said it like that had just occurred to her. "There's my hairdresser. And I sometimes talk to those nice girls at Foolscap and Vellum where I buy my bullet journals and wrapping paper, but I don't really know them." That was sad. Emile had at least ten places he could go if he needed somewhere to stay. Five of those wouldn't even ask questions. Apparently, Amy had not even one.

Well, she wasn't his problem. Even if she wasn't crazy, there was nothing he could do. Let Adam Fairly deal with her. What had he said? "We take care of our residents from first day to last—if there must be a last." Amy might not have signed any papers. Maybe she never paid any money—though he doubted that. But she'd been a resident. He might not have finished college, but he knew the definition of *resident*. *To reside.* She had definitely resided.

Now, how to get out of the room without looking like a dick? Was there a way?

She looked at her pocketbook, then picked it up and hugged it to her chest like it was her only possession. And it probably was.

Adam tossed him a frantic look, and Emile had his answer—there *was* no way to leave this room without looking like a dick, without *being* a dick.

He rose, took her arm, and urged her to her feet. "Come along, *chérie*. I will take you to my home." Because what else, short of a homeless shelter? He didn't know where to find one of those. Probably, Adam didn't either. It wasn't likely that had ever come up as one of the things that residents of Star View Towers needed, unless it was on a scavenger hunt list for one of those home association activities they did every few months.

"I can't let you do that," Amy said.

"Then what?" Emile asked. It was a valid question.

"Come along." He pulled her toward the door, and she let him. "I must go to practice. You will be alone to rest and think. You've had a shock."

How, how, how had this happened? He had no clue, but it had happened. He was in deep. This bastard Cameron Snow was in the wind.

But for now, he needed some ice under his feet.

CHAPTER SIX

It was easy to let Emile's décor distract Amy from the day's events. She didn't want to think about it yet.

Emile had let her in, quickly mixed a protein shake, and left again for hockey practice, drinking it as he went out the door. He'd said something about how she should make herself at *maison*. She didn't speak French, but she got the drift—*home*, though the French word sounded more like *mansion* than *home*. It would be a stretch to call Emile's condo a mansion, but it was a lot closer to one than hers and Cameron's—not that they had a condo anymore. Of course, she never had, not really. She'd just been squatting.

Amy beat the thought back. Obviously, she was going to have to think about it soon and for a very long time. Now that she knew Cameron wasn't hurt, dead, or kidnapped, she just needed a little grace period before letting her head tell her heart that he had left her because he didn't love her.

At that very thought, she wanted to slap herself. Why the hell was she thinking about lost love when he had not only taken everything she owned, but he'd also planned it in the most devious way? The bastard had made love to her just this morning knowing full well he was going to dump her in Beauford and hurry back to Nashville in time for the new owners to pick up her car. Still, she didn't want to think about it. Not now. So she walked from room to room, making herself at *maison*—not to the extent that she opened drawers or closets, but if a door wasn't locked, she figured what was on open display was fair game for looking.

The furnishings were surprising. If she had thought about it at all, Amy would have figured Emile would favor a modern, sleek, neutral design—not unlike Cameron's taste. Cameron might have liked Emile's brown leather sectional couch, but he would never have tolerated the rest of it—antique world globes, giant wall clocks with Roman numerals, pictures hanging from chains, pendulum lights with bubble glass, lamps with swing-out arms, and bookcases filled with baskets and branches in vases. There wasn't a single inch that wasn't covered with *something*.

Amy didn't dislike it exactly. It was certainly cozier than her former home, but it all seemed so, so … *canned*. It was like she'd seen it all before.

It was when she wandered into a guest bathroom with its raw pine, marble-topped vanity and ladder-like shelving unit with rolled up towels in wire baskets that it hit her.

Pottery Barn. He had bought whole catalog pages from Pottery Barn.

She began to laugh, though she wasn't sure why. Certainly today was not a day for laughter, but there was just something so endearing about the cast iron airplanes, kaleidoscopes, and brass hourglasses.

Hourglasses. *Time.* What the hell was she going to do next? A wave of cold went through her, and it wasn't the kind of cold that turning up the heat would help. Nonetheless, she chose a honey-colored throw from a big basket of similar blankets, sank down on the couch, and covered herself.

She needed to think of logistics. Money would be no problem. At least she had plenty of that—it was just accessing it right now. She needed to go down to the bank. Surely, as soon as she explained the situation in person, they would release her money.

But what to do until then? She poured the contents of her purse on the couch. For now, this was all she had in the world. Makeup bag with a few basics, sunglasses, bullet journal, zipper bag with about thirty pens in various colors, a phone that was no use, wallet with equally useless credit cards, and $84.38.

Where were her things? Her books, hairbrush, photo albums, and winter coat? Gone, along with her panties, English breakfast tea, and the pearl earrings her grandparents had given her for high school graduation. She didn't even have a change of clothes or a place to sleep tonight.

What kind of hotel room could she get for $84.38? Nothing within walking distance of here, but maybe at some place like a Comfort Inn out by the interstate. Emile would probably drive her there when he got home, but how would she get to the bank tomorrow?

She needed a plan. *If it works on paper, it will work in implementation.*

She picked up her bullet journal and quickly leafed past the Beauford pages. She couldn't look at them now, couldn't stand to remember how hopeful and happy she'd been this morning.

She chose her orange LePen because it was fall and orange was a cheerful color. She turned to a blank page in her journal and pondered what to title it. *How to Get My Life Back* was the first thing that popped in her head, but she batted it away. Her life wasn't gone. She just needed to straighten it out. So she wrote *How to Fix this Mess.* She was considering what rubber stamps and stickers to use to dress up the page, but then she remembered she didn't have any.

She needed her stuff back. That was something she would put on her list. Cameron had abandoned her. Okay. It was hard to swallow, but that was the least of her worries. He had no use for her things. Except for her car, surely he had just stashed them somewhere. She had to find him and find out where. The car was gone, but she'd consider that a life lesson and forget it. She could get another car as soon as she got access to her money. But that wouldn't be the first item on her list. Amy ran through her mind what she was going to put on the page so she would get it in the right order. She didn't like to make mistakes in her journal.

- Find a place to stay tonight.
- Go to the bank tomorrow and get new debit and credit cards.
- Get my phone working again or get a new one.
- Buy some toiletries, a suitcase, and a few changes of clothes.
- Check into the Hyatt or the Hilton downtown.
- Get a car.
- Find Cameron and get my things.
- Invite Emile out to dinner to thank him for being so nice, but make sure he knows it's not a date.

There were other things that needed to go on that list—things like:

- Tell my family what happened.
- Decide where I'm going to live.
- Go there, wherever that is.
- Make Cameron tell me why he did this to me.

But she wasn't ready to write that down yet. Suddenly, she was very tired. She laid her journal and pen on the table—the one with the rows and rows of little drawers—pulled the throw up to her neck, and drifted off to sleep.

CHAPTER SEVEN

Though it was unlikely that any of his teammates would have arrived yet, the Music City Ice Center was alive with noise and activity when Emile entered. There was always a lot going on this time of day—youth hockey practices, figure skating lessons, public skates. He paused to look through the door of rink D where the Junior Nashville Sound, the 16-20 year olds, were practicing. Juniors were the first level of elite hockey after youth hockey.

He'd loved his junior years as much as he'd hated his time in youth hockey, because junior hockey meant living away from home with a host family—not that he'd wanted to get away from his mother and sister. He'd just thought it would be better for everyone if he didn't live with them. After all, he was the one who infuriated Andre. Emile had thought with him gone, his mother and Gabriella would be able to live in peace. He'd been wrong about that. Emile understood now that a man like Andre was always going to have a punching bag—it was a just a matter of who. Turns out, he should have stayed and let it be him.

But he hadn't, and he'd hit the jackpot when he'd been drafted by the Buxton Ice Demons and Paul and Johanna Lindell had become his billet parents. Not every junior hockey player was so lucky, but the Lindells had provided him with a warm, welcoming home where clean clothes appeared like magic and he had the best food he'd ever had in his life. They treated him like family, but it was only after his son-of-a-bitch stepfather broke Gabriella's arm and knocked his mother down the stairs that Emile knew he *was* family. They'd taken Emile back to Canada for his mother's funeral, and when they found out that eleven-year-old Gabriella had no place to go, they'd gone through a mountain of red tape to bring her back to North Dakota to live with them.

Bad times. Good times. One always followed the other.

He wondered if the kids on the Junior Sound team had happy billet homes. The kid in the net wasn't bad. He'd stop by their practice one day next week.

When he entered the Sound locker room, he expected it to be empty, like it usually was when he arrived, but today he got a surprise—another one. The head equipment manager was not only there, but he was also fussing with things in Emile's stall.

"*Bonjour*, Packi," Emile said.

The weathered, gray-haired man looked up from hanging Emile's practice sweater in the oversized goalie stall. He'd played minor league hockey in the days when bloody fights were practically required but helmets were not, and he had the scars to prove it. Weathered and gray, he might be, but no one could accuse Oliver Klepacki of being wizened or weak. He was straight and strong, and Emile imagined a woman of a certain age would have said he was handsome. Maybe a woman of any age.

"*Cześć*," Packi said in Polish. Emile had learned his lesson about pointing out that Packi was a native of Milwaukee and had never set foot in Poland. Packi had given it right back to him; he cared not that Emile was a star and a two-time winner of the Vezina Trophy. Anyway, so what Emile if hadn't been to France—yet? He'd get around to it. On the other hand, Packi said he had no desire to go to Poland. He began to arrange Emile's pads.

"What are you doing?" Emile asked.

"I've decided to take care of you myself for a while. I sharpened your skates. I told Caleb and Marty not to touch them for the time being."

This stopped Emile in his tracks. Packi supervised two equipment managers and two locker room attendants. He ordered new equipment, made repairs on the bench during games, sharpened skates, and bossed his underlings around. He did not hang sweaters and put players' stalls in order—except when he did.

Every once in a while, Packi assumed taking care of a player when he needed a little extra care—sometimes when bad things happened, like when Jake Champagne was going through a divorce or when Mike Webber's mother died. But sometimes it was because of good things. He'd catered to Glaz when Noel was pregnant and to Mikhail Orlov when he, Sharon, and their three children were moving to a different house. Jan Voleck had gotten special care during the time leading up to his wedding to Krystal, the puck bunny who was seven years his senior—though no one could be sure if that was a good thing or bad. Probably bad, though Emile knew from personal experience she was good in bed—or really not so much in bed as up against the wall in the handicapped stall in the women's toilet at the Big Skate.

Glaz and some of the others swore that Packi had some kind of magical sixth sense, that he just knew when someone needed some extra help, but Emile didn't believe in that any more than he believed in superstition.

But there wasn't anything particularly good or bad going on in Emile's life, so why him and why now?

Packi handed him an insulated container and a fork. "You didn't have time to eat before coming here today, did you? Though you would have, if you didn't have to be the first one here. If I was guessing, I'd say you might have had a protein shake."

"How did you know?" Emile opened the container. It was his usual quinoa and wild rice with chicken on top.

"I know my boys. I know when there's something going on." He picked up Emile's helmet and began to polish it as if it were game day. "When you have this touched up, you should add something for the Stanley Cups."

Parfait! Why hadn't he thought of that?

"You are the wisest man I know, Packi."

Packi looked up and raised his eyebrows. "Because I thought of a new way to embellish your ego? Do you want to talk about what's going on with you?"

Emile took a bite of the chicken. "There's nothing going on with me." He pointed to the food. "But this is good. *Merci.*"

"Nothing going on? You sure?" He replaced the helmet on the shelf. "I cooked that chicken myself. I didn't just dump in a can of that stuff like you do."

"Maybe you should teach me to cook chicken."

"I could teach you a lot of things." Packi picked up one of Emile's skates. "Laces looking a little worn. I thought I'd change them."

"Good idea. You didn't tape my sticks did you?"

Packi sat down next to Emile in Swifty's stall and began to unlace the skates. "You know I never mess with a man's stick-taping unless he wants me to. You tape your own."

"Always." Emile finished his food and began to undress. He liked to stretch in the locker room and then again on the ice before anyone else arrived.

"I've heard that ballerinas sew the ribbons on their toe shoes themselves. It's kind of the same thing." Packi wove the new laces through the eyelets slowly and deliberately. Emile knew he could do it lightning fast with just as much precision. He'd seen him do it on the bench during games. A Sound player never missed his rotation during a game because of equipment failure.

"Really?" Emile was impressed. He'd been to the ballet. He'd wanted to like it like he wanted to like opera and modern art, but in the end he just didn't get it. "You know of ballet?"

"No. But I know of my wife. She likes to go, and I like her. Quite a lot. So, I go. Sometimes."

Emile had nothing to contribute to a ballet discussion, so he changed the subject.

"Tell me, Packi, what do you know of Cameron Snow?"

Packi looked up, surprised. "Voleck's agent? Not a lot. I've seen him around a few times. I didn't cotton to him. Too slick. You're not thinking of changing agents are you?"

"No. Miles suits me, and he has become my friend. In any case, I would not choose Snow. I am not sure of all the details, but I met his girlfriend today—or former girlfriend. It seems he has abandoned her and maybe taken all her money."

"And she let that happen? Is she stupid?"

"No. She's very smart." Emile wasn't sure how he knew that, but he was certain of it. "It's a mystery."

Packi gave out a gruff little laugh. "And you say you have nothing going on with you? Where is this woman right now?"

Chagrined, Emile admitted, "At my home. But it's temporary. By the time I return from practice, she will have figured out a plan." Probably she'll want to go to her family. Maybe one of them was en route, even now, to collect her. Certainly, if that had happened to Gabriella, that's where he'd be—even if it was the Stanley Cup finals. The Sound would have to make do with Case Cole, Emile's backup.

"So, she's good at figuring out plans?"

In truth, Emile didn't know. But if she wasn't, he was. He could buy her a ticket and put her on a plane to Georgia. Yes. That's what he'd do unless she had a better idea.

"Glad to hear there's nothing going on in your life." Packi finished lacing the skate and picked up the other one. "I hope she doesn't steal the silver."

"I don't have any silver." Though he would hate to lose the nice flatware set he'd bought at Pottery Barn. "She wouldn't take it. She's not the type."

"And you know this about her? You've known her how long?" Packi put down the second skate, picked up the first one again, and began wiping it down with a cloth.

"Not long." No way was he going to admit to anyone that he had left a woman he'd known four hours in his house alone.

"*How* long?"

"Four hours." Unless he was asked directly by someone he respected—and it was impossible not to respect a man who got tears in his eyes over a good win or a bad loss, and out-and-out cried without shame over a great win.

"Uh huh." Packi could confer more with an "uh huh" and head shake than most people could with entire French and English vocabularies.

"You're probably wondering why I know she wouldn't steal from me."

"I wasn't wondering. But why don't you tell me?"

"I am pretty sure she had some money. She said she'd sold her business and signed a non-compete contract."

"People don't usually sell their businesses without collecting money. What was her business?"

"She didn't say. It doesn't matter."

"It matters. Could have been a computer software company. Could have been a tattoo parlor or food truck."

"Do tattoo parlor and food truck owners sign non-competes?"

"Seems less likely than if she had a software company."

"I have considered getting a tattoo to match my helmet and mask."

"And your car. Don't forget that. And don't forget to add the trophies."

"If she's a tattoo artist, she could do the job."

"If you want to take your clothes off in front of her, just do it. From what I hear, you usually find a way."

"I wouldn't say usually. Only sometimes." And it seemed only with women who were interested in Goaltender Emile, but not the Emile who caught colds and wanted a Christmas tree. He had struck out completely with two women whom he could have imagined having Christmas Eve with him and Gabriella—Abby Whitman, who was a real hockey fan from the cradle, and Hélène-Louise Soileau, who could speak fluent French. They were both classy, sophisticated, smart, and educated. "Anyway, I don't want to take my clothes off for Amy."

"Amy? That's her name? You were telling me how you know she won't steal the silver?"

"Apart from the fact that I own no silver?"

"It's a figure of speech. Symbolic for your belongings."

"Right. I know because she found it so hard to accept that Cameron Snow stole from her. Only someone who would not steal wouldn't see it right away."

"Would you steal?"

"No. Why would I? I have plenty." He made eight million dollars a year, plus bonuses and endorsements. Right now, he had all that he and Gabriella would ever need—and he had a few more years ahead of him. There would be more hockey seasons and more underwear, wine, and chocolate commercials.

"Refusing to steal has more to do with the character of a man than what he's got. But regardless, you wouldn't steal, and you saw it," Packi pointed out.

"Not the same thing. I am an outsider. Uninvolved."

"Uninvolved? Uh huh." Emile didn't like it when Packi wouldn't look up from what he was doing when he said *uh huh*—like now, when he just kept wiping skates like a victory over the Blackhawks next week depended on it.

"That's right. But now that the shock is over and she's had some time alone to think, I am sure she knows. She will go to south

Georgia to her family. They will set things right for her. That's what family does." Or what they *should* do.

Though, Emile had to admit he was getting pretty curious about the whole thing. Maybe he'd find out what happened. Emile didn't have the inclination or skill to find Cameron, but he knew someone who did—at least the skill. And the fee he would be willing to pay Miles would provide the inclination.

Packi set the newly laced skates on the shelf. "Are you going to stretch or are you going to stand there all day in your underwear thinking about this woman who isn't impacting you?"

CHAPTER EIGHT

There was only one thing worse than waking and being unsure of where you were—waking in an unknown location and finding huge brown eyes staring at you.

Amy sat up abruptly. She'd slept hard without dreaming. Too bad she couldn't have carried on that way for a few days. Emile sat on the coffee table holding her bullet journal. He'd shoved aside a stack of books, a tray of candles, and a brass dog to make room for himself, and he didn't even try to hide that he'd been looking at her journal. In fact, he held it up.

"I like your little book. Is very beautiful—all the little pictures you have drawn of the stores in Beauford."

She reached for the journal. He didn't give any indication that he noticed she wanted him to hand it over. He closed it, laid it on his knee, but held on to it. His hand covered the entire book.

"You are very beautiful."

Surprise shot through her. It seemed an eternity since anyone had told her she was beautiful. When was the last time? Maybe back before she had moved in with Cameron, when he was still trying. She hadn't realized it had been so long, because being told she was beautiful wasn't something that she needed, that mattered to her very much. Still, it was nice to hear, so it must have mattered some.

She didn't acknowledge the compliment. If he could pretend he didn't know she wanted her journal, she could pretend he hadn't said she was beautiful.

"Do you always shove things to the side that are in your way?" she asked.

He frowned. "I don't know what you mean. My friends and my sister are important to me. I would never disregard them, even when they are sometimes not convenient. I try to remember that I am not always convenient."

Oh, good cow. A deep thinker. Just what she needed today—a philosophical discussion with a hockey player.

Amy shook her head. "I was referring to the things on the coffee table that you shoved to the side so you could sit down. And the scarecrow on the hay bale earlier."

"Ahh!" He threw back his head and laughed, displaying the whitest, most perfect teeth she'd ever seen. But wait. Not completely perfect. One of his bicuspids was the tiniest bit crooked. "*Oui.* In that way, maybe I do. They can be set right again." He glanced at the journal. "Though all things cannot be set right. You should draw your beautiful self."

"I can't draw people." If she could, she'd draw his mouth. "Only whimsical little doodles." There was nothing whimsical about that mouth.

"You drew Eat Cake. That is where my sister is an apprentice baker. She makes very fine cakes. Cookies, too."

Amy nodded. "I intended to go there." She had thought it would be a fun stop for a midafternoon snack for Cameron and her. Cameron liked a midafternoon sweet snack—maybe a little too much.

"But you didn't go to Gabriella's shop?"

"No. Piece by Piece was as far as I got. And we both know how well that went." She neatly folded the throw she had covered herself with and set it to the side.

He leaned forward, rested his forearms on his thighs, and let the journal dangle between his knees. When she reached out and captured the book, he didn't try to stop her or even take notice that she had taken it from him.

"I am very sorry this happened to you."

"I appreciate that, and I appreciate how much you have helped me."

"I haven't helped you." *No one can help you*, hung in the air. He might as well have said it, but Amy didn't believe that.

"Not true." She tried to sound breezy. "I might still be sitting on that hay bale."

He shook his head. "You would have found your way off that hay bale. So, no. I haven't really helped you. But I'm willing to."

"Thank you. I suppose you read my list of how to fix this mess."

He half closed his eyes and bounced his shoulders and head back and forth a bit. "Was hard not to read, especially the part about me."

"You?" What was he talking about?

"The one that said, 'Invite Emile out to dinner to thank him for being so nice, but make sure he knows it's not a date.'"

"Oh, right." She *had* written that down. "I do have another favor to ask."

"Yes?"

"Will you take me out by the interstate? I need to get a room for the night." If she was going to ask for favors, might as well go big. "And if it isn't too much trouble, maybe pick me up in the morning and drop me off at the bank?"

He frowned and bit his bottom lip. "I thought maybe you'd like me to take you to the airport so you can go to your family in south Georgia." He pronounced *south Georgia* very deliberately, enunciating each syllable.

Every muscle in her body tightened. "No. I can't do that."

"You do not get along with your family?"

"It's not that. I just can't go there." And God help her, she could not. They would welcome her, of course. But they'd never trusted Cameron, and they'd been right. They would have to know eventually that she and Cameron had broken up. She could take that. People broke up all the time. But her family didn't have to know that Cameron had abandoned her in a quilt store and sold her car, or that she had temporarily misplaced her belongings and her assets. That would be too much to endure. They wouldn't say they'd told her so. In fact, they *hadn't* told her so—not in so many words. But there would be no hiding that they weren't surprised.

He looked at her for a long time with a look that told her his mind was busy processing and trying to analyze the situation. Apparently that's what deep-thinking, philosophical goalies did.

He took her hand. "*Ma belle*, there is no need for embarrassment. There is no embarrassment with family. If this happened to my sister Gabriella, I would want her to come to me. I would comfort her and take care of her."

"Really? And if this happened to you? Would you want to go to her? Or the rest of your family?"

His expression froze. "It would not—" He stopped short but not short enough.

"To you? Are you sure?"

"I didn't mean that."

"Certainly you did. But it doesn't matter. I can't leave town until I get my money back. Going to the bank is my first priority."

"Not first. Your first priority is to get a place to stay tonight. I read the list."

"I'm aware."

He took a breath. "You can stay here tonight."

"No." Her answer was fast and firm. She'd never been surer of anything.

"Why not? I have seven bedrooms. You can choose the one you like. I am not asking you to my bed." He spread that mouth into a droll little grin. "I am not a killer. I am a famous goaltender with two Stanley Cup rings. I have never been caught breaking the law."

His dark eyes flashed, all flirty-like. How did he even do that? "Look me up on the Internet. You'll see that I've never been arrested."

She let out a long breath. "I don't have access to the Internet. Remember? No phone service. No computer. No tablet." Two more things she needed to add to her list. "Besides don't think I didn't catch that you said you'd never been *caught.* You didn't say you *hadn't* broken the law."

"Come now. Surely you go faster than the speed limit from time to time."

"No. I can't walk that fast and I don't have a car."

He tossed his head and gave her a sympathetic look. "Still, I might have jumped into a snowbank naked during my rookie year as a junior, but I am not a serial killer. You're safe here with me. You can sleep in Gabriella's room. There are some clothes in there. She is taller than you and not as—" He cupped his hands in front of his chest to indicate breasts. "But still. You could find something. She would not mind."

The thought of clean clothes was so appealing. It wasn't that she felt particularly dirty despite the amount of time she'd spent hanging out on a hay bale this morning. But it was as though all the bad of the day had seeped into the fabric of her clothes, and if she could cast them off, things would seem better. She would have burned them if they weren't her only worldly possessions.

No, that's not true, she admonished herself. She had things; she just didn't have them now.

Maybe she *should* stay here tonight. She wasn't sure her $84.38 would buy her a room, even at a Comfort Inn. Even if it would, it was certain that no Comfort Inn was going to provide her with clothes, though they could probably be counted on for a toothbrush.

He must have read her mind about the toothbrush. "In Gabriella's bathroom, there will be all the things you need for your bath and such."

He had a point. She had nothing to fear from him, and someone with only $84.38 and a cell phone/paperweight between her and the rest of the world couldn't afford pride.

"And if I am in your sister's room, where would she sleep?"

"She does not live here. She has an apartment above the pastry shop in Beauford. But she stays here on occasion—sometimes after a game if it's late."

"Well, if I stayed here, I wouldn't have to bother you to take me to the bank tomorrow." It was only a few blocks away. "And soon as I get a new credit card and access to my accounts, I can be out of your hair. I'll go first thing."

Emile dropped his eyelids to half-mast. "Amy, are you certain that going to the bank will benefit you? Do you think you will be able to get a new card and access to your money?"

Amy had always been taught that it was tacky to talk about money, but she had to make Emile understand that she was not without resources.

"Emile. I had a personal organizing business called Apple Pie Order. I started small but I did well. Last year, I sold it to a large organizing company. I don't pretend that I made as much as a professional athlete would make, but it was very lucrative."

"*How* lucrative?"

"Five million. Since then, there have been investments. It has grown."

Emile looked surprised but remained silent.

"I am not without resources. I have checking, savings, and investment accounts. I just can't access them right now."

"And you think going to the bank will solve this?"

"Of course." Why wouldn't it? "I just need to talk to someone face-to-face and explain it all."

"You must consider that Cameron may have stolen all your money—as he stole your car."

She wasn't ready to consider that, though not because she didn't think he was capable. He'd proven all too well what he was capable of. It was just unthinkable.

Emile ran his hand across his forehead, through his hair, and down the back of his neck. "*D'accord*. I must meet my friends Bryant and Jarrett at the gym later. But for now I am famished." He stood and held out his hand to her. "Please. Let's go down and get a bit of food at Eat In." He named one of the restaurants on the building's ground floor.

She knew from experience that a "bit of food" was going to cost more than her $84.38, but she'd return the favor and take him out soon.

When he paused to put the objects on the coffee table back in order, it struck her that she liked Emile. Maybe they would be friends.

CHAPTER NINE

Emile followed Amy out of the bank. He did not take her arm to steady her until they were on the street. Considering what she'd just been through, she would not have wanted to look weak in front of the bank employees.

It had been as bad as Emile had feared. That's why he had insisted on going with her—and insisted he had. She hadn't wanted it. He probably shouldn't have, but he hadn't been able to stop himself.

They were at the other end of the block before she spoke. "I suppose you're wondering how someone as stupid as I am could have earned five million dollars in the first place."

He steered to a stop in front of the Starbucks. "I wasn't wondering that."

"How could you not?" Even in Gabriella's ill-fitting clothes, Amy was beautiful. Her thick, shiny dark hair hugged her head like a sleek little cap, and those purple eyes were real. He knew because he'd asked her last night before bed if she'd needed contact solution. "I *am* stupid."

"*Non.* Cameron Snow was very crafty."

She shook her head. "You heard it all. All the accounts were joint *and* I signed a financial power of attorney."

It was true. As far as getting access to the accounts, there were no accounts to access. He'd closed them all.

Maybe she had legal recourse, but it didn't sound like it. Emile felt helpless, more helpless than he'd felt when he'd been a youth hockey Bantam and hadn't been able to stop anything in that final playoff game—the one that would have gotten them a championship if he'd been able to do what was expected of him. He'd known he'd have the worst beating of his life coming when he got off the ice, and he'd been right.

Amy turned her head and gazed inside the Starbucks.

"Would you like a coffee? Sheldon from *The Big Bang Theory* says one should offer a hot beverage in times of distress."

She closed her eyes and let out a sound that was half sigh and half laugh. "Wouldn't you know it? I don't even drink coffee. I drink tea." She gazed back inside. "Which sounds good, but I don't want to go in there."

Neither did Emile. There was standing room only. Then he got an idea. He couldn't solve her financial/breakup woes, but he could get her some tea. Breakfast, too. She'd barely eaten last night and not at all this morning, though he'd offered her chocolate milk and a granola bar.

"Come with me." He took her arm again and guided her across the street. "This way."

"Where are we going?"

"The Big Skate. It's—"

"I know. The sports bar where the Sound hangs out. Remember, I live in Sound Town, too. Or I did. And I also know they don't open until eleven."

It was barely ten. They had arrived at the bank as soon as it'd opened, but it hadn't taken long for Amy to face the music.

At that moment, they arrived at the heavy dark wood, brass, and glass door of the Big Skate.

"See?" Amy pointed to the hours etched in gold on the glass of the door. "Open at eleven."

"They will open for me." Emile rapped on the glass.

It was Carlo who opened the door a crack. Emile had hoped for one of the girls. Not that it would matter in the end. It would just go faster with someone he'd put in plenty of flirt time with.

"Mr. Giroux," Carlo said. "We open at eleven."

"That's what everyone keeps saying." He stepped inside and pulled Amy along with him. "Yet we are inside." He gave Carlo a smile, but he did not bother to bite his bottom lip. "See?" He swept his arm in an arc to indicate their surroundings.

Carlo looked around wild-eyed.

"Do not worry, Carlo. We will find our way to our seats. Please bring us bacon, scrambled eggs with cheese, and some of that ciabatta that you use for the jerk chicken sandwich, toasted. Orange juice. And a pot of tea for the lady."

Carlo opened and closed his mouth like a fish. "Mr. Giroux, we don't serve breakfast."

Emile put a hand on his shoulder. "Carlo, my friend. Think outside the box. You have bacon cheeseburgers, so there is bacon. Same for cheese. Every kitchen has eggs. We've already talked about the bread."

"It's all right, Carlo." Oh, good. It was Teresa, one of the managers—older than the wait staff and very sensible. "Go tell Griff to make the food." She turned to Emile. "If it's not the French Kiss out and about bright and early. So, you are having an egg emergency today?"

"No so much an egg emergency as a tea emergency. The eggs are extra."

Teresa nodded. "I'll just check and make sure Carlo remembered everything." She looked over her shoulders. "And let me warn you. We don't have a teapot. We only make iced tea, but we'll do the best we can."

Emile escorted Amy to his regular booth—against the wall but in the middle. He liked to sit directly under his framed autographed sweater that was surrounded by framed pictures of him in action.

Amy didn't even glance at his wall.

"Do you always get what you want?" she asked.

"*Non*. Not even today. I wanted an omelette with wild mushrooms and brie, but I thought that might be too much to ask."

"But insisting on eating in a restaurant that isn't open isn't? Do you do this often?"

"Never before." But never before had he wanted to please someone so much—and that was a scary thought. In the past, he'd just concentrated on pleasing someone if he'd happened upon them. He'd never gone out of his way to create a situation. At first, she had been an inconvenience. Beautiful, but an inconvenience. Then something had happened as he watched her in the bank this morning. She'd been so sure things would work out the way she wanted, because it was the right thing. But when it hadn't gone that way, she'd bravely accepted it and shook hands with the bank president and thanked him. She had blamed no one except herself. *Quiet grace* was the phrase that came to mind. "This is my first time to break in to a restaurant."

Amy fiddled with the silverware roll. "I guess pity will make a person do strange things."

The comment took him aback.

"Pity? You think I pity you? *Absurdité*. Why would I pity you?"

"Isn't it obvious?"

"*Non*. No." He translated just in case she hadn't understood and shook his head for good measure. "You are very beautiful. You are obviously smart and talented. You ran a business and made a lot of money once. You can do it again, if you like."

"Maybe. In five years. Well, more like four now. And there are those who might debate whether I'm smart."

"But those people are not here. If they were, I would make them leave." This time when he smiled, he did bite his bottom lip. She didn't seem to notice. "As for the four years, you have your whole life. How old are you? I would say not even thirty."

She grimaced. "Twenty-seven. And that's what Cameron said—that I have the rest of my life."

"Even a clock is right twice a day."

She smiled a little. "That's a *broken* clock."

"Yes. That. As time moves on, you will learn more skills and get better and better. I am the one to be pitied. The average goalie retires at age twenty-eight. I am thirty—already living on borrowed time."

"But some do play longer. Cameron told me that once."

"The second time the broken clock is right. *Oui.* Some do. Many do. They say my teammate Thor is closer to forty than thirty-five. He's been lucky. If I am lucky, if I stay healthy, if some eighteen-year-old wonder infant doesn't come swinging in on a trapeze, I figure I have five more years."

She nodded. "What would you do then?"

"Maybe finish college. Maybe become a chef."

"Can you cook?" she asked.

"Not yet." This time she seemed to notice when he bit his bottom lip. He could tell because she touched her own bottom lip with the tip of her tongue. Such a simple little gesture inspired a not so simple response in his groin. He wondered if he could make her do it again.

"Would you go back to France?"

"Back? *Non.* Not *back.* I might go *to* France for the first time."

She widened those purple eyes. "You aren't French? I don't understand."

"*Oui.* I am, but not the same as from France. I am *Québécois.*"

"Would you go back?"

"To Québec? No. Too cold. I knew nothing but the coldest of winters until the NHL. I played my junior hockey in North Dakota. I played at the University of North Dakota for only one season before I decided it was not for me and signed with the Blues. St. Louis. Not so cold as the places I lived before, but cold.

Then I came to the Sound. Best weather yet. My sister is nearby, baking her little things. I don't want to leave here, but I might."

"Oh?"

"There are rumors that the Sound could be sold to someone who wants to move us to Massachusetts." He sighed. "If they move my net to Bruin country, I must go tend it."

She looked surprised. "Cameron has a Sound client. He must have known this, but he never mentioned it."

"Cameron did not mention many things." Amy looked like she'd been slapped, and Emile regretted the remark. "I'm sorry. I should have not said that. We were having a nice conversation, even if it was about me."

"No." She busied herself with unwrapping her flatware and laying out her utensils. "It's true. I suppose he was too busy plotting how to get away from me." Amy arranged her napkin in her lap. "Why do you suppose he did it?"

Emile spoke before he thought. "I can't imagine. If you were mine, I wouldn't want to get away from you."

Surprise shot through him—not because he'd uttered the words. He said things like that to women all the time in the name of flirting. *Non.* The surprise came because he meant it. People always said that Emile fell hard and fast, because he gave the full court press to women when he thought they might be a possibility—like Abby and Hélène-Louise. But the truth was, he'd never fallen at all. He'd only wanted to. He wouldn't know how to behave if he really did.

He might have been disappointed when Abby ended up with Rafe Beauford and Hélène-Louise with Bennett Watkins, but he never exactly missed the women. He certainly never longed for them. He missed the hunt, the possibility, but not Abby and Hélène-Louise themselves. But he couldn't see how Cameron Snow could keep from missing Amy. Any man would.

He probably shouldn't have said that to her, but he reiterated it nonetheless. "No man in his right mind would want to get away from you."

Amy smiled, and her eyes darkened from deep purple to inky purple. "That's a sweet thing to say to a down-on-her-luck woman you've known twenty-four hours."

Good. She hadn't believed him. That was for the best. It was also for the best that, just then, Teresa and Carlo showed up with their food, because Emile didn't have to answer.

Teresa set a metal pitcher down. "It's sweet iced tea, heated up," she said to Amy. "It was the best we could do."

"Perfect," Amy said, though even Emile knew that wasn't how you went about making hot tea. He wondered if Amy always said things were perfect to make people happy. He had a lot to learn about her. Amy poured tea into her mug and added a slice of lemon, but she didn't drink. Instead, she wrapped her hands around the mug and met his eyes. "You evaded my question. You must have some idea why he did it."

That again. "Which part?"

"All of it. Left me without a word. Took my money."

"I'd say one was because of the other. He left you without a word to get your money."

She shook her head. "It doesn't make any sense for a couple of reasons. First, he makes plenty of money. He has a long client list, including Reynolds Fallon from the San Francisco 49ers, Saxon Creed from the New England Patriots, and Patrick Jackson from the Atlanta Falcons. Those are his big names."

They were big names to be sure, and based on the percentage that Emile paid Miles, that alone should have Snow sitting pretty.

"My agent only has hockey players. Unusual that Cameron would have hockey and football players."

Amy nodded. "Unusual but not unheard of."

"True enough."

"Besides he had a reason. He'd like to start an agency eventually. He wants connections with as many sports as he can get."

"Then there's your answer," Emile said. "He wanted your money to start this agency."

She shook her head. "Again, it makes no sense. I offered him the money to do just that. He said he wasn't ready yet—that he needed a basketball player and a baseball player at least before setting up shop and hiring other agents." She took a sip of her tea and didn't even grimace. Either she liked it or she was very dedicated to being a good girl who never expressed dislike or caused trouble. "Besides," she went on, "he could have just taken the money and stayed here. He's proven he can do it, and I've proven that I wouldn't know the difference."

"Did he ever talk about where he wanted this agency to be?"

She picked up her fork and set it down again. "Yes. He liked Nashville. Not too big, not too small. Pro hockey and football. Minor league baseball. Convenient airport. At least that's what he said."

"And there's the weather."

She nodded and took a bite of her eggs. "He must have wanted away from me really bad. I wonder if he knows I would have left peacefully."

But not without your money. Emile had enough sense not to voice that. He ate a piece of bacon and kept quiet.

"But I wouldn't have gone without my money." Now, that was uncanny. She sipped her tea again. "I still don't get why he wanted it so much."

"I doubt he had accumulated as much as you had. That job doesn't come without expenses. And for some people, no matter what they have, it isn't enough."

"Do you think he planned it from the start?"

"The start of what?"

"From the time we were dating. Not that I had it then. I was doing well, but we were dating before I had the offer. It's true he encouraged me to sell, but he couldn't have known that was going to happen."

Emile shook her head. "I don't know, Amy. But I do think you need to find out if you have any recourse."

"I'll get right on that." For the first time he heard bitterness in her voice. "I'll write a big, high-powered lawyer a huge retainer check so he can tell me what we both know: I put the power in Cameron's hands. I wasn't crazy, coerced, or tricked. I made what was mine his, basically because I was lazy and thought we were going to get married and have babies. That's what I wanted—for what was mine to be his, ours. To share everything like my parents do, like my grandparents do."

She picked up her teacup, gave it a look of disdain, and slammed it down again. Good for her. She wasn't going to drink bad tea to prove what a good girl she was.

"And do you know what I don't get? What I *really* don't get?" The anger in her voice made the hair on the back of Emile's neck stand on end—and it wasn't even directed at him. "Do you?"

He nodded. "I think so?" Was that the right answer? Maybe not. "*Non.* Why don't you tell me?"

"My panties! Why did he take my panties? Who would want my used panties?"

Emile had heard of vending machines in other countries where used underwear was sold, but he did not think he wanted to share that with Amy.

"And my bullet journals. There's nothing secret in them, but nothing interesting either to anyone except me—recipes, movies I want to see, gift ideas for my family. He took my *bullet journals!*"

As far as Emile knew, there were no such vending machines for these bullet journals. But what did he know? He'd never heard of the things two days ago.

"Wrapping paper, ribbons, my three-hole punch, and label maker. My chain-smoking great-aunt's crystal ashtray that I used for my loose change." She looked at her plate and continued to intone her lost belongings like she was casting some kind of department store catalog spell. "Stickers, rubber stamps, *Outlander* DVDs, high school yearbooks, the ugly bridesmaid dress from Lulu's wedding, toiletries. And my retainer!"

Amy looked up and met Emile's eyes. "For what possible reason in the name of the archangel Michael would he want my retainer?"

He wondered if he kissed her if she would calm down. Probably not.

She had paused, so maybe she even wanted an answer. "I don't know, Amy. But we can find out. We can also find out if you have any legal recourse. I've got a guy."

She went blank. "A guy? You've got a guy? Where do you keep him?"

"My agent. He's a lawyer, too. He will find out. I believe he is in Montreal, but I will call him. He will fly in. Miles can confer with you and look into this." He picked up his phone and began to scroll.

"No!" She placed her hand on his arm, and a little shiver went through him. No matter that she only touched him to get his attention and stop him from calling Miles. "I absolutely do not want to confer with a lawyer. I want to forget it and let it go. I didn't have sense enough to protect myself, but I've got sense enough to know when there is no recourse." The fire went out of her face, and then she just looked defeated. "I'll figure something out."

He'd already gone to the bank when she hadn't wanted him to, so he wasn't going to push the issue with this new, mad-one-second-and-defeated-the-next Amy.

"As you wish, *chérie*." Her hand was still on his arm. "You may stay with me a while longer—until you figure something out, as you say."

She removed her hand. "I can't do that. You've already done too much for someone you don't even know."

That might be for the best. "So, what then? Are you ready to go to your family?" She'd just spoken of parents and grandparents who shared everything. It sounded like a nice place to be.

But she physically shuddered.

"I understand," Emile said. "But what will you do? Because if you don't want to stay with me, where you are most welcome, or go to your family, where you would also be most welcome, I don't know what else. Maybe a homeless shelter."

He'd meant it as a joke, but her head snapped up and he could see the wheels turning. She was actually considering this! She looked hopeful.

"I could do that. Yes. They will let me stay there until I get on my feet—which I will do, because I'll get a job."

"A job? You said you could not do this organizing work for five years."

"Four, now," she corrected him. "I can't work as an organizer, but I can do something else. My parents were right. No one should sit around idle. I need to work at something. And that's what I'll do."

He put up his hands. "I cannot allow you to go to a homeless shelter. I was joking."

"*Allow* me?" Purple lightning shot from her eyes.

"Oh, *now* you get all up in the air about someone telling you what to do. You didn't have any trouble turning your life over to Cameron Snow." Emile slammed his fork down.

"You are not Cameron."

"Damn right I'm not. I am no thief and I'm trying to help you."

That stopped her cold. She looked at him without blinking as she sat silently. He didn't know if that was good or bad, but when she spoke again, her voice was low and tired. "Emile, I've explained it to you. If there is any other option at all, I cannot call my family and ask for a plane ticket. I cannot tell them I don't have so much as a change of underwear or a toothbrush."

"You have a toothbrush. I gave you one last night."

"But it isn't really mine."

"Do you think I want it back?" Though the thought of exploring her mouth was appealing, he had no desire to share toothbrushes. "I gave you another option. And you did not explain why you couldn't do that."

"Stay with you? Unacceptable. I've never freeloaded off anyone in my life. Even at the homeless shelter, I'm sure everyone pitches in to keep the place clean and make the meals."

Emile opened his mouth to tell her she had to go to south Georgia. Any idiot could see that that was for the best. But that wasn't what came out of his mouth.

"What if you stayed with me and 'pitched in,' as you say?"

"And do what? Be on the lookout for new Pottery Barn products?"

"Sure." He was pleased and impressed that she recognized his décor style. "I have my groceries delivered. The Star View staff arranges for my errands—dry cleaning, having my car washed, having the house cleaned. All that costs. I could pay the same to you. Not that I would expect you to clean or wash my car. Just oversee that it's done." He tried hard to think of something else. If he had a dog, she could walk it. Maybe he could get a dog. "I am not good at packing for road trips. I always forget something, and my clothes are always wrinkled. I bet you are good at packing."

"Actually, I'm very good at it." He was amazed at the joy that went through him when he realized she was actually considering this. Might as well face it—for whatever reason, he wanted her to stay.

"So, you would be helping me," he said. Maybe she would go on the road with him. Best not to bring that up.

"Nashville's public transportation isn't great, but I think I could work it out for running the errands."

"No need for that. You can use the Land Rover."

"Land Rover? You have a second vehicle?"

He shrugged. "Can't drive the helmet all the time."

"Is it … er … customized? The Land Rover, I mean."

"No. Not beyond being purple, like the purple and silver of the Sound. Like your eyes."

That got a smile out of her. Having abandoned the tea altogether, she took a sip of her orange juice. "If I did this—if I stayed with you—"

"Yes?" It was as good as done.

"I couldn't let you pay me. I would do the things you need in exchange for a place to stay."

He shook his head. "*Non.* That is slavery. I am not a slaver. I want to employ you as—what would you say? Personal assistant? Yes. You are my *personal assistant.* There are those who would say it would be an imposition for a personal assistant to be expected to live with her employer."

"There are those who have not been abandoned and left destitute and homeless."

"No matter. One man has taken advantage of you this week. I will not be the second."

"It wouldn't be forever," she said. "Only until I figure all this out."

"Of course." He'd made the save. Every goaltender knew to take care of one shot at a time. "Also, there are some things I have been wanting—Swiss Chalet sauce, Toffee Crisp bars, butter tarts, cheese curds. I'll bet you are good at finding things that can't be found."

She scoffed. "Oh, please. In the age of the Internet and overnight shipping, everything can be found." She screwed up her face like she was thinking. "I can cook, too. I can make your meals."

This was going to be even better than he thought. "Wonderful. Especially for game day. It has been a very long time since I haven't had to worry about my own food on game day." He rose and offered her his hand to help her to her feet. "I feel my life already getting better."

He would call Miles later. By the end of the week, he would have some answers about Cameron Snow.

CHAPTER TEN

Amy stood in Emile's kitchen and considered the boxes stacked on the counters. They had been delivered this morning before she and Emile had left for the bank, but there had been no time to deal with them. "Just some stuff I ordered," Emile had said.

After crashing the Big Skate, Emile had insisted on advancing her some money so she could buy "some little things that you must miss." She'd learned her lessons well during her teenage summers working at The Peach Stand, and it had gone against her grain to accept money that she hadn't earned—but desperation and those little things she missed won out over her lessons and her grain. What did that mean anyway—going against the grain? As soon as she had Internet access again, she would look it up. She checked the pocket of her skirt for the tenth time in as many minutes to make sure the five one hundred dollar bills were still there. Right before leaving to go "stretch," Emile had casually produced a fat, leather money clip, peeled off five bills, and handed them to her.

The money in her hand felt like comfort, though she had no idea how long it would take her to work off the advance. They had not discussed the terms of their agreement—an agreement she had accepted only out of desperation, because she had been sure Emile didn't have enough needs to require a personal assistant. She'd gone straight from relying on one man to relying on another and one she hardly knew. The very thought of being dependent on another man gave her a sick feeling in the pit of her stomach. She would never feel safe again until she could rely totally on herself, and right now, that time seemed like so far in the future that it might as well be a pipe dream.

But one thing at time. She transferred the money to her wallet, but then thought better of it. She left one of the bills there beside her $84.38, hid another in her phone case, and took the remaining three hundred dollars to her room and placed them in a drawer underneath panties that were not her own.

Better not to have all that cash in one place—though it was probably no more than a third of what Emile carried in his wallet, and he didn't have any problem with it. Why didn't he have it in the bank? But if she had been carrying her money in her purse, she'd still have it. She beat back that thought, as she wanted to beat Cameron in the face.

Anyway, was it physically possible for someone carry that much money around? What was the largest bill made? That was something else she'd look up when she had a working phone again, which meant buying a new one.

She'd used Emile's phone to call tech support and learned that her present phone was useless—a brick, the representative had called it. The man had been sympathetic, but had only been able to talk to her hypothetically, because she couldn't remember her password and her bullet journal that contained all her passwords and other pertinent information for her electronics was gone. The rep's best guess was that Cameron had reported the phone stolen, then changed the password and the ID number to a bogus one. He was sorry, but there was nothing he could do.

But there was something she could do. It lifted her spirits that she could correct this one thing in her life without any help, unless you counted the money Emile had advanced her. She reached in her pocket again for the keys to the Land Rover that Emile had given her.

Replacing her laptop and tablet were out of the question, but she could get an Android smart phone and have money left. Having money left was important, even if there would be more forthcoming—though that wasn't a given. How was she to know if Emile would get tired of paying her for all those things he insisted he needed help with? And suppose he didn't get tired? It couldn't go on forever. She needed a long-term plan in case Cameron didn't come back for her.

In case Cameron didn't come back for her—where had that come from? Denial, shock, or just plain crazy? Even if he did return, she wouldn't be fool enough to take him back—*unless* he had a good explanation for what he'd done. She cast about a bit for what that explanation could be, but came up empty. She tried to invent something that involved Russian spies, extraterrestrials, and television evangelists with mad brainwashing skills.

Unlikely. No, impossible. But hadn't Cameron selling her car, taking her money, and abandoning her in a quilt shop seemed impossible a few days ago?

When she entered the kitchen again to get her purse, she remembered the boxes that had been delivered this morning. Maybe she should deal with those before going out to buy a phone—earn some of the money before she spent it. What was in them anyway?

She needed a box cutter. Surely there was a junk drawer in the kitchen. But upon opening several, she found that they were all junk drawers—only not exactly. Every one contained a jumble of flatware, rubber bands, scissors, tape, mail, take out menus, and assorted kitchen utensils. There was no rhyme or reason to anything, let alone flatware trays and dividers to bring order to chaos.

She shuddered at the sight of the mess, but was elated the thought of straightening it out. There was definitely a trip to The Container Store in her future, and the feeling that gave her was not too far removed from sexual satisfaction.

But she needed to get into those boxes, and there was still no box cutter.

To hell with it. She found a Henckels knife under some tea towels. Using it to open boxes couldn't be any worse for it than rattling around in that drawer with jar tops, cell phone chargers, screwdrivers, novelty bottle openers, and a purple and silver flashlight with *Nashville Sound* inscribed on the side.

The boxes were from Zulily, BOXED, Jet, and Amazon Prime Pantry.

It didn't take long to figure out that all the boxes contained food—canned chicken, packets of precooked quinoa and rice, Clif Bars, microwavable pasta meals, shelf stable chocolate milk, granola bars, canned soup, Gatorade, and crackers—so many crackers of all varieties. And Jell-O, mostly orange, but plenty of strawberry and lime, too. This stuff might be good for an apocalypse, but not much else.

When he'd said he had his groceries delivered, this had not been what she'd envisioned.

Her first inclination was to throw it all away, but it wasn't hers to dispose of. Putting it away would be the thing to do, but first she needed to get the lay of the land.

Why had she expected the pantry and cabinets would be in better shape than the drawers? There was food everywhere, along with Pottery Barn dishes, mugs, pots, and pans, and it was all mixed together—canned chicken, crackers, Ziploc bags, and plates in one cabinet. Mugs, Gatorade, and Jell-O in another. The only things ingestible in the pantry were cases of Clear Valley wine and boxes of *Au Chocolat* candy—but there was a George Foreman grill still in the box, a blender, a milkshake maker, a toaster oven, a slow cooker, and a punch bowl big enough to bathe a baby. Really? No real food in the pantry, but a punch bowl? There wouldn't have been room for food anyway, for the piles of hockey pads and sticks. At least the hockey equipment was new and didn't smell.

She wondered if Emile was anything like his home—orderly and beautiful (if you liked Pottery Barn) on the outside but a mess on the inside. She didn't wonder long, because she had clutter to conquer. The drawers could wait, but the pantry and cabinets couldn't. First, she moved the boxes of food onto the floor against the wall. She would unload everything from the cabinets onto the countertops, put like items together, and put them away in an orderly fashion. Then she'd think about unloading the boxes—whether into the garbage or pantry remained to be seen.

Amy had just climbed onto the stepladder that she'd found in the pantry and unloaded cereal bowls, water bottles, and boxes of granola bars on the counter, when she heard the front door open. It seemed a little soon for Emile to be returning, but maybe not. She didn't know what "stretch" was, never mind how long it took.

But when Amy came off the ladder, prepared to explain to Emile what she was doing and why he needed to buy some things from The Container Store, she came face-to-face with a tall blonde with a flow of waterfall curls that fell almost to her waist. She wore a rose and moss-colored flowing silk tunic over amber leggings that gave her the ethereal look of a fairy—though she couldn't be. Magical creatures wouldn't be surprised, and she looked as surprised to see Amy as Amy was to see her.

This would be Emile's girlfriend, of course. Why had he not told her he had a girlfriend? Why had she not asked? For the same reasons she hadn't asked what was going on with her own finances. She didn't wonder enough. Or maybe *deep* enough. Maybe this woman wasn't Emile's girlfriend at all, but his wife. There was no reason to think he didn't have a wife, no reason he shouldn't. There was nothing between them. Still, the thought made her feel queasy and her face go hot. Now, she'd been caught sticking her nose in another woman's turf. She'd learned that even women who didn't cook—and no one could cook in this kitchen as it was—were highly territorial about their kitchens.

The woman set a small, square white box on the counter and looked Amy up and down. "So. Who are you?" She moved with the grace of a dancer—or a fairy who had wings to lift her up and help her along.

"Amy Callahan." She did not feel that she was in any position to return the question. "I'm a professional organizer. Emile hired me to"—she gestured to the mess around them—"organize."

The woman folded her arms across her chest. "Oh? That's a new one."

"I don't know what you mean." She could get out of here with the $284.38 in her purse, but she'd have to leave the $300 in the underwear drawer in the sister's bedroom—if there was a sister. That room could be filled with the wife's extra stuff. No doubt a rich hockey player's wife would have extra stuff and plenty of it.

It would be best to take what was in her purse and get out of here. If she left with Emile's $200, that would be stealing, since opening some boxes and unloading one cabinet was not $200 worth of work. But she'd do it. She could pay it back later.

The woman laughed. "You're no professional organizer. You spent the night here."

"What makes you think that?"

The woman looked even more amused—and why was that if she was his wife? Or girlfriend?

"You're wearing my skirt," she said. "And my sweater."

Relief that Amy didn't understand flooded through her. After all, she'd been caught in the woman's clothes, but no wife or girlfriend was going to laugh about that. "You're Emile's sister."

"Yes. Gabriella Charbonnet. We had different fathers, so different last names." She walked by Amy and seemed to know just which cabinets to open to find a tea kettle, mugs, tea, and sugar. The mugs were shaped like pumpkins.

"He has pumpkin mugs." She hadn't noticed them when she'd poked through the cabinets earlier.

Gabriella nodded. "Emile likes Halloween. He got them at Pottery Barn. Would you like tea?"

So this wasn't going to be a hostile exchange. Either that, or Gabriella was going to play with her like a cat with his mouse before she went in for the kill.

"I *would* like tea," Amy said. "Actually, more than anything."

Gabriella met her eyes and raised one eyebrow like Emile could do. "More than my brother?"

"I don't want your brother. I really am working for Emile. This is not how it looks."

Gabriella set the teapot on the Wolf range and turned on the flame. "It looks no particular way. You blushed earlier. I like someone for my brother who will blush."

Despite her long blond hair and blue eyes, there were some resemblances between the two—the big eyes, tall frame, and high cheekbones. But in no way was Gabriella's mouth as beautiful as Emile's.

"Really," Amy said. "There is nothing between Emile and me. I slept in your bed last night. I hope that was all right."

Gabriella put teabags in the Pottery Barn mugs. "Was it all right with Emile?"

It was clearly pointless to try to convince Gabriella that there was nothing between the two of them, so Amy changed the subject. "Your French accent is not as strong as Emile's."

"*Je parle Français, mais pas couramment.*" Gabriella poured boiling water into the mugs. "French is my first language, though I don't feel that it is anymore. We've been in this country fourteen years. Truthfully, my friend Hélène-Louise, who is from New Orleans, is better at conversational French than I am. I don't think in French anymore, but my brother works hard at being French."

"So, it isn't natural?"

"No. '*Non,*' as he would almost certainly say. It's natural. It's just that he's very aware of his French heritage. I have met Southerners who are the same. They work hard at being Southern. Do you take lemon?" She set the mugs and sugar bowl on the quartz-top bar.

"If you have it."

"I left some last time I was here." Gabriella crossed to the built-in stainless steel refrigerator and peered into the boxes of food as she passed. "Will you get us each a plate? I brought pastries. They're in the box. Emile isn't here, so you get his."

Amy found some takeout paper napkins and placed the pastries on the plates. "These are lovely. You made them?"

Gabriella placed the lemon slices on the counter and took her seat. "Yes. *Mille-feuilles.* Layers of *pâte feuilletée* and pastry cream. It was an experiment. Rather than finishing it with sugar icing and chocolate stripes, I topped it with marzipan and candied almond slices. I suspect my mentor knew the marzipan would be too heavy for the delicate pastry and the almond would overwhelm the favor of the cream, but she lets me try new things—even if they are certain to fail."

Amy took a bite. "This is delicious. I'm not sure how you call it a failure."

"Maybe not so much a failure as a work in progress. I have some ideas." Gabriella delicately touched her napkin to her mouth. "But enough pastry talk. Tell me about yourself, Amy Callahan."

Amy took a sip of her tea. "I really am a professional organizer, and Emile really did hire me. He's calling me a personal assistant."

Gabriella burst out laughing. "What are you going to do? Make his Jell-O? Put laces in his skates?"

"If that's what he wants. Isn't that what a personal assistant does? Whatever is asked of her?"

"You tell me. That's your new title. What became of professional organizing?"

"Long story. Let's just say it isn't working out for me anymore and I'm homeless."

Gabriella's mug stopped in midair and the smile left her eyes. "You don't look homeless."

"Oh, come on! I'm wearing a too-tight sweater and a too-long skirt with the ankle boots I wore with leggings yesterday because your shoes don't fit me."

Gabriella glanced at Amy's feet. "Gucci ankle boots." Then she let her eyes drift to the bar where Amy had left her purse. "And a Louis Vuitton bag."

They'd been gifts from Cameron last year, back when he'd been trying to impress her. She'd gotten the feeling he'd been trying to bring her up to "designer speed" so she'd present well to his clients and their wives.

"Well, there was a time …" Amy let her voice trail off on purpose. "But that was before I sold Apple Pie Order.

Gabriella frowned in a way that indicated she was trying to remember something. "Apple Pie Order, Apple Pie Order. Where have I heard that?" She seemed to be talking to herself. There was no way this woman could have heard of her business. But then the clouds cleared and comprehension dawned. "Did you organize Aubrey Jamison's tour bus?"

Amy reluctantly nodded. That had been right before she'd sold. She'd stayed with Cameron for the first time when she'd come to Nashville to do the job. It had been fun, and the country music star had been so nice.

"You know her?" Amy asked. "Aubrey Jamison?"

Gabriella shook her head. "No. I delivered a birthday cake for one of her band members. They were about to go on the road, and I delivered it to the bus. Her assistant took delivery and let me see the bus. It was really neat. She told me a company called Apple Pie Order installed all the little holders and racks and things."

Amy nodded.

"And you sold?"

Again, Amy only nodded. Asking a question that had already been answered was meant to prompt the sharing of information, but if Gabriella wanted to know anything else, she was going to have to come right out and ask.

But instead, Gabriella waved her hand, palm out, as she took a sip of her tea. "It's all right. You don't need to tell me things you don't wish to. In time, I will either know about you or it won't matter, because you'll be gone."

"I'll be gone. I'm only here until I figure some things out. But meanwhile, I assure you I will not take advantage of Emile." She glanced at the mess on the counter. "I also plan to tidy up a few things."

"I wasn't worried about that. Emile is a rescuer, and I would worry if he was only that, but he is also a survivor. It's easy to see you are in need of rescuing right now. No matter. Everyone needs rescuing from time to time. It gives people like Emile a reason for being. And more power to you if you can turn this into a real kitchen. I would cook here if it were workable."

It was interesting how Gabriella changed from an awkward subject to a neutral one without taking a breath. It was a relief—a pleasure, even—to discuss a neutral subject. Amy found herself liking Gabriella.

"Really? You'd cook? What would you do with precooked rice, canned chicken, and shelf stable chocolate milk?"

Gabriella closed her eyes and shook her head. "Don't forget the Jell-O. He loves Jell-O. It's awful isn't it? Our billet mom wanted to teach him to cook some simple things, but Jell-O was as far as they got. I, on the other hand, learned to bake from her."

Billet mom? "Your who?" Was that a French Canadian thing?

"Well, technically, Emile's billet mom. But they brought me to live with them a few months after Emile. I referred to Paul and Johanna as my billet parents, too, though they were actually my foster parents." And with that, Gabriella took a bite of her pastry, as if she hadn't said something that bordered on bizarre. No, not bordered on—full on bizarre.

"I understood nothing you said past Jell-O and that you learned to bake."

Gabriella frowned a little. "How much do you know about hockey?"

"There's a puck and a goal—which your brother defends. Oh, and hockey players keep their extra equipment in the pantry. I just found that out."

"Yes. That." Gabriella rolled her eyes. "So." She folded her hands and rested her elbows on the counter. "The best youth hockey players go on to play juniors. It's a huge leap. The very best of the best go on to play in top tier junior leagues. That was Emile. Since these boys are sixteen to twenty years old, they live with host families. The system is called billeting, so the boys are billet sons and the parents are billet moms and dads. Emile went to North Dakota to live with the Lindells the August he was sixteen." She looked at her plate and said the next words in a rush. "A few months later when our mother died, the Lindells brought Emile home for the funeral and took me back to North Dakota with them to live." She looked up and met Amy's eyes again. "So I learned to bake, and Emile made saves and learned to make Jell-O." She raised her mug, leaned over, and whispered with a smile, "And he makes it still. Mostly orange."

This woman was a brilliant communicator. With her body language and that last sentence, she had conveyed perfectly that she was not open to questions or comments about her mother's death or the whereabouts of their fathers.

Still a response was in order. "The Lindells sound like wonderful people. Are you still in touch with them?

Gabriella looked surprised that the question even needed to be asked. "Of course. I talk or text with them almost every day. Emile, the same."

"Emile the same, what?"

He had come in so quietly that he seemed to appear out of nowhere. Maybe these siblings *were* magical creatures. He reached out briefly and touched Gabriella on the shoulder with the barest brush of his fingertips. The contact seemed insignificant, but the look that passed between them was not. There was love there—and like. They were friends.

"Emile, the same as always," Gabriella said. "I have met your personal assistant."

"Good. Amy will stay here for a bit. It will be very helpful with the season starting."

"And I gave her your marzipan *mille-feuilles*."

"Just as well." He leaned on counter. "First game in five days. I have to start eating better." He reached into his pocket, pulled out a box, and placed it on the counter. "Your new phone, Amy. I went to the Apple store after stretch. Packi advised me that if I was to have a personal assistant, I should provide you with a phone. After all, I must be able to reach you."

"Oh, no." *No, Emile. And not in front of your sister who, despite what she says, probably thinks I'm a gold digger.* She pushed the box away from her. "You should take it back. I will take care of it tomorrow." And who was this Packi anyway? Another man who thought he could be in charge of her?

"*Non.* Everything is already set up for you. Here's your new number." He gave her a slip of paper.

"I was going to take care of it." In her own way, in her own control, and with a phone nowhere nearly as expensive as this one. "And I am the one who is supposed to be running errands."

"It was on my way. And how can I contact you if you have no phone? What difference does it make who procured it? You need a phone. You have a phone. It is right that I should pay."

Maybe he had at point, maybe not. Either way, he was paying—and either way, she was beaten—again.

He knew she knew it, too because he smiled triumphantly, as if he was so pleased with himself. "Who's hungry? I am. I will take a shower, and we will all go to dinner. Think, ladies, where you would like to go?"

And he disappeared down the hall.

"Does he always just announce what's going to happen?" Amy asked.

"Hmm." Gabriella closed her eyes and considered the question. "Yes. But you said it yourself. A personal assistant does what's asked of her."

CHAPTER ELEVEN

"It's not pretty." Miles said the words before slipping into Emile's usual booth at the Big Skate.

"I ordered you a rare cheeseburger, sweet potato fries, and a Blue Moon IPA." Like most Americans, Miles always got right to the point, while Emile believed in taking care of the niceties and the housekeeping first. The news was going to be the same ten minutes from now.

Miles smoothed his tie and grimaced. "That's what *you* always order."

"Not today. I am having the salad with grilled salmon, but I thought someone should have my meal of choice."

"Whatever." Miles didn't seem to ever care what he ate. "Do you want to hear about Snow or not?"

"Ah, here is the lovely Megan with our food." The waitress wore short shorts, white tennis shoes, and—like every other member of the wait staff—a purple and silver Sound jersey. "You wound me, *ma petite canard*. You are wearing Mikhail's sweater today. Why not mine?"

"I can't wear yours every day." She set the food before them. "I think Carlo is wearing yours today."

Emile didn't really care who wore his sweater, but they all expected him to pretend like he did.

"I will recover." He glanced at his water. "I have changed my mind. Will you bring me a glass of Clear Valley Vineyards Chardonnay?" He had never really learned to tell the difference in wines, but he was contractually obligated to drink Clear Valley Vineyards wine in public when it was available.

"Sure thing." Emile turned to watch her little bottom bounce as she walked away, but lost interest after about two steps. Odd. That didn't usually happen.

"Did you call her a little duck?" Miles shook catsup onto his burger.

"I like ducks, at least as well as any other water fowl."

"How about this little water fowl you have staying with you? Do you like her?"

"Of course. She is doing a good job for me. Yesterday, I went home, and she had put all of my kitchen cabinets and drawers in order—and though I did not ask it of her, she cooked a meal with salad and chicken not from a can." He'd had to insist that she sit and eat with him. For the first time ever, there had been something more than beer, water, and Gatorade in his refrigerator. "She bought cheese, chocolate milk, and fruit."

"You do realize that's how normal people live, don't you—even those who don't hire personal assistants?"

"*Merci*," Emile said when Megan brought his wine. He took a sip to fortify himself. "All right, tell me of Cameron Snow."

Miles leaned forward, looking like a wolf who was about to capture a goose. He lived for these moments.

"As I said, it's not pretty."

"So, is he really in California?"

Miles nodded. "San Francisco. And he's *married*."

"*Baise-moi!*" The words flew from Emile's mouth, louder than he intended. He had not seen that coming. "How? When? *Il a été marié tout ce temps?*"

Miles frowned. "Speak English, Emile."

"He has been married all this time?"

"No. He got married this morning."

"And you already know?"

"Twitter." He reached for his phone. "I made a few calls yesterday and found out he was in San Francisco. Then I followed him and some of his clients, just to see what would happen. I thought I'd have to make more calls, but there it was, like a gift."

Some gift. "You mean to say that this *salaud* put this on social media?" Did he think Amy would never have Internet access again? Didn't he know she would see it? Even though he knew she had not finished setting up her new phone yet, a part of Emile wanted to go rush back home, but he needed more information. A goalie might rely on instinct, but he never entered the net unprepared.

"No." Miles scrolled his phone screen. "*San Francisco Today* did, and they tagged everyone involved. Here." He handed Emile his phone.

The tweet read, "Super couple attend wedding," and there was picture of an attractive couple in party clothes.

"I don't understand," Emile said. "This isn't Snow."

"No. That's Reynolds Fallon and his girlfriend, Jules Perry. He plays for the 49ers and is Snow's client. She's that actress who was in the movie about the Vietnam war."

"I know who he is. I just didn't recognize him without his football uniform. I do not know her. So the wedding they attended was Snow's?"

"Yes. Snow married Fallon's sister."

"And you get all that from this?"

"Oh, I forgot. You don't know anything about Twitter. One of my assistants handles your account. You have to click through to the story. Here." Miles reached for phone. "I'll read it to you."

"I can hardly wait."

"*Super couple 49ers wide receiver Reynolds Fallon and Oscar winner Jules Perry attended the wedding of Fallon's socialite sister, Marley, to Fallon's long-time agent, Cameron Snow. The wedding was held at the Fallon family's Bay Area waterfront mansion. Reynolds and Marley Fallon are the children of Silicon Valley billionaires Joyce and Andrew Fallon. Sources say the newlyweds are expecting a baby in June.'* Here's a picture of the happy couple." Miles handed his phone back to Emile.

The woman—Marley—was pretty enough, though the dress she wore looked more like a nightgown than a wedding dress and she had nothing on her head. That was no way to get married, even to an asshole like Snow. If her parents were billionaires, it seemed like they could have gotten someone moving on that and gotten her a better outfit. The cake they stood beside was certainly big enough—at least five feet tall with bridges, towers, and all manner of other architectural gewgaws. How many people were they going to feed, anyway? Oh, well. Not his business. Emile had only seen Snow that one time when he'd given Emile his business card. Emile hadn't remembered what he looked like from then, but he recognized him from the picture he and Amy had showed around at Cracker Barrel. He was pretty nondescript with beady eyes, and he was running a hard race to fat. Maybe he was planning to eat the whole cake himself. Maybe that's why they'd paid more attention to the cake than the dress.

"I guess we know now why he abandoned Amy and ran off to California."

Miles wrinkled his forehead and squinted his eyes like he always did when he was about to broach something with Emile that he was dreading. The look put Emile in mind of someone who had seen a baseball headed for his face but there was nothing he could do about it.

"Emile, are you *absolutely* certain he ran out on this girl? That she didn't make the whole thing up?"

"I'm certain. I told you. I was there with her at the office at the Star View. I went to the bank with her. He stole her money and left her."

Miles nodded. "All right. I had to ask. It's my job to protect you."

"I understand, but I have nothing to fear from Amy—though she did take all my canned chicken and Nesquik to a soup kitchen."

"At least it sounds like she's got good sense about food, if not men."

"Do you think there's any way to get her money back?"

Miles shook his head. "Not if he's not willing surrender it. And I see why he took it. The Fallon family would be a hard one to marry into. He was probably trying to even the score a little—plus cut all ties with Amy. I doubt if the Fallons would be thrilled to find out he had a live-in girlfriend up until a few days before the wedding."

"Amy seemed sadder about the loss of her personal things than the money. She didn't understand why he took her things that meant nothing to anyone but her."

"Probably to cut ties. And remember, he needed the people at Star View Towers to think she was moving out, too."

"Do you think he might give her little things back?"

Miles shrugged. "Maybe. If he didn't dispose of them. He has no idea that Amy has allied with someone who knows him. He might turn her things over in exchange for a promise to keep quiet."

"We shouldn't keep quiet!" Emile could already taste the revenge he could bring about for Amy. "We should call newspapers and ESPN and tell on him. Everyone should know. Yes. Tell your assistant that I want to—what do you say?—tweet that."

Miles was already shaking his head, denying his fun.

"No, Emile."

"Why? Why should we save Snow?"

"We aren't trying to save Snow. We are trying to save you and your product endorsements—Clear Valley Vineyards, *Au Chocolat*, the Urban Under. They don't like messy. Involve yourself in a scandal, and they can terminate your contracts."

"I don't care. I have enough money—enough to pay you for your lost commissions from those endorsements."

"I'm not thinking about my commissions."

"How can you not?"

"I do. But I don't have to worry about my commissions, because I always put my clients' interests before my own. You know that. That's why I work for you."

Emile could not argue with that. "*Oui*. You do."

"But getting back to the question at hand," Miles said. "Do you want to ruin things with Open Hearts and Arms? Even if you aren't being paid for it, you were pretty pleased to be asked to be their spokesperson. The campaign launches the first of the year. All the TV spots and print with your face all over it has been done."

That gave Emile pause. This international child abuse and neglect prevention agency *was* important to him—and they'd made clear there could be no whisper of scandal associated with their spokesperson. But, still—Amy. Wasn't she more important? Open Hearts and Arms could find another public figure—a better one.

"Besides," Miles went on, "do you think Amy would want her name associated with all this? If I understood you correctly, she refused to tell even her family. Do you think she'd want them to find out this way? Wouldn't this be the ultimate humiliation?"

"I think she's already had the ultimate humiliation."

"Well, then the ultimate *public* humiliation—which is a thousand times worse than private humiliation."

All that was true.

"If you like, I'll fly out there and talk to him, try to get her personal things. He'll think it's a business meeting. I'll blindside him."

A jolt of possibility went through Emile. He would have his pound of flesh, after all.

"*Non.* I will go myself. Next week. We play the not-so-mighty Ducks and the Kings in California."

Miles looked amused. "California is a big state. Do you know how far it is from Anaheim to San Francisco?"

"*Non.* I am no good with American geography. But I don't care. I will make him come to me." Emile rose. "Thank you, Miles. I am in a hurry, but please finish your meal. Please tip Megan thirty percent and bill me. I must go tell Amy this news—before she finds it herself."

CHAPTER TWELVE

Except to buy some fresh food for dinner, Amy had not left Emile's condo for two days. But the kitchen was in order.

It was a hard fight, but she had won, and she'd made a list on a random sheet of paper of the things she still needed to do—order the food items he'd said he wanted, buy extensive groceries, make a packing plan, and talk to him about putting his closet and the drawers in his bedroom in order. But she didn't like random sheets of paper. She liked a bullet journal, though she was not willing to put his life in her journal, because he was temporary.

So that's how she came to be at Foolscap and Vellum—to buy a small journal exclusively for Emile's needs. Instead of taking the Land Rover, she'd walked the three blocks in the fall sunshine. It had been good to get out.

Maybe she'd have a cup of tea at the coffee bar there and finish setting up her phone. The change of scenery would be nice. Last night, she'd dreamed she was living in a Pottery Barn catalog, which was better than dreaming about Cameron—even if she'd been flat and someone had kept turning the page, leaving her in the dark until she appeared on the next page. So, come to think of it, the dream had been about Cameron.

But she wasn't going to think about that. Why bother? It was a waste of energy to think about things she could do nothing about.

Amy loved the sound the vintage silver bell made when she entered the shop. The owner, Chelsea Seymore, looked up from where she was arranging pumpkin treat bags underneath a banner that read Happy Halloween.

"Amy! We haven't seen you in nearly a week!"

Had it only been a week? Yes. It had been two days before her abandonment, as she'd come to think of that day. She'd come in to buy some fall rubber stamps and some gold, rust, and brown LePens. Of course, those things were gone now, still a bitter pill to swallow. Maybe she needed to pretend that there had been a fire and she was just lucky to have gotten out alive.

And she *was* alive. She didn't have a plan for the future, but she didn't need one yet anyway. She had a job to do for Emile and, whether he had known it or not when he hired her, it needed doing. She was itching to get into his closet and drawers, but that wasn't something she could do without talking to him about it. He might want to hide his porn.

"Hi, Chelsea." The shop was alive with displays of Halloween cards, masks, and party supplies, with vintage-look paper honeycomb jack-o'-lanterns, black cats, and ghosts hanging from the ceiling.

"How are things with you?" Chelsea asked.

"Same old, same old," Amy lied—but was it really a lie as far as Chelsea and her employees, Merry and Harper, were concerned? All they knew about her was she was a tea drinker, gift wrap hoarder, and bullet journaler. All that was still true, even if her gift wrap had gone up in metaphorical smoke.

"Can I help you find anything?"

"No. I know my way around."

Chelsea laughed. "That's true—maybe even better than I do."

It was almost sad how happy selecting the small dot grid journal made her—orange for the season. Then she thought better of it and exchanged it for Sound purple. Emile's first game was tomorrow night, and she had already discussed with him what she could do to make his game day go better. Maybe that's the first thing she'd put in his bullet journal. She perused the rubber stamps, looking for hockey-themed ones, when she noticed how expensive they were. She hadn't had to think about that before. Plus, all her stamp pads had been destroyed in the "fire." She chose a package of hockey stickers instead and was selecting a purple LePen when Chelsea appeared at her elbow with a cup of tea.

"Orange cinnamon," she said.

"How did you know I wanted that?" Amy asked.

Chelsea winked. "I know things. Would you like me to put your items at the register?"

"That would be great." Otherwise, she'd be tempted to start putting lists in the journal right away—and what she really needed to do while she had her tea was to finish setting up her phone. All she'd done so far was switch out her SIM card and put Emile in her contact list. She needed to reconnect with social media. And the first thing she intended to do was sever her connections with Cameron's clients. It wasn't her job to be his watchdog anymore. If they started posting naked pictures on Instagram and tweeting disparaging remarks about their opponents, let him find out the best way he could.

And when she finished that, she would shop for something for Emile's carb-up, night-before-the-game meal. She might make time to buy herself a pair of jeans, since Emile seemed to take for granted that she would attend the game tomorrow night at Bridgestone Arena.

She passed off her items to Chelsea. "You can go ahead and ring it up, if you like. That's all I need today." Or at least all she could afford, though the black and orange polka dot gift wrap and black ribbon with glitter skeleton heads were calling her name, calling hard.

She settled into one of the small tables in the coffee bar area. First, she texted her new number to the dozen or so people in her contact list who she actually wanted to be in contact with—her grandparents, immediate family, two cousins, a couple of high school friends, and two of her former employees who she considered to be friends and now worked for Order This in New York.

She could never remember her social media log in information, but at least all that was written in the journal that was in her purse at the time of the abandonment instead of the one with her other passwords.

First Facebook. One, two, three, in. Remember me. Easy peasy. There was a new batch of cinnamon peach cider available at The Peach Stand, her friend Lulu posted pictures of her little girl wearing a Halloween costume from *Frozen*, and her brother's best friend had changed his profile to a picture of UGA with "How 'Bout Them Dawgs?" underneath. She considered unfriending Cameron's clients now, but decided it would be more efficient to get all her accounts operational first. Then she'd make a master list and methodically sever ties with all of them.

Next Twitter. Why had she started following so many people? Probably boredom. It was mostly bullet journalers and things having to do with organizing and recipes. Nothing popped up of interest. Time to move on to Instagram.

But something stopped her. Did Cameron still have his Twitter account? Probably. She shouldn't look. He only tweeted things about sports anyway. Still … She needed to go to his account to block him anyway, and block him she would! He wouldn't care, but it would feel good.

One click and there she was. She didn't mean to look, not really, but there was a whole string of the same tweet: congratulations, congratulations, congratulations. For what? Being at least six million dollars richer? That had been her net worth the last time she'd noticed. Surely he hadn't tweeted that. Maybe he had a new client—that much-wanted baseball or basketball player. She had to know.

A scroll. A click—and her world fell apart, just when she thought it couldn't fall apart any further.

Married. Not only married, but married to Reynolds Fallon's sister. He'd gotten married today! Today—just about the time when she'd been labeling all the shelves in Emile's newly tidied kitchen so that maybe he could preserve the order when she was gone. The cinnamon in the tea that had been so soothing suddenly set her stomach on fire, and her vision blurred.

Why had she done this here, where she had to *maintain?* "We have to maintain, even when we don't feel like it," was one of her grandmother's favorite adages. No one had to ever ask, "Maintain what?" It was evident by the way Mimi held her mouth and the cadence of her words. Dignity. You must maintain dignity even when you don't get to be homecoming queen, your team loses the game in the final round, your cousin dies and you want to throw yourself in the open grave. And when the person you thought you were going to marry and trust for the rest of your life steals your money, abandons you in a quilt store, marries someone else, and—what else? If there was something else, she had to know right now.

She rubbed the blur out of her eyes and read on.

"Sources say the newlyweds are expecting a baby in June."

Well, hell. Hell and damnation. She didn't have the energy to think of worse words. But, then, theologically speaking, were there worse words, really? Than to literally be damned to hell—whether it was the fiery hell of fundamental Christians or the Arctic hell of Beowulf, wasn't hell the worst place a body could land? Even worse than sitting single at a table for two in a fancy, Halloween-bedecked paper store, forced to maintain, while the proprietor buzzed around and the billionaire socialite was probably off on her honeymoon to Greece or the South of France on *your* dime with the baby that was supposed to be yours in her womb?

Well. There would be no jeans bought today. And it was a good thing she hadn't taken Emile's Dinty Moore pasta meals to the soup kitchen yet, because that's what he'd have to carb up with tonight. There were limits to how long and under what circumstances one could maintain. Even Mimi knew that.

"Let it out, baby," she'd said to Amy when they'd finally returned from the funeral for her cousin Jayne Ann, who had been fine one day and dead of meningitis the next. "Cry. Scream. Throw every dish in the house. I'll help you." Mimi had had considerably less patience for the state football championship that didn't turn out like everyone had expected.

And what would she say about this? "I told you so?" No. That wasn't her style, but in terms of sympathy, it would probably rank somewhere below a certain Campbell High homecoming incident, when Amy did not bring home the crown, and above a bad haircut—and Mimi was particular about her hair. She didn't, however, have much energy for the antics of men who weren't worth it.

Amy's tea had grown cold, and her phone screen had gone to black. She brought the phone back to life and exited Twitter. Instagram and Snapchat would have to wait.

Why had she walked here? She knew without even lifting them that her feet weighed five hundred pounds each. How could she possibly pick them up to cross the small shop to pay for her things, much less make them take her the three blocks back to Star View Towers.

The bell above the door tinkled its sweet little song, and it was quickly followed by the sweeter sound of a little girl's voice and a mother's laughter.

That's what Amy had been holding out for. She wasn't sure she had fully realized until this moment that she wasn't going to get it—but Cameron was. He was going to have it all.

She was still holding her phone when it rang, and she almost dropped it. Emile. Duty calling.

"Hello?" So far, so good. Her voice was the voice of someone who could maintain.

"*Ma chèrie! Où es-tu?*" Clearly, Emile did not have a Mimi who expected him to maintain. He was obviously distressed and didn't care who knew it. The question was why. Maybe something was wrong with Gabriella. Maybe he was in trouble with the team.

"English, Emile." She knew he'd used a term of endearment, but after that, she had nothing.

"Where are you?'

"Foolscap and Vellum."

"What? I do not know this place."

"Stationery store next to the CVS."

"I know the CVS. I must come get you."

"Yes," Amy said. "Please." She took three deep breaths and made her way to the counter, where the mother was paying for a large quantity of party items, including the fox mask the little girl wore.

The child looked up at Amy. "Where's your little girl?"

Indeed, where? "I don't have a little girl yet. But I'd like to." Was that still true? Who the hell knew?

"Oh. It's my birthday on Halloween. I'm having a party."

"That sounds like fun," Amy said. "I see you're a fox."

The child nodded vigorously. "I bite people and give them rabies."

"Eva Caroline!" The woman took the little girl's hand and met Amy's eyes. "I'm sorry. Her daddy's fault entirely." But Amy could tell from the light in her eyes there probably wasn't much this child's father did that was displeasing.

"Thank you, Lucy," Chelsea said. "I'll ship the rest of your order as soon as it comes in tomorrow."

"Plenty of time. Thank you." Amy watched them go. A mommy, a daddy, and a little girl with a Halloween birthday. Such things did exist.

Chelsea would have chatted, but Amy paid for her things and went to wait outside.

As she stood on the sidewalk, she couldn't help but think of another sidewalk and another day when she was waiting for a man to pick her up. But before she could give it a second thought, the county fair ride car with the wolf on the hood screeched to a halt and double-parked in front of her.

Relieved, she started to move toward it, but Emile jumped from the driver's seat and was beside her in two bounds.

When he stood before her, his face wore such a mix of anger, compassion, and bewilderment that she no longer had to wonder why he was distressed. It was on her behalf.

Horns blared. Emile tossed an annoyed look over his shoulder, wrapped an arm around Amy's waist, and installed her in the car. And there was no other word than *installed* for it. If she'd had to move under her power, it wouldn't have happened.

They were in the elevator before he spoke.

"You know." It wasn't a question.

She nodded.

"I tried to find you, to tell you."

"How did you find it?"

"How did you?" He tossed the question back.

"Twitter."

"Well, there you go." The elevator doors opened. "Will your family see?"

Good question. "I don't think so."

"Good." And they were back in Pottery Barn, and it was a comfort. The shock began to wear away. They looked at each other for what seemed like a long time.

Emile raised his hands in the air. "I will see that he is ruined. People like me. I will spread the word. He will have no more clients."

"No," Amy said. "Please. I told you before. I want to let this die."

It was as if he hadn't heard her. "I will call Reynolds Fallon. We will get your money back. That family will throw him out. He will have nothing."

"Emile, no. I am telling you—this is my business. I want you to stay out of it. Do you hear me? I let it happen."

"Are you saying you deserve it?"

"No. Maybe."

"How could you think it? That you deserved what he did because you trusted him? *Non. Non.*" He spread his hands before him and shook his head. Then he stepped forward and put his hands on her shoulders. "Amy, this man must not be allowed to get away with this. I know you think you would be embarrassed, but you wouldn't be. You would be triumphant."

"Emile, are you listening to me? I said *no.* I want it left alone. I want you to stay out of it. Triumph might be important to you, but it's not to me. And there is more at stake here than whether I am or am not embarrassed. There's a child to consider."

"And you think this *fils de pute* would be a fit father?"

Ha! She used to think so. "That's not for us to say. The fact is, good or bad, he's going to be a father. If his wife and family find out what kind of man he is, so be it, but I'll have no part of it."

Emile half closed his eyes and he seemed to be thinking. "One question. Did he ever hit you?"

"Hit me? Of course not. Why would you think that?"

"Why wouldn't I? But at least there's that. Forgive me for my rant, but I am very, very angry that this man has insulted you like this in addition to his other evildoing."

There was no doubting his anger. He wore it like a full-length cloak. If this man, this good man she knew so little of, but who had been good to her and loved his sister, could be angry on her behalf, she could be angry, too. She let it move in and take hold.

If she had been writing in her journal, she would have written:

- I was good to Cameron.
- I loved Cameron.
- I helped Cameron in every way I could.
- I trusted him.
- He betrayed me in the most deceitful, calculating way possible.
- I might have brought some of what happened on myself, but he has no justification.
- I do not deserve it.

Emile spoke again. "You've had a shock. I don't have hard liquor in the house, but I have wine. I'll get you some. Please. Go sit and I'll bring it. Then we can talk. Or not. Whatever pleases you."

But she didn't sit. She followed him into the kitchen and leaned against the counter and watched him open the refrigerator.

It was when he bent over to get the wine that everything changed.

She was thankful that Clear Valley Vineyards had sent such a large variety of white wines and that she had chilled one of each, because as he riffled through them intoning the names as he went, his Lululemon-clad bottom remained on perfect display—and perfect it was. Round, muscular, and beautiful. How could she have not noticed it before? And his powerful thighs? His mouth was a wonder of the world to be sure, but that athletic body was a wonder of a universe full of worlds.

She wanted him, wanted him right here on this kitchen floor. And she wanted Cameron to *not* be the last man who had touched her.

Without thinking, with nothing to guide her but her feelings, she quickly moved behind him.

"What do you think, *chérie?* Moscato, Sauvignon Blanc, Riesling," he muttered.

All sweet, but not as sweet as those thighs.

And she put her arms around him, placed her hands on the inside of his knees, and slid her palms up his legs, relishing the feel of his muscles as she went.

His breath caught. "Amy?"

"Yes. It's me. Who did you think?"

"It's not who, so much as *what?* What is going on here?"

"You said whatever pleases me. You please me and I want you." When she slid her hands up the legs of his shorts, she found that he was erect and hard before her hands closed on him.

She had never been so bold before, but she'd never been gutted before, so maybe one thing followed the other. He was paralyzed, maybe from shock, maybe from desire. Impossible to say which, and she didn't care. She played and stroked with both hands, enjoying the fullness of him and the sounds of his breath coming hard and fast.

Damn Lululemon and that infernal lining. There was too much fabric there, and she couldn't find her way around it. Finally, she reluctantly removed her hands, but when she reached for the waistband of his shorts, he let out a moan that was a mix of frustration and regret.

"Amy. No." He placed his hands over hers to stop her.

No? He was saying no to her!

He turned to face her and placed his hands on her shoulders.

"*Non.* I want you. Of course I do." He spread that beautiful mouth into a smile that had an element that she had not seen before. She couldn't identify that element exactly, but it was a look that any woman would be elated to have directed her way. Sex. Lust. Secrets. All of that. Then the smile faded and the light in his eyes dimmed. "I think you felt how much I want you."

Yes, and she wanted to feel again, would die if she didn't get to.

"But I cannot," he rushed on. "You are hurt and vulnerable. I cannot take advantage."

His words lit and fueled something she hadn't known she had. The cry that escaped her was part animal and part woman possessed. "Vulnerable! Listen here, Excellent Wolf, French Kiss, Goalie Man. I am *not* vulnerable. I am mad, but I am strong. And I know what it feels like to be taken advantage of, but this is not it! I am not weak. Or defenseless. Or afraid to say what I want. That's who I've been too damn long, but no more! I've lost a lot, but I haven't lost everything. I'm still me. No. I'm a better me. If you don't want this, fine. Say so. But if you do, I'll make my own decision, and I'll have you right here and right now!"

His lips parted. "I did not know," he said quietly, "that you knew that I am an excellent wolf."

"You are excellent," she whispered. "Very, very excellent."

He only looked at her wide-eyed for half a beat before he nodded.

And finally, she knew the feeling of that mouth on hers, those thighs against hers, and her hands on that magnificent, muscled bottom.

CHAPTER THIRTEEN

"As long as you're sure," Emile said against her mouth. But he knew she was sure, and not just from her words. She really wanted this—wanted him—to try to be so bold, emphasis on *try*. It was endearing, but he'd been with plenty of assertive women, so he knew true bold when he saw it. But this was playacting. Amy thought if she played the role of an aggressive woman, she would be that woman. Yet somehow, this was much sexier than the smoothest, practiced woman who'd done this a thousand times.

"Do I feel sure?" She rolled her hips against him, making him harder than he'd thought possible, harder than he'd ever been.

"A good goalie is never surprised, but you have surprised me, *chérie*." He teased her bottom lip with his tongue.

She pulled away the barest bit and smiled. *Smiled!* She had not smiled in a week. So, so beautiful. He trailed his hand down her cheek.

"Are you saying you are no longer a good goalie?"

"*Non*. Or *peut-être*. We will find out tomorrow night." He had asked Packi to have one of his old sweaters ready for him to pick up at morning skate tomorrow. Packi had said it was a bad idea to give her his sweater, but Packi didn't know everything. "I am not thinking of my goaltending proficiency now."

"What are you thinking?" She ground her groin against him.

Mon Dieu. "I am thinking that I have wanted you for days."

"Days? I've wanted you for about four minutes, and I don't want to want to wait four more." And she pulled back and put her hands inside his shorts, skin on skin.

"*Doux Jésus, je soufflé dans vos mains.*" He was breathing like an out-of-shape senior citizen in a marathon.

"What did you say? Speak English."

"Come. Let me take you to my bed."

"No. I want you right here and right now. You can take me against the refrigerator. Or I'll sit on the counter." She put her hands on the waistband of his shorts but stopped. Then a look of alarm came over her face. "Wait. Condom?"

Baise. For the first time ever, *ever* since he'd had sex for the first time at fifteen years old, he would have forgotten a condom. That scared him, but it didn't scare him off.

"*Oui.* Of course."

"Then get it." She blushed and looked surprised at her words.

He smiled and bit his bottom lip. Maybe this assertiveness was an experiment. But he was happy to participate. What wasn't to like about it? It'd gotten them to this place, after all. Besides, it was as exciting as hell, the demands mixed with blushes.

"Maybe you will put it on for me. For *us?*" He reached into his pocket for his wallet, found the little packet, and handed it to her.

She took the package, turned it over, and studied it intently— clearly looking for directions. Maybe she would write the steps down in her little book. Maybe it wasn't such a good idea to let her do this until she had done that.

He took the packet and laid it on the counter. "Let's unwrap something else first."

"What?"

"You." And he peeled off her sweater and stepped back to admire her. "Your breasts— *charmant.*" And they were—beyond lovely. Luscious, full, exquisite. He moved toward her, anxious to remove her bra, but thought better of it. Better to let her playact at being bold. "*Ma chérie*, you are so beautiful. Remove your bra for me so I can see more of your beauty."

She hesitated, but barely. He thought of asking her to touch herself, but thought better of that, too. There were limits to what Bold Amy would be able to do. But just the image of that shot a fresh lightning bolt of desire straight to his balls.

When she reached behind to unhook her bra, he eagerly slipped his hand underneath the band. She shuddered, dropped her bra, and let her head roll back, clearly enjoying his touch. He gently lifted, stroked, and squeezed until she moaned. "So good." Encouraged, he repeated the movements, but a bit rougher this time, and rolled her nipples between his finger and thumb. She slammed her pelvis harder against his and cried out.

He would have tasted her nipples then, but she said, "My turn," and peeled his shirt off. "I want to touch you." She ran her hands up his arms, over his shoulders, and down his stomach. "You look so strong."

"*Non*. You are the strong one—so strong." And it was true. That she could even walk around after such an ordeal was amazing.

"We're both still wearing shorts," she said.

"Then let's not." He reached to remove hers, but she was faster and pushed his off his hips and settled her hands on his penis, stroking the shaft and teasing the head, driving him insane.

"It's beautiful," she said. Then she giggled. "And *huge*."

He laughed, too. "Now you." He pushed her shorts and panties off at the same time. When he brought his hand between her legs, she gasped and her knees buckled. He caught her, bent his head to her breast, and took her nipple in his mouth. When he sucked, she moaned. "When I do that," he said, "do you feel it *here?*" He stroked the mouth of her vagina and slowly brought his finger to massage her swollen little bud, all the while his mouth tasting her nipple, pulling urgently with his lips and tongue and biting lightly.

She closed her legs tightly around his hand. "Please, please Emile. Don't make me wait."

And suddenly, he couldn't wait either. "*Je veux être à intérieur de toi.*"

"English, Emile. Tell me what you said."

He squeezed between her legs and whispered against her ear. "I want to be inside you."

"Yes!" She backed against the refrigerator and spread her legs. "Here. Now!"

He reached for the condom and peeled it on as he took a step backward, away from her, smiling and biting his lip. "I do not need a refrigerator, a wall, or a counter." He held his arms out. "Come to me, *chérie*" He squatted a few inches. "Here, spread your legs and straddle my thighs."

She looked doubtful. "I'm not sure …"

"I am very, very sure." With that he lifted her, sheathed himself inside her, and stood up, fully erect on his feet and fully erect and pounding inside her. She wrapped her legs tight around his waist, drawing him deeper. "Yes, that's right, *chérie.*"

"You're *huge*," she repeated. "And you feel so good."

"You're not huge," he said. "You're tight … and wet. And *you* feel so good. I want you so much. Put your arms around my neck. I'm going to make this good for you."

He cupped her bottom and moved her up and down against him and around him, making sure that her clitoris received equal attention with each motion. She cried out. "Oh, yes. Slow. Again. Hard."

He laughed against her ear. "Hard is right, *ma chérie.* No one has ever made me so hard." He could have come then, but he fought it, fought it harder than he'd ever fought to keep any puck out of any goal he'd ever tended.

It was only after she came and he let her rest a moment, then brought her back to full desire and made her come again, that he indulged in his own release.

And what a release it was. He shuddered and cried out her name as he emptied inside her. But still, he didn't let her go or put her down. He stood strong and erect until they both calmed. Then he carried her to the couch and lay down beside her.

"I need a moment," he said. "But I must have you again."

When he began to fondle her breasts, she didn't hesitate. She began to caress him, bringing him back to life. She seemed no longer like someone pretending to be bold, but rather like a woman who was going to take what she wanted.

And he was happy to give it.

CHAPTER FOURTEEN

Amy's first thought upon waking the next morning was *I hope he doesn't have a girlfriend.*

Not because she wanted him. Hell no. If she ever wanted another man, it wasn't going to be any time soon. Still, no matter how good the sex had been—and it had been mindboggling, life-changing good—she would not have wanted to be a party to Emile cheating on someone.

Then why didn't you ask? a little voice inside her demanded.

Actually, there were reasons—good and bad—she hadn't asked. Though it was a given that a rich, excellent wolf, goaltender with a mouth and body like Emile's would have lots of women, Amy had never seen evidence of any since she'd been living in his condo. If there was a particular woman, she would have been around before now. That wasn't necessarily true of the harem he no doubt had. That was the good reason she hadn't asked. As for the bad: she hadn't been thinking—or really caring—about anything except getting him inside her to wipe away the pain and bad memories.

But it'd turned out to be so much more than that. Never had she known, or even imagined, such pleasure. She'd *wanted* him, wanted him badly. The memory of him standing firm and powerful, sliding her against him and setting both of their worlds on fire, made her nipples prickle. Even now, she wanted him, although her good sense told her it shouldn't happen again. But she also knew if she'd gone to his bed to sleep there, like he'd wanted, she'd be reaching for him right now. Instead she reached between her legs and quickly soothed the ache that the thought of Emile had evoked.

Three times they'd had sex—once in the kitchen, another time on the couch, and the third (last) time on the floor, where he'd demonstrated that he was not only strong, but oh, so flexible, too. Something about goalie butterfly style. He'd been like Gumby with an erection, playing World Champion Twister—except she'd been the board and he'd bent in ways that no man without wires for bones ought to have been able to. His mouth here, a hand there, and who knew a knee could be so useful for *that*.

Afterward, he'd reached for her hand. "Come, *chérie*. Let's go to bed."

But she'd declined—had reminded him he had a game the next night and he needed to rest. And, by the way, she had been reading up on what a hockey player needed to do to get ready for game day. Shouldn't he eat? She hadn't shopped for ingredients for the fresh marinara she'd meant to make, but she could get creative. So in the end, after she'd grilled some chicken and dressed some pasta with olive oil, garlic, and cheese, it seemed best to take herself off to bed while he ate—alone.

She looked at the clock. Time to get up and make the three-egg omelette with cheese, whole grain bagel with peanut butter, fruit, and yogurt.

Just as she finished slicing the strawberries and banana together, Emile appeared dressed in workout clothes, his hair damp from the shower. He looked at her for a long moment, and she got the feeling he was considering kissing her.

That was no good. Well, not that exactly. It would be good, but it would come to no good.

"I have your breakfast." She removed the omelette from the warming drawer and set it on the bar with the bagel, fruit, and yogurt.

"What is all this?" He looked at his food on the bar and gave her a sweet smile. "You made this for me? You must like me."

"I'm a good personal assistant. I looked up on the Internet what you should eat for breakfast on game day. What would you like to drink?"

"Water. Always water and only water on game day. I'll get it." He turned and took a step toward the refrigerator, but she got there first.

"No, let me." No good would come from him bending over. "You sit and eat." Yes, much better that he should sit on his butt, not display it for her viewing pleasure. She set two bottles of water in front of him. "What time would you like your pre-game meal?"

"Will you eat with me?"

She hesitated. They had been eating together, and there was no reason to change. It was best to pretend it had never happened.

"If you like."

"*Oui.*" He nodded. "After morning skate, there are meetings. I will be back about noon. Then I nap for two hours. Then to the rink by three."

She nodded and slid onto the barstool beside him. "I'll have it ready. Your blue suit is fresh from the cleaners, and I ironed your shirt."

"Amy, you do not have to do these things."

"I do. This is what you hired me for—to make your life easier."

"Ah, yeah," he said like he'd just remembered that. "Thank you then. You do make things easier."

"I read you should take a snack to the rink."

"True. A small snack." He smiled around the spoon in his mouth. When he removed it there was a bit of vanilla yogurt on his mouth. It was hard not to look at it. "You have been reading a lot."

"It comes with being organized. I read that an apple and a peanut butter and jelly or honey sandwich on whole wheat—"

His smile froze, and his eyes went dark and dead. "*Non.* No sandwich. No peanut butter and jelly. Ever."

What on earth? Was he allergic? She glanced at the bagel. It had peanut butter, and he'd already eaten more than half. She got the feeling she'd said something very, very wrong.

"I'm sorry. I didn't know ..."

His face relaxed, and he shook his head. "*Non.*" He put his hand on her arm. "Nothing to be sorry for. You researched the best things for game day. You made me this beautiful breakfast. I am grateful. For my snack I like a Clif Bar and a protein shake." He smiled. "But the apple? A good idea, and I thank you for it."

What was that about? Or maybe it hadn't meant anything. Maybe it was just game day weirdness.

• • •

There were a half dozen guys milling around when Emile entered the locker room. *Baise-moi, merde, and all the rest of it.* He had hoped the other early arrivers would be late. He'd overslept by a half hour. Not since he'd played juniors, when his billet mom sometimes had to literally shake him awake, had he slept so hard. He should have set an alarm, but that was something he had never had to do in his adult life. He simply told himself the night before when he needed to wake, and it happened. But had he told himself last night? Maybe not. He'd been distracted—and tired.

"Hey, F. K.," Mikhail Orlov called from across the room. "You'd better not mess up our mojo by not being the first one here. We are not losing our first game of the season."

"No such thing as mojo." He stepped up to his stall and began to undress. "And we are not losing. You just put that puck in the right net and let me worry about my net."

Packi appeared at his elbow. "Here's your breakfast." He handed Emile two protein cereal bars, a can of peaches, and a bottle of water.

"*Merci.*" Emile laid the items on the shelf and reached for his compression pants. "I ate breakfast already." How could he not have? Amy had read up on what was a good game day breakfast and made it so nice with matching dishes and a placemat that he didn't know he had.

"Yeah?" Packi leaned on the stall next to Emile's. "It's not like you to mix it up on game day."

"It's no big deal what I eat. Or when I eat." *Except for that pregame snack peanut butter and jelly sandwich.* He'd not meant to react so strongly, but Amy had taken him by surprise—again. Only unlike last night, today's surprise hadn't been pleasant. "Packi, my friend, did you get the sweater for me?"

"Hanging between your practice jersey and game jersey."

Emile moved his black sweater aside. Yes. Two identical purple game sweaters, except he'd be wearing a new one tonight, and Amy would have the one that had been worn. It would be huge on her, but that was the idea. She'd have an authentic sweater with his name and number to wear to the game tonight.

"Again, thank you, Packi. Did you arrange things with the ticket office?"

"Not yet. But I will, if you still want me to. I hope you've changed your mind about that."

"Why should I change my mind?"

"It's not where she should sit, and you know it. That section is for wives, girlfriends, and family. She is none of those things. You've known her one week."

"There are no rules about it, so why shouldn't she sit there? She has had a very bad week. It's a comfortable place to sit, with a good view and nice food and drinks provided."

"It's tradition and you know it."

"I rate tradition and superstition the same. Good sense is best."

"And you think this is good sense? It's not as if the rest of Bridgestone Arena is a hellhole with tree stumps for seats. I would not waste my time telling you all this again except for the good of the young lady. The wives and girlfriends don't like outsiders. You know how they reacted when Voleck let Krystal sit with them. They will never accept her, even though she's married to him now."

"They will not accept Krystal because she was a puck bunny and slept with half the team. Amy has slept with no one."

Packi opened his mouth to speak but stopped short and narrowed his eyes. "She slept with *you.*"

"No," Emile said emphatically. "She did not." And it was true. She had refused to go to his bed to sleep—probably a good thing, considering he'd wanted her again and he'd overslept as it was. But it had still bothered him.

But Packi was onto him. "Okay. So, you didn't *sleep.*"

Best to change the subject. "If you do not want to make the arrangement, I understand and respect that. I will call Charisma in the ticket office. She likes me."

"You are being belligerently obtuse and stubborn. You know I don't mind making the call. You just don't want to listen to me." Packi began to walk away.

"Where are you going?"

"To call Charisma."

"Her name is—"

Packi waved him off without turning around. "I know her name. You've said it often enough. I'll see you after you skate."

Emile sat down, raised one leg, and began to ease on his compression pants.

Bryant Taylor—Swifty—approached his own stall and began to strip. Maybe he hadn't heard.

"So, you're screwing that girl." He'd heard.

For some reason, Bryant's wording didn't set right with Emile, though he couldn't fault Bryant. The two of them were best friends, and they had said that and worse many times about the puck bunnies that drifted through their beds. But Amy wasn't a puck bunny, and he didn't like that kind of talk about her. But to take issue with Swifty would be an admission, and he didn't want to admit that he'd slept with her. It was private.

"Packi doesn't know anything."

Swifty laughed. "Since when? I admit he may not know everything, but he knows you've got a hickey."

Impossible. Emile's hand flew to his neck. "I do not. I haven't had one of those since I was a teenager."

The big defenseman removed the last of his clothes. "You've got one now—on the inside of your thigh."

Emile finished jerking up his pants and put his leg down. Damn. That would have been when they were on the floor. She'd given the insides of his thighs lots of attention while she'd worked up the courage to do what followed—what he'd been doing to her. He pushed the thought away. Wouldn't do to think of that now. Compression pants left nothing to the imagination.

"If you're not careful, your 'personal assistant' is going to be a permanent fixture."

Maybe that would happen if he were careful ... and very lucky. Where had that come from? But would it be so bad? He must think on this. He'd known her a short time, but what did time matter?

"Can she speak French? You always say you won't marry someone who can't speak French."

He did say that.

"Put some clothes on, Bryant. We've all seen your cock more that we want." Emile finished dressing. "I'm going to stretch."

CHAPTER FIFTEEN

"I brought you this to wear to the game tonight." Emile held out a purple and silver Sound jersey. His eyes were bright, and he was talking very fast. It reminded Amy of her brother when he was in high school and was pumped for a football game.

"Thank you?" She took it from him. "I think." He expected her to wear this? It was huge. And when she turned it around, she discovered to her horror *Giroux* was plastered across the back above the number 30. "This is yours?"

"*Non.* Yours, now. It was mine, but it's for you now," he said proudly.

"*Non* is right. If it was mine, it would have my name."

Emile laughed. "Silly Amy. You do not play hockey."

"Then maybe I shouldn't wear a jersey."

"Have you never been to a hockey game before? Everyone wears the sweater of their team."

She thought back to the one game she had attended with Cameron. She didn't know about everyone, but there had been a lot of jersey-clad people.

"But it has your name."

"Right. Most have to buy their sweaters in the Sound fan shop. They are replicas. You have a real one—my sweater that has been in a game." He pointed to some little holes. "See? It is a bit worn where it rubs against my pads. No blood though. Sorry about that."

No blood? And he was sorry?

"Noel has a sweater with Nikolai's bloodstains. Sharon, same, except it is Mikhail's blood."

"That's … charming."

"I seldom bleed on the ice. Goalies are protected and must get out of the way when there's a fight. When goalies do fight, it is usually with each other when a mass fight breaks out. But that doesn't happen much. And I do not participate if it does. I don't hit people. Hitting is barbaric, for savages."

Her head was spinning. Blood … wives with bloody jerseys … and he wanted her to wear his?

"Emile, I'm not sure I should wear your jersey. Does it … signify something?"

"*Oui.*" He nodded. "It signifies that you know me and I gave you a jersey. People will be jealous. And they will see that there is someone there to see *me* play."

Surely he did not read more into what happened between them than was possible. "But you were talking about women wearing their husbands' jerseys. I'm not your wife. Or your girlfriend. Or anything. I work for you."

Was it her imagination, or did his smile dim just a bit?

"*Oui.* I know. But you are my friend. Do you not feel that we are friends?"

"Well, yes, but …"

"And it isn't only wives with sweaters. Gabriella has my sweater. So do my billet parents from my junior days—Paul and Johanna. They wear them when they travel to see me play."

"I see. I guess it's okay then. Is Gabriella coming to the game tonight?" Maybe they would sit together.

"*Non.* Usually she comes, but there is a big party. She must make cakes and pastries. She will be at the game tomorrow night."

Amy had not realized there was another game so soon. Would he expect her to go to that one, too? And if he did, would she? There was a thin line between doing the job he'd hired her for and putting herself in his control. But whether she went or not, she had another game day ahead of her. It was a good thing she had plenty of supplies for it. She needed to write the schedule in the purple bullet journal she'd bought yesterday.

But she'd think about all that later. "Your lunch is ready. You'd better come and eat so you can get on with your nap."

"What am I going to eat?"

"Caesar salad, grilled chicken, and quinoa and brown rice, not from a microwavable pouch."

"Perfect," he said happily. "Everything is perfect. Nice. Johanna always had everything ready for me on game day. I worried for nothing. This is the same."

What now? First, he likened her to his teammates' wives and now to a mother figure. What did that mean? Or did it mean nothing at all? Amy decided to go with the latter.

"I made you some Jell-O, too."

•••

The traffic around Bridgestone Arena was insane. Amy didn't remember it being like this when she'd come before. Maybe it was because this was the season opener. She finally found a parking place in the deck, climbed out of the Land Rover, and made her way inside the building.

A ticket was to be waiting for her at the box office near the main entrance, and she was to ask for Charisma.

Emile had told her all this when he'd appeared after his nap looking like a gorgeous dream in his suit and tie. She'd almost forgotten herself when he'd smiled and said, "A little kiss for luck," but she'd remained strong and turned her cheek just in time. Problem averted.

The line was long, but it moved quickly. When she reached the window, Amy said, "I'm Amy Callahan. I'm supposed to ask for Charisma."

"Yes," the young man at the window said. "If you'll step to the side, she'll be right with you."

An older woman wearing a blazer with an in-charge look about her appeared. "Miss Callahan?"

"Yes?"

"You will have to forgive me in advance, but I'm going to need to see some ID."

That was odd. She hadn't shown ID when she and Cameron had come before, but maybe this was because she was getting a free ticket. She fished her driver's license from her wallet and showed the woman.

"Good. That's fine." She reached into her pocket and pulled out a lanyard with an ID holder. "Again, sorry. But you have no idea what some of these people will do. Here, put this on."

The card in the holder was printed with her name and *VIP* in big purple letters.

"There must be some mistake. I'm not a VIP."

Charisma smiled. "You are tonight. But I like your style." She looked over her shoulder. "Anthony, you can take Miss Callahan down now."

What in the hell? An escort? And why?

"Miss Callahan, come with me."

"Wait. I was supposed to get a ticket."

"It's okay," he assured her. "Come this way."

She expected to go through one of the doors directly into the arena, but Anthony unlocked a door with the words "staff only" and led her down a long, empty hallway that seemed to go nowhere. Her heart began to race. There was no one around. What if he was taking her back here to rob, rape, and kill her? After Charisma had handed her off to this Anthony, she'd gone about her business. Maybe this Anthony was new and he'd sought this job out for the sole purpose of robbing, raping, and killing?

"Are you sure I'm supposed to be back here?" she asked.

He laughed. "It's fine."

Finally, they came to an elevator, and he used a key card to open it. Surely they wouldn't give criminals key cards at the Bridgestone Arena.

She got on. Why had she done that? She'd felt uncomfortable to the point she'd questioned her safety, but what had she done? Toddled off after this boy/man because he'd told her to. She'd kept following him because it would've been impolite to refuse.

And now she was on an elevator with him, and it was too late to get off because he'd pressed the button. They were going down.

It was Cameron all over again, except this time she might end up dead. Would she never learn to take responsibility for herself?

She stepped closer to the elevator door so she could get out as soon as it opened—if it opened. She glanced at Anthony to gauge his reaction at her moving.

He just smiled and nodded. "Looking forward to the game?"

She relaxed a bit. He *was* going to let her live. But wait—why would she assume that? Because he indicated that she was going to see the game? Well, Cameron had *indicated* that he was going to marry her, not steal her money and wrapping paper, and come back and pick her up from Piece by Piece after getting coffee. Instead, he'd sold her car, gone to San Francisco, and married the mother of his love child.

Love child? She must truly be insane. Wasn't that an archaic phrase? Or was it just one she'd never had occasion to use before? Who the hell cared?

But Anthony had asked her a question.

"Yes," she answered. "It should be exciting. Will you see the game?"

"Some. We'll close the box office about an hour after puck drop. Then I'll go watch."

"That's good."

He smiled again. "Mr. Giroux is nice. He brings us boxes of that candy he advertises."

"*Au Chocolat.*"

"Yes. I suppose they give it to him, but it's still nice that he thinks about us." The door opened. "Here we are."

There was noise—noise of an arena. That was good. She wasn't in the bowels of the arena about to be tied up and left for dead beside an antiquated boiler that could blow at any minute. She could see the ice.

"Just there." Anthony pointed. "That's the WAG suite."

"The what?"

"The WAG suite." He walked her to the entrance, where an attendant stood. "Yvette, this is Mr. Giroux's guest."

Amy turned to Anthony. "Thank you." *For not killing me.* Should she tip him? If so, how much? Oops. Never mind. He was gone.

"Enjoy the game," Yvette said. "If I can get you anything let me know."

Damn, damn, damn. Where was she? Not in a narrow, plastic, fold up seat, that was for sure. This enclosed area had big, plush chairs, and there was a restroom and a little kitchen in the back. Some of the seats were already taken, and there was a group of women milling around in the kitchen area—some with children—visiting and eating from a small buffet. Some wore jerseys and jeans, and some were dressed like they were going to a Paris fashion show—or had been to one.

Did she really belong here? At least no one had noticed her yet. And if this *was* where she was supposed to be, which seat was hers? How could she tell since she had no ticket? Should she just sit down? Maybe there weren't assigned seats, but this crowd seemed to all know each other. Maybe it was like church—no assigned seats, but everyone knew not to sit in Johnnie Ruth Hovater's pew. She'd been sitting there since the day she was christened eighty-six years ago.

But there were no eighty-six-year-olds here. No men either, unless you counted that toddler in the miniature jersey with Orlov across the back.

Orlov. Amy knew that name. He was a teammate of Emile's.

The WAG suite, Anthony had called it. Suddenly it came to her. *Wives and girlfriends!* Oh, she was going to kill him, kill him dead. She *didn't* belong here. She was no one's wife or girlfriend. Maybe there was a jilted-girlfriend-former-millionaire-personal-assistant-suite. She could get on board with that. Of course, it wouldn't have a kitchen or a restroom. It would be more like a plastic fold up chair for one, because there was no one else in this arena stupid enough to be that person.

Her stomach tied itself in knots until it was the size of a marble. And just when she thought it couldn't possibly get any worse, a voice called out across the way, "Noel! We were beginning to wonder if you were going to make it!"

Oh, damn. Now her humiliation was complete—or would be when someone finally noticed her and she had to face the woman who'd witnessed the moment her life started to unravel.

A sweet bit of laughter rang out. That would be Noel. Amy remembered her laugh. "Miss the first game of the season? Not a chance. Anna Lillian needed to be changed just as we were about to leave."

Amy didn't dare look, but she could imagine the scene from the erupting sounds. Squeals. Coos. Gushes.

"Let me see that sweet baby!"

"Let me hold her!"

"She has Glaz's eyes!"

More coos. And squeals. Gushing all around.

"Noel, she is so beautiful!"

"And look at her little jersey with Glaz's name!"

"And that precious quilt with the Sound musical note and her daddy's number!"

Gush. Squeal, squeal, squeal. Gush some more. Coos for days.

Amy took a deep breath. She had to get out of here.

Then she got a break—the first one she'd had in what seemed like a millennium. The place went dark, the ice turned purple, and images of spinning silver music notes danced across the ice.

She slipped out as unnoticed as she'd entered.

CHAPTER SIXTEEN

A win was always good, but the only thing better than a season-opening win was a championship win.

The reporter interviewing him in the tunnel, Kelton Reeves, was one of his favorites, though Gabriella said they were all his favorites because he liked to be on TV. That wasn't completely true. He hated them all after a loss, but loved them all after a win. Tonight was a night of love.

"You must be feeling pretty good after the 3-0 shutout in the Sound season opener," Kelton asked.

"*Oui.* Is a happy moment for the team and the fans."

"And a happy one for you as well. You were on fire tonight. What do you attribute your outstanding performance to?"

"Always the leadership of Coach Colton and our captain, Nickolai Glazov. Tonight, the excellent defense deserves much credit." Emile had learned early on to never take personal credit. "Taylor, Champagne, Voleck—they make a goaltender's job easy."

"You're modest. What about your personal performance?"

"I don't know. Sometimes things just go better than others."

But he did know. He'd played better because Amy had been there watching him.

She'd been shy today, and after last night, he understood why, but he was really hoping to get her *in* his bed tonight. In the kitchen, on the couch, and on the floor had been more than incredible, but he was hoping for even better tonight. He was too pumped to sleep, and he wanted sex like he'd never wanted it before. Or was it that he wanted sex with Amy?

Interesting.

Emile grabbed a Gatorade and went to the stationary bike for his cooldown. He pedaled and pondered. In the best of all worlds, she'd sleep with him and they could have a marathon night with naps in between.

Swifty saddled up on the bike beside him. "You didn't suck tonight."

"Neither did you. But you stink."

"We all stink." And that was the truth. Johanna had always said there was no smell like hockey smell.

"What do you say we unstink ourselves and go to the Big Skate? I could use a burger and a beer."

"Not tonight," Emile said. "But tomorrow night after the game for sure." He would ask Amy to come.

"Here comes your nursemaid, F. K.," Swifty said.

Packi was headed toward them, towel in hand. Emile laughed. "You're just jealous because I'm the special one right now."

"Totally," Swifty said. "But it won't last."

Packi said, "Great game. Both of you. Emile, Vinnie is ready for your massage."

Emile briefly considered foregoing the massage, but knew if he did, he'd be a stiff as the tin man left out in the rain.

Packi tossed Emile a towel. "How did Amy like her seat?"

"I haven't talked to her yet, but it was great. No reason it wouldn't have been."

"Hmm. See you tomorrow."

"Sounds like he knows something you don't," Swifty said.

"There's nothing to know." Emile climbed off the bike and wiped down with the towel. "I'm going to get this done and get out of here."

Usually after showering and dressing, Emile hung around as long as an hour signing autographs and posing for pictures, but not tonight. He did just enough so he wouldn't look like Thor, who never signed autographs and was proud of it. Then he begged off, saying it had been a long night—though it hadn't been. Not yet, but he could hope.

He couldn't wait to get home.

Once in the car, Emile was always tempted to loosen his tie, but he never did. It had been drilled into him from a young age that that there were certain things hockey players did and did not do, and dress correctly on game day was a big do. As an older youth player, that meant dress pants, shirt, shoes, and a tie for arriving at and departing from the rink. But from juniors on, it had to be a full-blown suit. Ridiculous as it was, Emile could never shake the fear that if he loosened his tie when there was even a minute chance that he might be seen, Andre would know and find a way to break out of prison and beat the hell out of him.

But he did loosen it once the Star View Towers elevator passed the thirteenth floor.

He opened the condo door and called, "Amy?" but was met with silence and the light of one dim lamp.

What the hell? Where was his hero's welcome? His celebration? Hadn't she seen him go into full side splits and throw himself on the puck belly-first? Hadn't she been impressed when the puck had sailed over his shoulder and he'd come up from the butterfly position in a fraction of a second and caught it in his glove?

Maybe she was hiding, waiting to surprise him—maybe naked in the kitchen. That would be sweet. But no. There was a note written in big letters on a legal-size piece of paper taped to the refrigerator. "FOOD IN WARMING DRAWER," it said.

He opened the drawer. There it was, and it was a thing of beauty—penne with alfredo sauce and what looked like blackened salmon. She must have noticed that he had ordered blackened salmon the night they went out to eat with Gabriella.

But where was she? It would be too good to be true if she were waiting for him in his bed, but sometimes too good to be true happened.

He went to his room.

Baise-moi, merde, and all the rest of it! No Amy, but what was this? At first, he thought it was a pile of purple ribbons, like for a little girl's hair. Then he took a closer look and realized to his horror the sweater he'd given her was on his bed, and it had been cut into narrow strips—hundreds of them! Why would she do this thing?

He grabbed a handful of the carnage and stomped down the hall toward her room. He didn't care if she was asleep, but she wasn't—not unless she slept with the lights on.

But he beat on the door with his fist as if he needed to wake a vampire from midday sleep. The way he was feeling, no polite little knock would do.

"Amy! Are you in there?"

To his surprise, she immediately threw open the door, looking every bit as mad as he felt.

"What is the meaning of this?" He waved the purple strips in the air. "You destroyed my sweater."

"Yeah, how about that?" She leaned on the doorframe and crossed her arms over her breasts. She was wearing a nightgown—Gabriella's no doubt. Pink with little flowers and wide straps on the shoulders. The only thing provocative about it was that it was a nightgown.

But this was no time to be distracted. "Why? I gave this to you." He held up the remnants again.

"Are you aware that you look like a cheerleader shaking a pom-pom?"

He looked at the mass of purple in his hand. "Bah! I could have won the Stanley Cup in this sweater."

"Did you?"

He hadn't. He'd donated that one to Open Hearts and Arms to be auctioned. But she didn't know that.

"Would it have mattered?"

"Not one bit."

"I don't understand."

"You don't *understand?*" She uncrossed her arms from her chest and put her hands on her hips. "You arranged for me to sit in the wives and girlfriends section! Without so much as one bit of warning! You knew I was apprehensive about wearing your jersey, afraid it would send the wrong message. But you sent me right in there to sit with all those women who had a right to be there."

Merde! Packi had been right, but Emile wasn't giving in. "You had a right to be there. I said so. What I say matters. Sometimes."

"I am not your wife. And I'm not your girlfriend! Did you even stop to consider how embarrassing that might be for me?"

He had not thought of her as his girlfriend. Had he? But what if he had? After last night, it wasn't a completely illogical assumption.

"Many would not be embarrassed to be my girlfriend. Many would have been happy to see me stop the puck with my crotch."

"You're changing the subject. We aren't talking about your crotch. We are talking about that WAG suite and how I had no business there."

"It's not always only wives and girlfriends in the suite."

"True enough. There are also the offspring of players, of which I am not one."

"And sisters. When Gabriella is there, that's where she sits. Same for when Paul and Johanna come to see me play, and the parents of my teammates."

"Emile, even the Bridgestone staff calls it the WAG suite. Don't you stand there shaking your purple pom-pom and tell me you didn't know that."

He threw his sweater ribbons against the wall. "It is not the official name. It is called the Player VIP Suite."

"You're missing the point entirely, and you're doing it on purpose."

"You worry about embarrassment overmuch. There is no reason to be embarrassed."

"Easy for you to say. You weren't there."

His gut sank. What was it Packi had said? *They don't like outsiders.* "But the women? They were nice to you?"

"I didn't stay long enough to find out. When I figured out what was going on, I left."

"You *left?* You didn't see the game? You didn't see me get the shutout?"

"That's right, Excellent Wolf." And damn it all to hell, she smiled, and not a happy smile either. It was mean. Smug.

Emile wanted to slam his fist against the wall, but he'd need his hand tomorrow. Instead, he slammed the disappointment deep inside him.

"Well. That's too bad. You missed a great game. You missed it because you were afraid of being embarrassed. Those women would have been nice to you. They like me."

"Which is why they wouldn't have been nice to me."

"Sharon and Noel—they are my friends. They are nice women. Sharon even welcomes me to her home for holidays when I cannot go to North Dakota. You have no reason to think they would not have welcomed you. This makes no sense to me."

"Then let me explain it to you. Let's take Noel. I met her a week ago—"

"Eight days."

"All right. Eight days. I was engaged at the time—"

"Except you weren't. No ring."

"Okay. I thought I was engaged, ring or not, because I thought I was going to marry Cameron. I referred to him as my fiancé. Then I tried to buy a three-thousand-dollar quilt from her, and my cards wouldn't work. I told her I would return for the quilt when Cameron came back for me and everything was straightened out. Only he never came back, and for all I know, that quilt is still sitting wrapped up waiting for me. I'm sure she thought I was lying or delusional or both."

"You're making it sound worse than it was." It would be best if she never knew he'd considered the delusional possibility.

"I'm making it sound exactly like it had to look to Noel. Then here I come into the WAG suite—wearing your jersey—the girl with no money who was engaged to someone else a week ago."

"Eight days. And you were not engaged. Snow was engaged—and not to you. If you think you were engaged, you *are* delusional!"

She raised her hands and growled like a furious animal. "You are not listening to me! You're the most stubborn man who ever lived."

"*Calmez-vous. Drame! Drame! Drame! Tout sur rien. Je déteste drame!*"

"Give me strength!" She put her hands to her head and closed her eyes. "Would you please stop speaking that devil's spawn language to me? You know I can't understand you! It's rude."

Rude! He'd never been rude a minute in his life. He was charming! It had said so just last week in *Sports Illustrated. Sports Illustrated* did not lie!

"*Vous pensez que vous ne pouvez pas me comprendre? Vous êtes la reine de la confusion!*"

Her face went from red to white. "I swear, if you don't stop, I'll—"

"You'll what? Destroy my sweater? Leave the game and refuse to see me play?"

"You just love yourself so much, don't you, Mr. French Kiss?"

He gave her his best smile—the one he used in the chocolate commercials. "Ah, you would like a French kiss, would you?"

He'd meant it as taunt, of course, another way to win this argument. But all of a sudden, with the thought of his tongue in her mouth, winning didn't matter anymore. His balls tightened and his cock sprang to life.

When he looked into her face, her eyes, he thought he saw his own feelings reflected there. Her purple eyes were dark velvet, and her mouth parted the tiniest bit. He let his eyes drop just in time to see her nipples rise and show against the fabric of her chaste little gown. *Doux Jésus*, he wanted her.

She took a deep, shaky breath, further evidence that she was feeling what he felt, but he couldn't be sure. In the net, his instinct was nearly perfect. He could tell what an opposing forward would do by the rise of his shoulder and dart of his eyes. He never lost track of the puck's location.

But his instincts outside the net? Not good, in general, especially with women, and non-existent where Amy was concerned.

Funny, it had never mattered before. He'd always just plowed on, bumbling as he went. Sometimes it worked out, sometimes not. But this time it mattered. He'd made so many mistakes with her, he needed to be sure.

He put his fingertips to his mouth, kissed them, and slowly brought them to her lips. And waited. The look she gave him was one of conflict and—he was pretty sure—of desire.

At last, she sighed a sweet little sigh and brought her own fingers to her lips and brought them to his mouth.

That was all the encouragement he needed. He closed his eyes and relished the feeling for just a moment before drawing her into his arms and laying her head back so he could look into her lovely, lovely face. "*Tu as de beaux yeux.*" He stroked the corner of first one of her eyes and then the other and said, "Beautiful," just so he could be sure she understood.

"*Merci*," she said in slow south Georgia French. It was one of the most endearing moments of his life.

"Now, about that French kiss," he said.

Her mouth was open and eager when he bent his face to hers. Their tongues tangled together, slow, sweet, and wet. She made a little sound low in her throat that spoke of satisfaction and need all at the same time. His cock pounded, and he longed to rub it between her thighs and caress her breasts, but he wanted her to feel good and kissed first.

Finally, it was she who broke the kiss. She placed a hand on his cheek, and his heart skipped a beat. There was nothing sexual about the gesture, but it excited him all the same, though not so much in his cock as in his heart. He couldn't think how to describe her touch. Sweet? Tender? Caring? Yes, all of that.

Her voice was raspy when she spoke. "I can't not want you."

"I'm right here." He let his hand graze her breast as he picked her up. "I'm taking you to my bed."

"Mine is closer."

"*Oui*, but the condoms are in my room." And that was true—his only condoms. For the first time since he was fifteen, he had not replaced the condom in his wallet—hadn't even thought about it. And he knew why.

He had no intention of having sex anywhere except this condo with this woman in his arms.

CHAPTER SEVENTEEN

When Emile jerked the comforter from his bed, purple ribbons flew everywhere.

"Purple rain," Amy muttered, as he lay her down. How had she gone from furious with Emile to such a different kind of hot in a matter of seconds? Or maybe she was still furious with him. It was hard to tell, turned on as she was.

He looked confused. "Purple train?"

"Never mind. I guess you don't know Prince."

"No." He smiled and dropped his eyelids. "But I know a princess."

He stood before her, his hair a mess, still in his suit with his tie barely loosened. He looked so good that she considered asking him to leave it on, to just undo his fly and come to her—but she changed her mind when he stripped off the coat, tie, and shirt at what seemed like the speed of sound. She caught her breath at the beauty of him.

"Another time, I will want you to undress me," he said, "but tonight there is no time."

Another time. She knew there shouldn't be another time. He'd already assumed too much. But she'd known there shouldn't be another time after last night, and here they were. If she stayed in his home, it was going to happen again and keep happening.

He kicked his shoes off without untying them, and when he dropped his pants, his penis sprang out, hard and huge. "Ah. Is a relief. It was getting crowded in there." He gave it a light little stroke, and Amy felt a fresh rush of moisture between her legs. What she felt must have shown in her face, because he did it again. "You like to see me do this? But you are much better at it than I am."

"Then come here." She held out her arms to him.

"In time. Will you take off your nightgown for me?"

What? Sure, she could take it off, but was he expecting a striptease? Even if she knew how to do that, she didn't have enough clothes on to do it effectively. So she just shucked it over her head and tossed it to the bottom of the bed.

She had not expected the moan that escaped from him or the expression of lust that came over his face. After all, he'd seen her before.

"*Mon amour*, you are not wearing underthings."

"Of course not. I was dressed for bed—not your bed. Bed for sleeping."

"Turns me on so much. Will you go without your underwear tomorrow? In the day? In your regular clothes?"

"No."

"Even though it would please me?"

"Even though. But I will try to please you tonight."

"Ah. Well. I guess I will take that. You are very beautiful. It pleases me to look at you."

Apparently it did, because he was still standing beside the bed like a statue of a Greek god, albeit a bruised one, and still had made no move to touch her since that kiss to end all kisses.

"I am coming to you very soon," Emile said. "But first, do one thing for me."

"Yes?"

"*Yes* as in consent or a question?"

Dear St. Cuthbert and all his followers! Could he not just get on with it? She needed to feel his hands on her—and his mouth.

It wasn't only beautiful; it was also magic. And he was willing to kiss parts of her that Cameron never had.

"It sounded like a question," he pressed on.

"Tell me what you want, and I guess we'll see."

"Ah, my clever girl. Touch yourself for me."

She was surprised, not so much at his request, but that she didn't recoil. Yet, she hesitated, unsure of exactly what to do.

"Please?" he coaxed.

She almost asked where, but to hell with it. She'd just go for it and hope for the best. She ran her fingers over one nipple and then the other as she stroked her inner thigh with her other hand. It was the look on his face, rather than her own hands on her body, that made her breath come faster and her blood boil a little hotter.

"I know what you meant now," Amy said.

"About what?"

"You are better at this than I am."

And that did it. He moved like a released spring that had been wound too tight, and he was beside her, naked, warm, and reaching.

"You're fast."

"Gotta be fast to stop the puck." And with that, his mouth was on her breasts, his hand urging her thighs apart and slowly massaging, stroking, and squeezing there.

"Roll on your side," she said. "I can't reach you … I want to touch."

He never stopped arousing her but rolled the two of them so that they were facing each other.

When she reached for him, his penis jerked against her palm and he groaned.

"Yes, that's right. Slow … lightly. *C'est bon!* Oh, sorry. No French. It's good." And he went back to her breast—gently sucking one nipple, then the other, running his tongue between them.

"Do you want to know the truth?" Amy asked.

"Always. Mmm, you taste so good."

"It turns me on when you speak French."

"*Ouais?*" His head popped up, and he inserted a finger into her. "*Belle chatte. Je ne peux pas attendre pour souffler en vous.* This talk? It turns you on, *ma belle?*"

"Well, maybe not as much as this." And she rolled her pelvis against his hand and cried out.

He removed his hand and swung around to sit up. "It's time."

"Yes." Past time. She rolled to her back and parted her legs.

"*Non.* Tonight I have something special for you." He reached into the bedside table drawer. "But first, I teach you to put on the condom." Had he been able to tell last night that she didn't know how to do it? "It's much more fun this way." He handed her the packet. "Open it. Be careful not to tear it with your nails. Yes. Now, stroke my cock a bit."

She was happy to comply. "But why?"

"To get it hard."

"Could you be any harder?"

He laughed. "Then for fun. Okay, now pinch the tip a bit. No, not there. The tip of the condom."

"I'm not that stupid. I wasn't going to pinch your penis."

"But it was funny. Put it here." He guided her hand to the head. "Leave a little space. That's right. Now, roll it on all the way to the base. Yes. Stroke it as you go."

"For fun?"

"Wonderful fun." He took her in his arms and kissed her slow and deep for a long time. "Now." He sat against the headboard and, to her amazement, stretched his legs until they pointed almost straight on either side of his body, putting his hard erection on magnificent display.

"I had no idea you could do that."

"It's useful in defending my goal. You would have known if you had stayed for the game."

"That again."

"Never mind." He held out his arms. "Come to me, *mon amour*. Kiss me." With his tongue deep in her mouth, he parted her legs and stroked there until she moaned and pressed her thighs against his hand. He ended the kiss. "You are ready?"

"Yes, please."

"I try to please. Kneel in front of me. As I lift you, part your legs. Yes." He grasped her hips and lifted.

"I'm not sure this is going to work." He might need a gymnast or a trapeze artist.

"It will work. I am very strong. Legs wide apart." And he lifted her high, grasped his penis, and settled her opening over the head—and held. "You feel it? Do you want more?"

More than anything, she wanted more. "All of you."

"As you wish." And he lowered her onto him until they were belly to belly and he was fully sheathed.

"It's very deep."

"Yes." He barely thrust inside her. "Very deep. Feel it. Stay still for as long as you can. Savor it there." And he thrust again, the tiniest bit for emphasis. "I am going take your nipple into my mouth now." This time, he did not dart from breast to breast, teasing and nipping first one and then the other. He sucked slow and hard, drawing more of her breast into his mouth with each pull, letting his teeth come into play from time to time.

She had never realized until having sex with Emile that there was a direct current from her nipple to her genitals. Or maybe there hadn't been. Maybe he invented it.

"You're making it very hard for me not to move."

He grasped her hips and held them fast. "That's the idea." He came up for air and switched to the other breast, giving it the same miraculous pleasure. He continued to hold her still, which only increased the pressure in all the right places.

She gritted her teeth and ran her hands over his torso and back, willing herself not to move, concentrating on how his mouth felt on her breast and his beautiful body felt against her hands.

Finally, he released his hold on her hips and threw his head back. "You win! I have to …" And he began to thrust hard, slow at first, then faster, with his hands on her hips moving her with him, lifting her higher each time.

He muttered a muddle of garbled French into her neck. She had no idea what he was saying, but it didn't matter. His body was speaking volumes, and she understood it very well.

Then he said a word she did understand. "Come, *mon amour.* Come for me." And he pressed her hard against his pubic ridge. "Come, come, come …"

And she did, with a splendor that bordered on violence. It had never been this good for her, not even last night when she had thought she'd reached the acme of all that was good.

When her spasms subsided and the cries quieted, he thrust in her again. "It was good, *ma belle?* Enough?"

"Enough. For me."

She resumed the rhythm he had set, and he urged her back a bit with his hand. "Lean back a bit. Just a bit. I want to see your beautiful breasts and face." He lightly stroked her breasts, increasing the speed of his thrusts. Then he grabbed her and hugged her hard to his chest. "Amy, Amy, Amy … *A présent. Je vais souffler!*"

She could only assume that that last part meant he was going to come.

Because he did—in what seemed to be the most satisfactory way.

For both of them.

CHAPTER EIGHTEEN

Emile dreamed he was starving to death in a desert, and when he woke, he discovered it was true—except for the desert part, and he probably wasn't going to die.

When he'd gone to sleep, Amy had been in his bed, but when he reached across the mattress she was gone. He sat up. "Amy?"

"Here." She came out of his walk-in closet. She'd put on her gown again. Too bad.

He rubbed his eyes. "How long have I been asleep?"

"Not long. Twenty minutes, maybe."

"Why are you in my closet?"

"I was putting your clothes in the bin for the drycleaner."

"You don't have to pick up my clothes because we had sex."

"I'm not picking up after you because we had sex." Laughing, she picked up a pillow from the loveseat in front of the fireplace and threw it at him. The only reason it hit him was because he let it. "I'm picking up after you because I'm the one who sees to it that your clothes get to the cleaners." The laughing was a good sign. She rolled up his tie, placed it on the dresser, and came to sit on the side of the bed. "We need to talk."

If he ignored that last thing she said, it might go away. There was a purple ribbon stuck to his chest. He pulled it off. "I forgive you for cutting up my sweater."

"That's good of you, since I'm not sorry."

"Not sorry?" After all they'd just done?

She shook her head. "Not one bit." She sighed. "We need to talk." It had not gone away.

"*Non.* We don't need to talk. No good ever comes after someone says that. We need to *eat.* I'm hungry." She was about to tell him no more sex. He knew it. He was going to distract her as long as possible. She could still forget. Maybe.

"You can eat in a minute. I made you some food."

Right—the salmon and pasta. His mouth literally watered at the thought.

"I saw the food in the warming drawer. There's something I don't understand. Why did you make that beautiful meal for me, if you were so angry?"

She shook her head and raised her hands. "For the same reason that I picked up your suit. It's my job. You seem to forget that you hired me to do a *job.*"

She wasn't wrong about that. He did lose sight of it, but come to think of it, he hadn't given her any money since that first $500.

"Right. I need to pay you." The question was, how much? A thousand? Two?

"No. We never discussed salary, so I did some research on what personal assistants for pro athletes make. After I read some job descriptions and took into account that I have no experience, I decided that twenty dollars an hour is fair. I've been keeping up with my hours, and I haven't worked off the advance you gave me yet."

What the hell? He'd just had the best—the *best*—sex of his life, and she was talking about an hourly job. Why couldn't they just not worry about that? She could do what she wanted to help him, and he could give her all the money she wanted and get her a credit card.

She pressed on. "Does that sound fair to you? Twenty dollars an hour? Maybe it should be less since you are giving me a place to stay and feeding me. I can show you my work log."

"*Non.*" He waved his hand. "Is fine. Perhaps more …" Something told him not to bring up his good idea about the credit card and all. She wouldn't go for that. Then he had another thought. "But you must have charged more when you had your business."

"Yes. But I was charging as an experienced professional organizer. I am working now as an inexperienced personal assistant."

"But you are organizing for me. I should pay you for that."

"I cannot work as a professional organizer. I signed a contract."

"Then we will call you a personal assistant, but I will pay you what you charged before. There are no rules about that."

Fire shot from her eyes. "More is not fair. *I* have rules. I am not a prostitute."

"*Baise-moi!*" Why would she say such a thing? "Who would think such a thing?"

She closed her eyes briefly. "I need you to understand that if I have sex with you, it's because I want to. It has nothing to do with our work arrangement."

He sat up straighter and took her by the shoulders. "Amy, I would never think that of you."

She nodded. "Good. I am a grown woman. I can do what I want. The fact is, I like having sex with you. It's my right to do it, so long as you want it as well, so long as neither of us is deceiving anyone or each other."

She waited with a question in her eyes. She wanted him to answer some part of that, but hell if he knew which. He didn't want to mess this up, because it sounded like she intended to continue to sleep with him, and that was the best news since the shutout.

"Yes," he said. "I agree with all that. You are right about all of it."

"I thought last night that having sex was a terrible idea and we shouldn't do it again—"

"*Non!* Was the best of ideas." Was she going to shut this down after all?

"Well. Regardless, as long as I'm here, it's going to happen. People don't stop doing what they want." That was a relief. "And as I said, we're both adults. We understand there are no strings."

"No strings?" He picked up a handful of purple ribbons from the mattress. "There are strings everywhere."

She laughed.

"So …" He bit his bottom lip. "You will come to see me play tomorrow night? Maybe I will have another shutout?"

She looked at him for a long time, but finally nodded. "I will. But on my own terms."

"Terms? What terms are these? Because I've got to say, I will be unhappy if you plan to cheer for the Bruins."

"I'm serious. First, I will not sit in the WAG suite."

That made no sense. "But it's nice. With food, drinks, nice chairs. And Gabriella will be there. She will keep company with you. You will see that Sharon and Noel will be your friends. Some of the others, too."

She shook her head. "I won't do it. And I'll buy my own ticket—"

"What? This is crazy talk! I can get you a seat—a good seat for free. Not as good as the suite, but fine enough. These tickets are expensive. You don't know."

"I *do* know. I have over half the money you advanced me, plus my original $84.38. I bought a few clothes and a pair of shoes, but it was all on sale. I will buy the ticket I can afford."

"That's crazy. The ticket I get—I do not pay for. It is a perk."

He'd almost rather her not go than spend what little money she had on a ticket—but only almost. Cameron Snow was the cause of this. If he were here, Emile might be willing to change his rule. Maybe hitting someone who deserved it so much wasn't barbaric. Maybe it was the most civilized of behavior.

"Those are my terms. I will never put myself in anyone's control again."

He didn't see how getting a ticket for her would put her in his control, but he nodded. "I'll get you another sweater—though I hope you will not cut it up this time."

She shook her head. "I'll wear my own clothes."

She had almost no clothes. But there was nothing he could do. "Understood?"

He nodded. "*Oui*."

She rose and held out her hand. "Then come on. You need to eat—protein and carbs. And I made you some Jell-O."

"And after I eat?"

"Yes?"

"Will you come to my bed? To sleep? With me?"

"Yes. I'll do that."

He followed her to the kitchen.

CHAPTER NINETEEN

The next morning, there was no one in the locker room when Emile entered to get ready for morning skate. Not even Packi—though he'd been there. Emile's stall was in perfect order.

It was good that there was no one here yet. Being late yesterday had discombobulated his day—and what a day. Good and bad parts. But this was a whole new day. Last night's win didn't matter anymore; it was over. There was a whole new win to capture tonight.

He drank the bottle of water Packi had left for him and sat down to tape his stick.

"Stand up. Let me look at your bruises from last night."

Emile jumped. How did that man appear out of thin air? "Good morning, Packi. Thank you for putting my things in order. I cannot show you my bruises."

"Why not?"

"I am taping my stick. Once I start, I do not stop."

Packi sat down in Swifty's stall. "I can wait. Do you need breakfast?"

"No, thank you. I had a nice breakfast. Scrambled eggs, some grits with cheese, blackberries, and yogurt." He hadn't used a spoon for the yogurt or eaten it from the container. Amy had made an exceptional and erotic serving vessel, and his tongue an adequate eating utensil. Amy had seemed to think it was more than adequate.

There was no need to mention any of that to Packi.

"I never learned to like grits. Never even saw any 'til I came South to work for the Sound. That's one thing I won't miss if we end up in Massachusetts."

Emile didn't want to talk about the possible sale of the team. He preferred to talk about grits. "A good whole grain carbohydrate. That's what Amy said."

"Amy. Did she enjoy her seat in the WAG suite?"

Damn. Why had he had to bring up her name? But it didn't matter. If Packi wanted to know something, he didn't have to be reminded. Emile considered lying, but there was no point. Packi would probably know it, and if he didn't, he'd nose around until he found out she hadn't stayed for the game.

"Not so much."

"That so?" Packi took his time taking a sip of his coffee. And waited.

Emile cut the tape at the heel of his stick. "No. She was not enchanted to be there."

"Uh huh. What did she think of your game?"

There was no way to keep from telling the whole story. "She had no opinion. She left before puck drop."

At least Packi had the decency to look surprised, though Emile doubted that he was. "Before puck drop? You don't say. So she didn't see you play at all?"

"*Non.*" He rubbed a puck over the newly taped blade of his stick without looking up. "But she will see me tonight."

"Yeah?"

"*Oui.* But she will not wear the sweater. There is no sweater anymore. She cut it into little pieces."

Packi began to laugh. "Is that so? Does she know what it would have sold for on eBay?"

"*Non.* I doubt it. I think she would not sell something on eBay that she wasn't sure was hers to sell. She has scruples. Too many scruples." He wasn't sure how destroying it was different from selling it, but it was.

"Can someone have too many scruples?" Packi handed him the stick wax, though Emile didn't know how the man had known he was ready for it.

"Thank you." He opened the wax. "Maybe not too many, but unnecessary ones. She insisted on buying her own ticket tonight. And she won't accept another sweater."

Packi nodded. "Good. I like this woman. I had wondered, but she really is in love with you—or at least well on her way."

Emile's head snapped up. "What? *Non.* There is nothing. She works for me. That's all." No matter that it didn't feel that way to him. She'd reminded him often enough.

"Yet she's sleeping with you."

That didn't sit right with Emile. "I will not speak of that, and neither will you. She is a lady—a very fine lady." Like Gabriella and Johanna. Like Noel and Sharon. Like his mother must have been before life beat her into the ground.

Packi nodded and smiled. "Most excellent. You're growing into the character that I know you have."

"I don't understand what you mean."

"It means that you love her, too."

Did he? "Bah. *Non.* I have not known her long enough for that."

"It doesn't take long. I was nineteen playing in the minors. My wife was eighteen. She came up to the table for an autograph. It wasn't even mine she wanted. She was in Brucie Holland's line. They all were. Top hatter that season, but you couldn't begrudge him the attention. Great guy. But anyway, she never did get Brucie's autograph. We looked at each other, she jumped into my pitiful little line, and it was all over. We got married four months later. People said it wouldn't last. We're still waiting to see if that's true. It's been thirty-nine years now."

It was a nice story, but you only ever heard about that kind of thing. It never happened to you. "Even if I did love her, what you say is wrong. She does not think of me in such a way." He wanted Packi to deny it, even though the man couldn't know the truth of it.

"Sure she does. She may not know it yet, but she does."

"I wanted her to sit in the suite wearing my sweater tonight. I wanted her to at least let me give her a ticket. She is doing none of that."

"But she *is* coming to your game."

"Yes, but if she—as you claim—loved me, she'd do what I want."

Packi laughed. "If that's what you think love is, you have more to learn than even I thought." He sipped his coffee. "Are you through taping that stick?"

"Yes."

"Then stand up and strip. I want to see your bruises and make sure there's no broken skin."

• • •

Emile did not get a shutout, but the Sound won 4-1 so maybe that would be enough for him.

From where Amy sat, the team looked like a swarm of purple ants, but it had been fun to watch. She loved the music, the air horns, and the way the players on the ice, when they scored, swarmed together to hug and then skate by the bench to celebrate with their teammates.

It hardly seemed fair that Emile was the only one who never got a break. She hadn't realized that teams didn't usually change goalies. And he played so hard he had to keep a water bottle in the top of his net.

She'd promised herself that she would watch the whole game, but again and again, she found herself only watching Emile. And it was amazing—the way he contorted himself, rising to his feet and dropping to the ice on his knees or into full splits, and back up again, in a fraction of a second.

It was, well … arousing. What would it be like to press him against her in all his sweaty glory? The realist in her laughed at the thought. That might *sound* sexy, but it was sure to be a mood killer.

She waited until the Sound had skated off the ice to start making the long, long way down from the next-to-the-highest row in the arena.

Buying the ticket had been humbling. She'd been feeling so good about sticking to her guns about paying her own way and finding such a good price online. But then she'd realized she had to have a credit card to purchase it—something she'd taken for granted for years. It was a dilemma. She could wait and take her chances at the door, but what if the ticket was too expensive, if she could even get one? There was no getting out of going. She'd promised Emile, and also, Gabriella had called and made arrangements for them to ride together since the traffic and parking could be difficult.

So she'd waited until Emile returned home from morning skate and his meetings and asked to borrow his credit card.

She'd been fully prepared to have a fight on her hands about reimbursing him, and she'd been all right with that. She could win a fight. But when she'd counted out the bills and held them out to him, he'd only closed his eyes and sighed. "*Ma chérie*, if I argue, will I win?"

"No. But you might win later tonight if you don't."

That had gotten a smile out of him, though not much of one. But he'd folded the money and put it in his pocket. And then she'd had to ask to use his laptop so she could print out the ticket.

At moments like that—when she couldn't be completely independent—she still felt frustrated and furious with Cameron, but not so overwhelmed. She was going to be all right.

Somewhere along the way, her mind had stopped going immediately to, "I must get on my feet and get a job." She had a job. It wasn't permanent, but it wasn't bogus either, like she'd first thought. Emile worked hard every day, and he needed help. He'd rescued her at a time when she'd had no options, and she couldn't just turn around and leave him now that the season was just starting.

She felt useful; she *was* useful. Though she hadn't planned it and she certainly hadn't been ready to talk about what Cameron had done, she'd told her family just this afternoon that she was working as a personal assistant to a pro hockey player. She hadn't said who and they hadn't asked. Like most Southerners, they didn't know much about hockey and a name would mean nothing to them, but they'd probably assumed it was one of Cameron's clients. They were just happy she was doing something constructive. And so was she, even if it was out of desperation.

Now, she was on her way to meet Gabriella at the main entrance—and there she was, wearing an authentic Emile Giroux jersey. Not a lot of women could get away with silver metallic leggings, but a lot of women weren't six feet tall with legs up to their armpits and waist-length blond hair. Gabriella had urged Amy to come with her to the suite but hadn't pushed when Amy had firmly declined.

"You beat me here," Amy greeted her.

"You had farther to come than I did. Did you enjoy the game?"

"I did, though I don't understand a lot about hockey. I suppose that would have been one advantage of watching from the WAG suite. I might have learned something." Amy followed Gabriella out the door.

"Don't count on it. And careful who you listen to."

"I don't think I'll have occasion to listen to any of them."

As they approached the parking garage, Gabriella said, "Just remember this: It's organized chaos. The object of the game is to get the puck and put it in the goal. That's it."

"Unless you're Emile. Then it's to keep the puck out of the goal."

Gabriella laughed and clicked open the locks on her BMW crossover. "He's very, very good at it. He's won the Vezina Trophy twice."

Amy climbed in the vehicle. "I don't know what that means."

"It means he's very, very good at defending that goal." Gabriella started the car. "It's a little chilly. You have a seat warmer and your own temperature control."

"I'm fine. This is a nice car."

"A birthday present from Emile. He's very generous. He tried to buy Paul and Johanna a new house last year and couldn't understand why they didn't want a new one. And imagine that— not wanting to give up a house that's been in your family for three generations, even if it isn't grand. But he did update their kitchen."

"Sounds like my house," Amy said. "Or the house I grew up in. I suppose it technically belongs to my grandparents, but we all live there together. It's just an old farm house, though there's plenty of room for all of us. But it could use a kitchen update."

"Don't tell Emile," Gabriella said, "unless you want your family blindsided by an architect and interior designer showing up at the front door ready to go to work. It would take me a long time to tell you what Johanna had to say to him about that."

"But ultimately, she let him have his way."

Gabriella nodded. "Most people do." She put her hands on the steering wheel. "So. How about it? Are you hungry? Big Skate? The guys will be along in about an hour."

Amy laughed. "Is it open?"

Gabriella wrinkled her nose and nodded. "Of course. Why wouldn't it be?"

"It's just that Emile took me there one morning. He pounded on the door and made them open. Then he demanded eggs and bacon, even though they don't serve breakfast."

Gabriella's eyes went wide. "You're kidding. That doesn't sound at all like Emile."

"It doesn't?"

"Oh, don't get me wrong. He's certainly arrogant enough. And he's plenty willing to spend money on people he loves, but he doesn't go to *that* kind of trouble for anyone." She put the car in reverse and began to back out. "Or, he never has."

• • •

Good. She was here—in his regular booth seated across from Gabriella.

He turned to Swifty. "You can sit beside my sister, but don't touch her." Swifty had taken his tie off and unbuttoned his shirt collar, but Emile was still tricked out like a show pony in a first class rodeo. Or would that be a horse show? He'd never been to either.

"Why don't you sit by her if you're so worried about it? I'll sit beside your personal assistant."

Like hell. What was wrong with him? He was cursing in his head in English, like an American Southerner. Gabriella slid out of the booth as soon as she saw them. She hugged Emile. "*Tu étais formidable.*"

"I was wonderful, too," Swifty said. "I know because four puck bunnies and a preschooler told me so." And he winked at Amy— winked at her! And offered his hand. "Hi. I'm Bryant Taylor, aka Swifty. Number five. Chief Sound Ass Kicker."

Amy laughed like a music box and shook his hand. "I'm pleased to meet you."

Emile maneuvered Swifty out of the way, unbuttoned his jacket just like that manners lady Johanna had sent him to had taught him, and slid into the booth beside Amy. "Do not say *ass* in front of the ladies. And you are not the chief ass kicker. That would be Thor."

Swifty threw his jacket off, rolled up his sleeves, settled in beside Gabriella, and put his arm on the back of the booth. "No. He is the Ultimate God of Make You Hurt. I'm just the Chief Ass Kicker."

Emile turned to Amy. "So, you watched tonight? Did you see me stop the puck and shoot it to Glaz? Then he scored on the breakaway. I got an assist. Goaltenders do not often get assists."

She nodded. "That's great. How many goals have you scored?"

Gabriella and Swifty laughed.

"What?" Amy looked around wide-eyed. "Gabriella said you'd won that Verizon trophy thing twice. I thought you must have scored a lot of goals."

"Vezina," he said. "And goaltenders do not score goals." Though it had happened. Just not by him. "As a rule."

Gabriella reached across the table and squeezed Amy's hand. "I love you. You have no idea how much."

There sure had been a lot of love talk tossed around today. He went to put his arm on the back of the booth, with a mind toward gradually sneaking it down around Amy's shoulders.

But she turned and gave him a death stare.

Got it. I can do whatever I want to you in bed, but no public affection. Wouldn't want to make people think we like each other.

But there was no time to give that any energy. Just then, two girls in generic replica Sound sweaters approached the table—and giggled.

"French Kiss! Swifty!" the redhead said. "Could we get a selfie with y'all?" Wasn't it getting a little cold for shorts at night, even if they had kept their tans?

Usually Emile enjoyed this kind of attention and was the first to jump to his feet and say yes. Refusing was not possible or appropriate, but tonight he was in no mood. Maybe it was because he could feel the warmth radiating from Amy, even if she wouldn't let him touch her.

"Sure can." Swifty ambled to his feet. "Though why two lovelies like you would want to clutter up a picture with a couple of ugly old hockey players like us is light-years beyond my understanding."

Gabriella rolled her eyes at Amy like they were sharing a joke.

"Yeah, right," Amy muttered almost under her breath.

The fan girls didn't notice the exchange for their giggling. It was true that people said Swifty was the best looking of all the Sound players, but Emile did not like his sister and his … his … *Amy* making jokes about it.

"*Oui!*" Emile quickly rose and buttoned his jacket. "You are very kind to notice us." He tried to put extra enthusiasm in his voice to make up for his hesitancy.

When the blonde pulled a selfie stick from her big bag with the writing on it, Amy gracefully slid out of the booth.

"No need for that. I'll be delighted to take your picture."

The girls cheerfully handed over their phones. "Could you get one for both of us?" the redhead asked.

"Of course. I'll take several so you can be sure to have a good one," Amy said. "Okay." She held up one of the phones. "Ladies in the middle, gentlemen on each side. Emile, put your arm around her."

What the hell? He'd gotten the death stare when he'd tried to put his arm around *her*, but she was pimping out his arm to this other woman? Great!

"Yes," Amy went on. "That's good. Everyone lean in like you like each other. Say *hat trick!*"

So, she knew what a hat trick was but not that a goaltender wasn't expected to score goals?

He wanted to run through the place turning over tables and pouring beer on people. But he only smiled and leaned his cheek against the top of the blonde's head.

He did not like feeling so angry. He didn't understand it. But at least he didn't want to hit anyone.

But later—after many autographs, many photos, a rare steak, and more beer than he probably should have had, Emile and Amy returned home together, since Amy had ridden with Gabriella and his sister had opted to return to Beauford rather than spend the night.

They had been quiet in the car—Emile, because he was still nursing his anger, and Amy, because … Who knew? Not him. He didn't even know why he was angry or how long it would last.

But he didn't have to wonder long. As soon as they entered the condo, she caught him by the arm. He drew her to him—hesitantly, because he wasn't certain she would allow it. But she did.

"I like your sister," she whispered, "but I'm glad she didn't stay over, because if she had, I couldn't do this here and now. She pushed him into the nearest chair, knelt before him, and reached for his zipper. "I seem to remember an episode this morning with you, me, and some yogurt."

Yes. He replayed it in his mind, which was probably what she intended—her writhing against his mouth and then her urging him to plunge into her and take his pleasure quickly, because there wasn't much time and she was beyond satisfied.

"*Tu me rend si dur.*"

"You were incredible tonight," she said. "Just relax. You don't have to do anything. For once, take. You don't have to give anything."

And he didn't. He leaned his head back, closed his eyes, and waited for her sweet mouth to close on him.

He didn't have to wait long. His anger was a distant memory.

CHAPTER TWENTY

"I would like for you to go to a little party with me."

"What?" Amy looked up from where she was packing Emile's bag. It was Wednesday, and the team was flying out on Thursday afternoon for three away games beginning in Anaheim on Friday and ending in San Jose on Sunday, with Los Angles in between on Saturday.

"A party. Tonight. It is Sharon Orlov's birthday on Saturday, and Mikhail is making a little party for her. Nothing very big. Just a few people at a restaurant. Maybe ten. It will not go late, since we fly out tomorrow."

"Thank you for asking, but no." She counted out eight pairs of boxer shorts and began to roll them into compact little cylinders. It would be like stepping into that WAG suite all over again when she wasn't a wife or girlfriend.

He sighed and sat down on the bed. "I would like it if you would. I know you are shy about being around Noel, even though she would be nice to you. But I inquired. She and Glaz are not coming. Noel is at a quilt festival, and Glaz will be home with baby Anna Lillian."

He smiled. Bit his lip. Let his eyes sparkle. He wanted her to go—and a part of her wanted to.

He must have sensed her wavering. "You would have a nice time. And this is a nice place. You have cooked so many good meals for me and made game days so much better. You should have someone cook for you. I know you worry for the cost of things, but this is a party. We are all invited as guests of Mikhail."

"Where is it?"

"A place Mikhail says everyone is speaking of. The Butter Factory. Though that makes no sense to me. I thought a cow was a butter factory."

Well. That clinched it. She had no decision to make now. There was no way she could go there. "I can't, Emile." Cameron had taken her there once, back when he'd still been trying, which she understood now was back before he'd started wooing his new wife. "I don't have anything to wear. It's a jacket required, or at least jacket suggested, kind of place." Nashville was casual, a boots and jeans kind of city. They wouldn't turn someone away, but it just wasn't the kind of place where one wore jeans and a sweater—especially for a birthday party.

Emile looked confused. "I have jackets."

"I know you do. But I don't."

He laughed. "Funny, Amy. *Jackets required* only means men. Not ladies."

Was he really that obtuse? "I know, Emile. But I don't have the equivalent. I have the leggings and tunic I had when you took me in and the clothes that I have bought since—one pair of jeans, one pair of corduroy pants, two knit turtlenecks, a sweater, and a white button-down shirt." She realized as she enumerated her wardrobe that she sounded as though she was poor-mouthing. "And I am very grateful to you that I have this job that allowed me to buy those things. I am only explaining that none of that is appropriate for the Butter Factory."

His face clouded. "Grateful to me? That you have these few things? I can buy you a dress … any dress you want. Or some kind of other outfit. I don't know what. Some kind of fancy pants? With a jacket? Maybe with sparkles? That would be good for this restaurant that should be called Cow?"

In that moment, it was almost impossible to not throw herself into his arms and stroke his adorable face. On second thought, why not do that? If she could lick him head to toe, she could do that.

Thinking he'd won, he smiled and brought her to sit on his lap. "So, is a good idea? To get an outfit for the party? It's not noon yet. Plenty of time to shop."

She rose from his lap and pulled her hand from his. "No, Emile. I cannot let you buy me clothes."

"I don't understand you. You only need these sparkle pants because of this party I want you to attend. You let me buy all manner of containers, labels, and such to put my drawers and closets in order."

"It's not the same thing."

"Then wear something of Gabriella's. She does not mind. She likes you. She *loves* you. She said so."

"I know. And I appreciate that she was so generous before I got some clothes of my own. But her things don't really fit me." There was no point in even trying to explain to him why she could not get away with what a tall, ethereal beauty who should be strutting down a Paris runway could. "I *am* sorry. Really. But you don't have to go alone. You must not feel that just because we ... enjoy ... each other that you can't ask someone else to go." As she said it, she realized how much she didn't want that to happen. And that was a scary thought. It was a good thing he was leaving for four days. She'd have time to get her bearings back.

He set that beautiful mouth in a hard line and crossed his arms over his chest. "If Cameron Snow had not taken all your things, would you have this dress? These sparkly pants?"

"Well, I don't believe I had any sparkly pants, but yes. I did have outfits appropriate for a party at the Butter Factory."

"*Je méprise ce putain bâtard!*"

"Apart from proclaiming him a bastard, I don't know what you said, but I agree." And she did. She wanted to go to that birthday party, but not enough to let Emile buy her clothes.

"I could advance you—"

"No," she cut him off. "I told you. I'm keeping up with my hours. You won't owe me again until you get back from your road trip." Anyway, she couldn't afford to buy party clothes that she would wear once. She was going to need a winter coat soon—plus in a euphoric moment of wanting to surprise Emile by speaking French, she'd downloaded a Rosetta Stone subscription to her phone. It might have been unwise to spend the money, but she didn't regret it, and she intended to use his time on the road to master at least a few phrases. He stood and ran his fingers through his hair. "You confound me. But I must go to stretch. I am meeting Swifty, Thor, and Mikhail."

"Emile," she called after him. "Do you need a birthday gift for Sharon?" He'd given her a credit card to use for household purchases. She left the receipts on his desk, but she couldn't tell that he ever looked at them.

His eyes widened in surprise. "Yes. I did not think of it. You can get something nice? And wrap it pretty?"

"Oh, yes. That's well within my skill set—especially the wrapping." She'd get that autumn leaf paper she'd seen at Foolscap and Vellum and embellish the package with moss green velvet ribbon, a cluster of artificial acorns, and some dried wheat. Perfect for a fall birthday. As for the gift—maybe some lovely linen napkins or a crystal liquor decanter. Emile said Sharon invited him for holidays, so she must like to entertain.

"See? You are so good at doing the things I need done. I should give you a gift—a bonus. Perhaps of sparkly clothes. *Oui?*

"*Non.*"

"If you change your mind, you have the card."

"I won't."

"I tried." He turned to go but called over his shoulder. "*Ma chérie?* I will be going alone."

And I'll be waiting for you when you come home. But she wouldn't have dared to speak those words aloud.

•••

By the time Emile got in his car, he was firm in what he was going to do. First, he found Snow's website and dialed the number listed. It went straight to a voicemail message that informed Emile that Snow would be out of the country until November, but he would return all calls then. Just leave a name and number.

No fucking way. He was Emile Giroux, best goaltender in the league according to *Sports Illustrated*, and *Sports Illustrated* didn't lie. He wasn't leaving a damn thing.

Out of the country. Even better.

"Miles?" he said as soon as his agent answered. "Get me Cameron Snow's private cell number."

"Emile, are you about to do something stupid?"

"No, my friend. I am going to do something very smart."

"I've told you," Miles said. "He had every legal right to the money. It sucks, but it's true. She did it to herself."

"You're right about the money. I know that. But I'm going to get Amy's belongings back. They are hers, and she had a right to them."

"Does she *want* you to interfere in this?"

"She wants her things back." Technically, Amy had told him to stay out of it, but as long as he didn't rat the bastard out to his wife and new in-laws, Amy would be all right with it—especially when she had her things back.

Miles was quiet for moment. "You didn't answer my question, but all right. I'll get back to you."

"Text me the number. I'm going to stretch." Not that he intended to go into class until he took care of this. He just didn't want to talk to Miles about it again.

His mind was made up, and he was surer that he was right than he'd ever been in his life. The very idea of Amy only having—what was it? Five? Seven garments? Garments that she was grateful to have!

Sure enough, just as he pulled into the parking lot of the yoga studio, his phone signaled that he had a text. *Most excellent*, as Packi would say.

If he was quick and lucky, he wouldn't even be late for the class. He could be quick, but lucky was out of his hands.

But luck showed up. "Snow, here."

"*Bonjour*, Cameron. We met last year, and you gave me your card. This is Emile Giroux."

This was met with silence.

"I am a goaltender with the Nashville Sound. You are the agent of my teammate, Jan Voleck."

"I know who Emile Giroux is. I'm just trying to decide if this is someone pulling a prank on me."

Yes, it is—but not as you think, connard.

"I have no time for pranks. I am late for stretch, and I go on the road tomorrow."

Snow laughed. It was not a pleasant sound. He had no right to laugh, to feel happy. "Sorry. This is a surprise, a welcome one to be sure. What can I do for you?"

"I wish to meet with you. We play the Ducks tomorrow night and the Kings on Saturday. I can give you a half hour immediately after the game either night. You may choose."

"Well, the thing is …"

"Yes?" Emile said impatiently.

"I'm not in California. I'm in Milan. On my honeymoon."

"I see." He'd be damned if he'd congratulate him.

"So I can't make either of those days."

"Ah," Emile said shortly. "I understand. Have a good day. Or evening. I do not know of the time in Milan. Goodbye." Or care. It was too bad that it didn't sound as if he'd wakened him.

"Wait! Wait." The sound of desperation in his voice was sweet.

"*Oui?*"

"I will make meeting with you my first priority when I get back in the country on November first. I can fly straight to Nashville, or wherever you are. Or any other time and place that is acceptable to you."

"The times and places that are acceptable to me are after my games tomorrow night and Saturday night in California."

There was silence.

"I must go now," Emile said.

"Wait. I'm thinking." There was another moment of silence. "All right. I'll be at the game in L.A. You say right after the game?"

"*Oui.* Directly." He intended to meet him sweaty and in full pads. "Meet me in the tunnel."

"Wouldn't you rather go someplace where we can sit and have a drink? There are some good restaurants in the Staples Center. You'll be hungry."

Hungry to see the look on your face when you find out I know Amy and what I have to say to you. "No time for that. I will have to get on the team plane and leave for San Jose. I will be fed." Did this man know nothing of how a hockey team operated on the road? "It will be fine. I've done my homework. It won't take long for us to come to an agreement."

Snow laughed in a very satisfied way. "Glad to hear that. Thank you for tracking me down. I look forward to our meeting Saturday night."

"I assure you, no more than I. *Au revoir.*"

Emile chuckled. Never once had he said he was looking for an agent.

CHAPTER TWENTY-ONE

Emile was waiting on the steps when Amy pulled up in front of the Music City Ice Center at a little after 3:30 p.m. He'd skated at two o'clock and was to board the bus for the airport at 4:30 p.m. Originally, he'd planned to come home, change clothes, and get his luggage, but he'd called to ask if she could bring it. He'd come off the ice with a sore calf muscle that needed some treatment.

"Are you all right?" she asked after popping the back hatch.

"*Oui*. It is nothing. I'm just careful to not let nothing become something." He slung his leather carry-on over his shoulder and set his suitcase on the pavement. "Packi and one of his assistants, Caleb, took my car home. Packi offered to collect my things, but I admit it. I wanted to see you before I go."

That pleased her probably more than was healthy. "Your phone charger is in the side pocket of your carry-on, and your headphones are inside, on top." She reached into the back seat and removed the suit bag. "Here are your dress clothes. Are you sure two suits will do?"

"*Oui*. There is an arrangement with the hotels to have them dry cleaned and returned to us quickly."

She nodded. "Your ties are in your jacket pockets, and I put in an extra shirt. Just in case."

He took the bag and smiled. "Just in case of what, *chérie?*"

"Just in case of marinara."

He touched her arm lightly with his fingertips. "It could happen. You make me laugh." His smile faded. "Well …"

His mouth went into kiss mode. She knew the look. No public displays of affection. That was her rule. Just now, she'd forgotten exactly why she'd made that rule, but it was a good one. She was sure of it.

He leaned in. She put a hand on his wrist and squeezed. "Have a great trip! And good luck."

"Amy, I—"

But Emile's voice was drowned out by a gruff, angry bark of a voice from behind them. "I don't want to see any slacking off in there today!"

Emile tensed and let his gaze follow the voice.

As young hockey players and parents streamed into the rink, a father and son stood still ten feet away from Emile and Amy. The boy could not have been more than fifteen, and he carried a huge goalie bag.

"Dammit, Chase, did you hear me?"

The boy nodded.

"What did you say?"

"Yes, sir." He set his bag on the ground.

"Pick up that bag!" His voice rang out so loud, so angry, that several people turned to look. Amy's stomach recoiled. Clearly, this man did not care that he was publicly humiliating his son.

The boy slung the bag over his other shoulder.

"Thousands, *thousands* of dollars, I spend for you to play this sport. And what do you do yesterday? Go out there and dick around. How many got past you?"

"I don't know."

Emile stood motionless, taking it all in. His face was completely neutral. How could that be?

"You don't know! How can you not know?"

"It was practice, Dad."

More people slowed and looked at them. By the logos on the boys' bags and their ages, it was clear that some of them were this boy's teammates. Why didn't one of these parents stop this?

"And you call yourself a hockey player! Maybe you ought to quit. Get yourself a set of toe picks and try to join the Ice Capades. Because with an attitude like this, you've got no prayer of even making juniors, forget a higher level."

The boy looked as miserable as Amy had ever seen a person look.

"Dad, just let me go get dressed and go to practice. You've said all this before! That's all I heard last night and in the car coming here!"

The man raised his hand but put it down again. "If we weren't in public …"

"Can you hold this please, *chérie?*" Emile handed Amy his suit bag and set his carry-on at her feet. "And excuse me."

Amy's heart beat faster. Thank God. Emile was going to defend that child and put this man in his place!

As Emile approached the pair, he turned on the charm. "Hello! Chase is it? You play for the Ice Griffins."

The boy looked up, eyes wide. "Yes, sir."

Emile reached to shake the boy's hand. "I am Emile Giroux. I play for the Sound. We share a practice facility."

"Y … yes …" the boy stammered. "I mean, I know. I know who you are."

Amy stole a look at the father. He looked as impressed as the boy.

Emile extended his hand to the man. "Emile Giroux."

What? He was supposed to be defending this boy—*not* sucking up to that bully from hell.

The man laughed and shook Emile's hand. "Fine games against the Blackhawks and the Bruins. Chase, I'll bet Mr. Giroux here knows how many pucks—if any—get by him in practice."

Emile laughed. "*Non.* No. And I assure you, there are plenty. Now in a game, I know. But only because it is lit up on the scoreboard for the entire world to see. Practice? It is just that."

Emile leaned in companionably toward the father. "I often watch the practices of the junior and youth hockey teams." He laid a hand on Chase's shoulder. "You have a fine budding hockey player here. Much promise, much promise. And I give credit where credit is due. Parents are the backbone of hockey. The money, the time, the getting up at dawn, all the driving. It's a hard life, but a good life. Worth it don't you, think Mr. …" He laughed a bit, continuing to pour out the charm on his new best friend. "I'm sorry. I don't remember the last name."

This can not be happening!

"Allen," the man said. "Charles Allen. Call me Chuck." And the man had the nerve to clap his son on the shoulder. "Worth it for sure."

Emile turned to Chase. "I saw you and wanted to say hello. Come to a Sound practice soon and wait for me. We will skate together a bit, no?"

"Really?"

"Of course. We are goaltenders—brothers of the net."

"Could we get a picture?" Chuck Allen waved his phone in the air.

"My pleasure."

Amy stood astonished as the two took turns posing with Emile. How could Emile have done that? Praised a man who was clearly a lunatic? When father and son walked away, Chuck had his hand on Chase's shoulder.

Emile briefly leaned his head against his hand and sighed before turning and walking back toward Amy.

She didn't know what to say, but unlike Emile, she could not pretend any of this had been acceptable. She took a deep breath. "That man is a monster." Amy could hear the quiver of fury in her voice.

Emile nodded. "*Oui.* The worst kind."

"Then I don't understand. I thought you were going to tell him to leave his son alone, to stop humiliating him in public. How could you stand there and praise him?"

"And if I had chastised him? What do you think would have happened? I will tell you. That boy would have gotten the beating of his life when he got home. It would have become the boy's fault for causing the man humiliation." Emile put up a hand. "No. People are well meaning when they interfere, but they say their piece and leave. It is the boy who must go home with the father."

It wasn't the words that Emile spoke as much as the look on his face that told the story.

"Emile, who beat you? Who treated you like that?"

He shrugged. "Andre. My stepfather. When I played poorly, he beat me for embarrassing him. When I played well, he beat me for not playing better, he claimed, but really because he was jealous that my talent surpassed his. Sometimes he would get me up in the middle of the night, lock me out of the house, and make me run for miles in the snow."

The thought of the beautiful child Emile must have been, outside in the cold in the middle of the night, made Amy want to take him in her arms and promise him that no one would ever hurt him again. Would he have been allowed a coat? Would he have been bleeding from the beating?

"Dear God. Where was your mother?"

He shook his head. "Beat down. Sometimes she tried, but it never worked. And she stopped trying. Andre might have meant well in the beginning. He played on a minor team—not very good, him or the team. He taught me hockey. I remember being happy with him on the ice. He used to make me a peanut butter and jelly sandwich before games and tell me how he always had the same for luck. That's why I don't believe in luck—or peanut butter and jelly. Andre was a very good-looking man and people liked him. Gabriella's beauty came from him. He had much to be thankful for. But by the time I was seven, he was working at the rink, driving the Zamboni and cleaning the rink—playing men's pickup and reliving his glory days. Not that they had been glorious. It made him mean."

"Where was your biological father?"

"Dead. Skate to the neck before I was a year old. I like to think things would have been different."

Was there no end to what he'd endured as a child? "And your mother died, too."

He nodded. "Not long after I left to play juniors. I had many offers, some close to home. But I thought if I went away, the household would be peaceful for Gabriella and my mother. I thought I was the cause of all the unhappiness. But Andre was a savage; he wanted to hit. I never thought he would hit his own child, but he broke Gabriella's arm. When my mother tried to intervene, he knocked her down the stairs. Her neck snapped and she died immediately, without pain. At least that's what they told me. Andre went to prison, and it was over."

Was something like that ever over? Amy's gut twisted into a thousand knots. It was no surprise that Emile and Gabriella had had a hard childhood, what with missing fathers, a dead mother, and Gabriella's broken arm, but she would have never imagined such horror. How did they endure and achieve? How did they smile every day? This made her problems seem miniscule.

"Emile … I can't even imagine. I am so, so sorry."

"We were lucky, Gabriella and me. Johanna and Paul loved me from the start. I don't know why. I did nothing to deserve it. But they loved me so much that they took Gabriella—and they loved her, too."

"I'm not sure deserving and love have much to do with each other."

"Ah, well." He looked at his phone. "A discussion for another day. But, I know of what I speak. When I pandered to the ego of a man who was trying to live through his son, I bought the boy a few days of peace. But it is frustrating, to not do more. All I can do is skate with him and tell his coach to keep an eye out. And those things, I will do. I was asked to be the face of Open Heart and Arms—the abuse prevention agency. The ads and commercials are done, and the campaign launches in January. I was glad to donate my time, but do those things help? I don't know."

"I don't know either, but it certainly can bring about awareness."

"Yes. So that well-meaning people chastise monsters who will take it out on the child? Is it a circle? I don't think men such as this one will see Emile Giroux on TV and say, 'This great hockey player says I should not hit my child. So, I won't.'" He ran his hands through his hair. "But I must go. I have to change clothes."

The smile he gave her was full of heartbreak, but something else too—triumph.

"You are so strong." And she didn't think twice. She took him in her arms and brought his mouth to hers. It was a different kind of kiss, not one meant to ignite a fire, but to convey warmth and give comfort.

When they broke the kiss, he spoke quietly. "Amy. I know it has been a short time, but I care for you. Do you think—?" He stopped, maybe because he didn't know the words that should come next. But she didn't need the words to know what he meant.

"I don't know. I don't know anything anymore. But it bears considering."

He smiled. "Then we will consider. When I return."

"We will consider." *And maybe I will be able to speak a few words of French to you.*

He picked up his luggage and began to walk away.

"Emile?"

"*Oui, ma chérie?*"

"Have you really watched that boy play?"

He shrugged. "Perhaps. Probably. I do like to watch the young ones practice. But not to know who he was, *non*. But I will."

She watched him go. Such a good man.

Maybe that was the first point to consider.

CHAPTER TWENTY-TWO

Emile stripped off his jacket and tie as he entered his hotel room in L.A. The trip from Anaheim had been a short one, but it was late and he was still on Tennessee time, so it felt like two hours later.

The 3-2 win over the Ducks hadn't come easy, and tomorrow night wouldn't be any better. The Kings had lost two or their first three games, and they were hungry for blood—Stanley Cup-winning blood on home ice. Emile understood that only too well. He'd been there and would be again. But everything had a place. He'd consider that and consider it hard. That was mandatory for mental preparation.

But first he would consider this Snow business one more time.

Looking at this from one view, it was all rather pointless. Emile could replace everything Amy owned with a few swipes of his credit card and never miss a dime. But that wasn't going to happen. She'd insisted on giving him a five-dollar bill and some pennies for an eyelash curler that had accidently gotten rung up with the groceries she'd bought with his credit card. He was surprised she didn't calculate what she ate and try to pay him for that. Ridiculous—but admirable, too. Which made him all the more determined to restore her belongings.

Plus, Christmas wasn't far off. The next time he wanted Amy to go to a party, he wanted her to have something to wear.

On the long flight from Nashville to Anaheim, he'd come up with a good plan, but he needed to go over it one more time in his mind. Once he was sure he had missed nothing, he'd put it away and fully dedicate his mind to hockey and the game tomorrow night—or later today as it were.

Emile knew his limitations—always had. As a kid, he'd learned early on that he had little talent for putting the puck in the goal. But he could stop that same puck from entering the net—oh, yes he could.

He wished it were different, and he had thought about it from every angle, but he'd had to face that he would not be able to get Amy's money back. That pained him; returning home the complete hero would have been sweet, but getting her possessions back was going to have to be enough. Partial heroism was better than none.

He'd considered many vehicles for achieving his purpose— bribery, threat of bodily harm, and appealing to Snow's sense of fair play, if he had any. But in the end, Emile knew it had to be bluffing and blackmail—bluffing because he had to threaten to go public with what Snow had done, and Emile wouldn't do that. Though he believed that the baby would be better off with no father than one like Cameron, Amy had been adamant on that point. And maybe she was right. She'd said Snow had never hit her, and like *Sports Illustrated*, Amy didn't lie. So at least, the child would probably be safe from physical harm.

One could argue that Amy had also been adamant that Emile not interfere, but he was sure if he could accomplish this without Snow's new wife and in-laws learning the truth, she'd be fine with it—happy even, happy enough to take that into account when she was "considering."

But here was the thing with bluffing—the person being bluffed could never be sure if the bluffer would carry though on the threats, so there was only so much Snow would be willing to give up on a maybe. Emile figured that Snow would be glad enough to send back Amy's little bullet books, sparkly pants, and the panties she had been so concerned over. After all, what would he do with them? Emile was more than sure the only reason he'd taken those things in the first place was because he'd had to get out of the condo without calling attention to the fact that he was abandoning Amy. He only hoped Snow hadn't dumped the little things in a landfill somewhere.

But that was all he would be able to get away with. A few boxes of clothes and such were one thing. Five million dollars was another. Snow would be more willing to risk the blackmail for the money and would immediately plan a preemptive strike.

In short, Emile had to be perceived as a pest, not a true threat to anything that mattered.

Which brought him to the question Snow would ask himself if he had any brain cells at all: why would Emile demand Amy's things and not the money? That was sticky, but Emile had decided to just pretend he didn't know about the money. He simply wouldn't bring it up, and Snow certainly wouldn't. The way Emile saw it, he had two major things going for him: (1) Snow would be completely blindsided, and (2) Snow had no idea Emile had any connection with Amy.

There. He was prepared for Snow the best he could be.

Now, he needed to switch gears and get ready for the Kings, and that would start with sleep. He stripped to his boxers, got into bed, and reached for his phone to set the alarm.

It was late, later still in Nashville. But he had not spoken to Amy since leaving yesterday, since she'd said she would "consider." He would wake her, but he couldn't stop himself, didn't even try.

Her phone rang only twice before she answered.

"Hello." Her voice was so sweetly sleepy.

"*Bonjour, chérie.* Are you sleeping in my bed?"

She hesitated. "Yes."

"*Bien.* I like picturing you there."

"Why are you awake? You have a game tomorrow night."

"I am awake, waking you."

"I noticed." She lowered her voice. "It wouldn't be the first time."

"Were I there, I would have woken you in a different way—a much more pleasant way."

"Would you now?" She laughed.

"Would you like me to tell you about it?"

She was quiet for a beat. "Yes. I think I would. But in English, please."

He turned the light off, lay back against the pillow, and did just that.

• • •

"It was fun to watch the game together last night. I'm glad we're going to do it again." Gabriella brought in the tray of guacamole, pimento cheese sandwiches, and hot artichoke dip that they intended to make a meal of. "Thank you for making all this lovely food."

"It's been fun having you here and eating party food for meals. I might dream for the rest of my life about those chocolate croissants you made for breakfast this morning." Amy brought in a bottle of wine and two glasses.

Gabriella had dropped by yesterday afternoon to pick up a coat she'd left. They had started talking, and she'd been here ever since. One of the things they had talked about was what had happened with Cameron. While she hadn't pushed Amy, Gabriella had opened the subject, and Amy had found herself telling her the whole sordid mess. Gabriella had a way of directing the conversation the way that she wanted it to go.

But she was a good listener. While Amy had told the story, Gabriella had simply listened, nodded now and then, but had never interrupted.

"Good," she'd said when Amy had finished. "It is good when women are rid of bad men."

"Your reaction is very different from Emile's."

"Of course. Emile and I *are* very different. I am sure he wanted to fix everything. I recognize that some things can't be fixed, but I try to look at the positives. This Cameron is the lowest of lowlifes—a cunning thief who plotted to do what he wanted without so much as having the decency to face you. He is not worth anyone's anger. And what he took from you was wrong, but you must look at what he didn't take—your skills, your intelligence, your work ethic, your good heart."

Amy wasn't sure she deserved Gabriella's high praise or, considering the short time they'd known each other, if her opinion was even valid, but it had felt good.

Amy turned the television on to the hockey channel. "Ten minutes until time."

Gabriella took a bite of artichoke dip. "This might be the best thing I have ever eaten. Is your recipe a secret?"

Amy laughed. "That recipe has been in every Southern church and community fundraising cookbook published in the last thirty years. I'll write it down for you."

"There is a reason things become popular. When Christmas comes, we will make saffron buns together."

Christmas. At no time had she envisioned being here at Christmas, though she hadn't thought about where she *would* be. Her family would expect her home for Christmas—Thanksgiving, too. Surely by then, she would have gotten the courage to tell them what had happened. But she had told Emile they would "consider," whatever that meant.

"Saffron buns were the first thing Johanna taught me to make when I got my cast off—I had a broken arm when I went to live with them. She and Paul are third generation Swedish Americans, but they have preserved their heritage. The buns are Johanna's secret recipe, but she won't mind if I share it with you."

And there it was again—Gabriella's uncanny talent for flitting from one subject to another like a magical fairy kissing the dew from flowers. That she'd had a broken arm was buried under so many other layers that it was not up for discussion. Amy wondered how she'd feel if she knew Emile had told her about their abusive past. But Amy wouldn't mention it. She would address the thing that Gabriella clearly wanted her to ask about.

"How do you know Johanna wouldn't mind my having the recipe? If it's a secret?"

"Because you care for Emile."

Care for. That was the phrase Emile had used.

"I work for Emile."

Gabriella gave her a knowing look. "I watched you watching my brother play last night. It was good to see. Don't tell me there's no attraction. It wasn't lost on me that you went to his bed to sleep last night, like that's the bed you always go to."

Horrified took on a whole new meaning for Amy. How could she have been so stupid? To have trotted off to Emile's bed like it was hers? But it hadn't occurred to her to sleep anywhere else. Besides, she liked the smell of his pillow. But what Gabriella must think of her.

"I—" She had no idea what to follow that with, so she just closed her mouth.

Gabriella laughed. "Don't be embarrassed. I know you are not the kind of woman to go to a man's bed lightly."

But wasn't that exactly what she'd done? Told herself that it was just sex, that she was taking what she wanted because she could? But was that still true, if it ever had been?

Amy put her hands in the air. "This is so crazy."

"Why is it crazy?"

"To even consider that Emile and I might have—or be headed toward—some kind of relationship. You know what a short time we've known each other."

Gabriella shook head. "Time means nothing. My mother knew my father—and Emile's— from the time they were toddlers, all skating on the pond together almost before they could walk. And look what happened there."

Amy's head snapped up. "You know I know?"

She nodded. "Emile called me this morning and told me he told you."

"I hope you don't mind that I know."

"I don't mind. That still doesn't mean that I want to have any deep heart-to-hearts about what happened. I'm not like Emile. He says refusing to talk about it doesn't mean it didn't happen. He had a lot of baggage for a long time, but he has moved past it."

"How about you? Do you have baggage?" Amy asked tentatively.

"Ah." Gabriella smiled. "That would be the beginning of a heart-to-heart. I like you very much—I love you for my brother. But no thank you on the heart-to-heart."

"I will respect that."

"Thank you."

"But about this 'for your brother—'"

"Do you deny the attraction?"

"No. I don't." Nor could she deny the warm feeling that came over her when he came into the room or gathered her to him to sleep after sex. It had never been like that with Cameron. He had always been reaching for his phone and tablet practically before he finished ejaculating, never mind where she was in the process.

"Then what does the time matter?"

"But there's more than just the time factor. I will never—and I mean *never*—put myself in a man's control again. It is insane that I would even consider—" Yet, she was considering it.

"You should not try to make Emile pay for what Cameron Snow did to you. He would not do such a thing."

"I don't think he would. But he does want his way."

"I am probably as well aware of that as anyone on this planet. But that isn't the same thing as having you in his control. From what I saw about where you sat at that game with the Bruins, you can handle him pretty well—maybe even out-stubborn him, and that is a great feat."

She thought of the cell phone he'd bought her, how he'd insisted on going to the bank with her that day, the pass for the WAG suite, and how hard he'd tried to buy her clothes and take her to that birthday party. Wouldn't there come a time when she would just tell him yes because she was tired of saying no? But at least he'd stayed out of her business concerning Cameron. "I don't want someone I have to fight so hard to handle."

Gabriella poured them glasses of wine. "Good luck with that unless you want no one at all."

And that's exactly what she'd thought she wanted. Why did this have to be so confusing?

"It's time," Gabriella said.

"Time? We've only known each other two weeks."

Gabriella shook her head and pointed to the television. "Time."

And Amy sat forward, waiting for a glimpse of him. Yes— skating out with his stick held high over his head, around the goal twice clockwise and twice counterclockwise, tapping the posts with this stick.

And what was that?

"Did he kiss the crossbar of that goal?"

Gabriella laughed. "Every game, every period."

Lucky goal.

Apparently, Amy had missed seeing this ritual when she watched before. She concentrated on the television screen, determined not to miss a thing.

CHAPTER TWENTY-THREE

Win over the Kings, 4-2. Check.

Celebrate with the guys on the ice and bench. Check.

Now if he could exit the ice without a reporter waylaying him. Ah, good. Glaz, Thor, and Swifty already had microphones in their faces. Emile slipped on by without any problem. Small wonder. They were the stars tonight.

Now for the next matter on the list.

It had never crossed his mind that Snow would fail to show up, and there he was—standing behind a security guard in a Staples Center uniform. *Baise-moi*. The *bâtard* was wearing a Sound sweater.

Emile shed a glove, took his helmet off, and put it under his arm. He was careful to address the guard first.

"Many, many thanks for all you do. But it is all right. He's here to see me."

Emile gave him his best smile and extended his hand for Snow to shake. He would have resented the gesture if not for the stench of his hands. A hockey player's gloves stunk like no other part of his equipment, and that was saying a lot. Snow would have a souvenir of this meeting for days.

Just then, something happened that Emile had not anticipated but should have—Packi stopped in front of him. He frowned and barely shook his head, as if in disbelief. Emile caught his breath and waited for Packi to speak, but when he did, he only said,

"Here you go," and handed Emile a water bottle and towel, took his helmet, gloves, and stick, and headed toward the locker room.

Emile drank deeply from the bottle and slung the towel around his neck. "Great game! Brilliant saves!" Emile hated Snow all the more for saying that. His performance had been solid tonight, but not great and certainly not brilliant. No crazy, reason-defying saves. As for the Kings's goals—the best parts of Dominik Hesek and Patrick Roy combined could have done nothing about one of the pucks that got past him. The other, he should have stopped. He'd work on that.

"Let's step to the side." Emile moved against the wall, but though he was exhausted, he was careful not lean on it. Snow had a leather messenger bag over his shoulder, no doubt containing a contract with a big red X where he was supposed to sign. There would be a pen, too. At least he had better sense than to wave the contract around first thing.

But Snow did want to get down to business. "I know you need to cool down and hydrate. Do you have any questions for me?"

Determined to look relaxed and happy, Emile smiled and nodded. "*Oui.* Do you still have Amy's personal possessions?"

Emile had never seen a face go from giddy-smug to utter shock so quickly. When Snow's head whipped around, Emile noted that his hair was getting thin on top. Emile brushed his own full locks off his forehead.

"Wh-What? What did you say?"

Emile leaned in and said very carefully, "Do you still have Amy's material belongings? For your sake, I hope you have not disposed of them, because you are going to send them back to her." He was no longer smiling.

"I don't know what you're talking about. I don't know any Amy. I certainly don't have her things."

Emile laughed. "I was right. I thought that was the tack you would take. Had Amy gone public, I'm sure that's what you intended to tell Reynolds Fallon and all his family, including your new wife. It might have worked on them, but don't waste my time. As you say, I must cool down, hydrate, and get on a plane. I have no interest in ruining your marriage or your life. I have no interest in you at all. But you will send Amy's personal possessions back to her, or I will call your brother-in-law and tell all. He may not believe me at first, but he will look into it, and you will not survive the scrutiny."

Snow's face was now white and red blotched. "This ... this is what you interrupted my honeymoon for? You said you were interested in signing with me."

"*Non.* I did not. I never said what I wanted. I just called you here, and you came like a stray, mangy dog hoping for kibble. There is no kibble, unless you count my willingness to keep your secret."

Snow took a deep breath, no doubt assessing how to proceed. "How do you know Amy?"

When Emile shook his head side to side the sweat from his hair landed on Snow's face. He gave another vigorous little shake. "Doesn't matter. You will crate her things up and ship them back." If Emile were guessing, they'd never been uncrated but were sitting in a storage unit. When enough time had passed, Snow would cease to pay the rent, and the contents would be sold. But he'd phrased it that way because he wanted to make it seem as if he didn't know about the money.

Indeed, Snow did look the barest bit relieved. "But you have to understand. Things had not been right with Amy and me for a while. I tried—"

Emile put up a hand. "*Arrêtez.* Stop before you lie. I have no interest in you or your motives. I have interest only in seeing Amy's clothing, books, and all the rest of it returned to her. Do it. And make sure you don't leave anything out—not a little bullet book, ribbon, rubber stamp, or pair of panties. Leave something out, and the deal is off."

"All right. Okay." He closed his eyes and shook his head. He looked like a man who had lost something that cost him nothing. "I'm flying back to Milan tonight. I'll do it when I get back."

Emile had not anticipated that. No matter. "*Non.* You will do it now. Her things will arrive tomorrow by end of business. She will wait not one second longer than that." Emile would be home in the wee hours after the San Jose game. He was determined this be done before then.

Snow's eyes widened. They were bloodshot. "That's impossible! I don't think you realize how much there is. There's a storage unit half full! And my wife is expecting me back."

Emile studied a blooming bruise on his forearm. "That's a personal problem and not mine. You are a resourceful man who has proven he has the talent to act quickly. Utilize that talent. Send them to her attention to Star View Towers. Fourteenth floor. I'm sure you know the address."

Just when Emile was certain a man couldn't look more dumbfounded, Snow turned a lovely shade of purple and his eyes bulged. "She didn't go back to Georgia? She's living with *you?*"

Emile pivoted on his skates and walked away.

Snow must have thought he was out of earshot when he sneered, "That didn't take her long."

If Emile had allowed that to sink in, he would have turned into the savage he'd sworn he would never be.

He just waved over his shoulder without looking back. "Just do what I said."

•••

Later on the plane, Emile had expected Packi to quiz him, but he hadn't. He'd delivered Emile's chicken parmesan, asked if he needed anything, and made some small talk about the game, but he hadn't mentioned Snow. Emile didn't even wonder why. He was just relieved. It was done, and he didn't want to think about it anymore.

However, he did have to think about it again—at least briefly. After the meal, most of the team had put on headphones and settled back to chill out or sleep. Emile was about to do the same when Jan Voleck stopped in the aisle beside Emile.

"Yes?" Emile was always very careful to never speak French to the young Swede. He had enough trouble with English.

"Hello, Emile."

"Hello."

"I saw you, I think, in the tunnel. You were speaking with my agent? With Cameron Snow?"

Oh, great. The kid was about to ask him if they were going to be agent-sharing buddies.

"Yes," Emile said hesitantly.

Jan looked perplexed. "Hmm. I thought it, but then I wondered and thought, can't be. Sometimes people can look similar."

"What? He didn't talk to you?"

"No," Jan said. "He did not."

Odd that the guy's agent had been at his game and not so much as said hello. Miles would never do that. Of course, Snow had been rattled—that, and he had to arrange to ship some boxes.

"I don't know, Jan."

Jan set his mouth and nodded. "Thank you." And he walked to the back of the plane.

CHAPTER TWENTY-FOUR

Amy returned from shopping midmorning.

There was no denying it. She was excited that Emile was coming home. She missed him. Though she hadn't known it before, she had never missed Cameron when he'd traveled. Sure, she'd looked forward to his return, but it was because she was lonely, not lonely for him.

She had not been lonely over the weekend. Gabriella had left early this morning to go to work, but she had been here most of the weekend. She'd been great company—but through it all, Amy had never stopped missing Emile.

She set about putting away the groceries she'd bought for his homecoming—smoked salmon; some lovely pears; and free-range eggs, fine herbs, wild mushrooms, and brie for an omelette. She didn't know if he'd want food as soon as he got home, but even if he didn't, this was a meal she could put together quickly when he got up tomorrow—whatever time that might be. When he'd called in the wee hours after the Kings game, he'd said Tuesday and Wednesday were off days for the Sound, though he would go work out. Then Thursday, back to business with Saturday and Sunday game days at home. Ottawa and Carolina, though Amy wasn't sure of the order.

The housekeeping service had come on Friday, but she intended to freshen up the master bath and put the new sheets she'd bought on the bed. The Pottery Barn sheets were nice enough, but the new ones were thousand thread count Egyptian cotton. The price didn't even give her pause. He wouldn't care, and after such a hard few days on the road, he deserved the most comfortable bed possible. It wasn't as if she'd bought them for herself. Well, maybe a little. Lying on those sheets would be like sinking into mounds of whipped cream. She could just imagine how they would feel against their entwined naked bodies.

The twinge in her groin reminded her how spoiled her body had become.

Yes. She'd definitely missed him. Her phone rang, and she dove for it as if there were a thousand pound sleeping tiger in the room that would eat her whole if it was disturbed.

"Hello." She kept her voice neutral.

"*Bon matin, chérie.* Did I wake you?"

"No. I've been up for hours."

"After talking to me so late? Perhaps you will take a nap this afternoon."

"Maybe. I wouldn't want to fall asleep during the game tonight, though I suppose if one of has to fall asleep, better me than you."

"That's why I will have a nap. I am hoping you will have some energy for me when I come home."

She laughed. "I hope that, too."

"So, you have missed me, as I have missed you?"

"I can't answer that. I don't know how much you've missed me. But I have missed you, yes. Will you call me when the plane lands so I will have an idea of when to pick you up at the rink?"

"*Non.* It will be very late. Jake Champagne also lives in the building. He has his car. I will catch a ride."

"It that doesn't work out, call me."

"All right. Don't wait up." Then he laughed. "No need. I will wake you." And they both laughed. "I must go," he said. "The bus leaves soon for morning skate."

"I'll be watching tonight."

"I never doubted."

He never doubted. After she hung up, she thought about that. There was a huge gulf between being trusted and taken for granted. She used to think they were the same.

Then all of a sudden it hit her. Why was she contemplating considering whether they should pursue a relationship? That ship had sailed. Whether it had been two weeks, two years, two decades, or two seconds, it was done. They were five steps into a relationship. It had happened while she fretted about whether they should. Oddly, it didn't scare her.

She went into the laundry room to put in the new sheets to wash.

Why should she be scared? She'd lost everything she owned, but not only was she living and breathing, she also felt happy. *Happy.* Why toss that away because it might not work out?

And it might not. If it didn't, she could walk away—or he could. Either way, Amy knew if it came to walking, it would be done honorably. There might be pain, but there would be no cowardice, no stealing, and no taking advantage.

And it might work. Why not find out?

Once the washing machine was going, she went into living room, picked up her bullet journal, and wrote, "Reasons It is a Good Idea to Find Out."

- Emile is a good man.
- We make each other laugh.
- The sex is incredible.
- He is considerate of me.
- He appreciates what I do for him.
- Gabriella and I get on well.
- He cares about others.
- He is generous.
- He is friendly and kind to everyone.

- When I asked him not to interfere where Cameron is concerned, he complied.
- Emile is a really good man.

That last one was important enough to mention twice.

Seeing it all written before her gave Amy comfort and relaxed her—and she knew why. *If it works on paper, it will work in implementation.* This time, she wasn't going to worry about engagement rings and baby blankets. She was just going to *be*. It had been easy to get this far. Maybe it would keep being easy.

However, she was going to get a job—a job where she got a paycheck and not a wad of bills from Emile's hand. That didn't mean that she would stop taking care of Emile. But it was important that she do that because she cared for him and not because he paid her. He'd fight her on it, but she would win. She had to earn her money somewhere else.

But she knew she would have to bend a bit. She might not be ready for the WAG suite this week, but if they were in a relationship, there was no reason she shouldn't accept a ticket Emile got for free. And she'd work up to the WAG suite and going to Beauford and telling Noel what had happened and why she had never come back for the quilt.

So many realizations, so many decisions. It made her tired, but it was a good tired, like when you'd worked hard all day but knew you'd done a good job.

It was only just noon, but maybe it wasn't too early for that afternoon nap. She'd have plenty of time after waking to do her chores and make herself some dinner to eat while she watched the game. And she couldn't wait to watch Emile play.

She'd barely laid her head on a Pottery Barn pillow and covered herself with a Pottery Barn throw before she was sound asleep.

• • •

It was her phone that woke her. *Emile*. She smiled before she even opened her eyes. She answered without looking to see who it was. "Hello."

"Ms. Callahan?" Not Emile—a woman's voice.

Amy sat up. "Yes?"

"This is Lila from downstairs. There is a delivery for you. I was just checking to see if you were in before sending it up. Is this a convenient time?"

"Sure. It's fine."

She wasn't expecting anything. All the Canadian food and snacks Emile had requested had already arrived, and she thought she'd canceled all the standing orders for canned chicken, pouches of precooked rice, and shelf stable chocolate milk. Maybe it was some of that wine, chocolate, or underwear that Emile endorsed.

After hanging up, Amy checked the time. Almost 2:30! She'd slept for more than two hours, though it felt like five minutes. She fluffed the pillow and put away the throw. She had just fetched some cash for the tip when the doorbell rang.

Amy expected to open the door to a Star View courier carrying, at most, a case of wine. Nothing could have prepared her for the small army that trooped in with carton after carton, and none of them small.

"Where would you like it?" asked the young man leading the line.

"What is all this?" she asked.

"We don't know, ma'am."

"Of course not." Her first thought was that Emile had a standing order for food that she didn't know about—but so much? Then she thought hockey equipment. "Just put what you can in the kitchen and breakfast room. Put the rest in the dining room." They never used the dining room, or hadn't yet. Maybe that would change as things progressed. But things weren't going to progress that fast before tomorrow. "Actually, put it all in the dining room please." It would be out of the way in there. She'd have her work cut out for her unpacking and putting all this stuff away—whatever it was—and there was no way it would all happen today.

"Here you go, Ms. Callahan." The courier handed her a clipboard. "Fifteen boxes. Do you want to count them?"

"No. I'm sure they're all there." And if they weren't, even better. Fewer to deal with. She scribbled her name and looked at the bills in her hand. Not nearly enough. "Just a moment. I need to get …" Her voice trailed off, and she went to her purse for more money. How much? Fifteen boxes and they looked heavy. Should she tip by the person or box? Maybe person. She counted heads. Six. "I don't have change." She handed the guy with the clipboard three twenties. "Can you get change and share this?"

Maybe she could get a job in this building delivering boxes.

He smiled broadly. "Call us if you need anything." They always said that.

After they'd gone, she looked at the stacks of boxes and felt more overwhelmed than curious and more hungry than overwhelmed. She went to the refrigerator, poured a glass of milk, and drank it with a few cheese and crackers while standing up. That would do for now. She threw the sheets in the dryer and brushed her teeth before getting the box cutter from the toolbox she'd bought and stored in the utility room.

With any luck, it would be hockey equipment, in which case she would leave it alone until Emile returned. In fact, if the boxes were marked Bauer, CCM, or Easton, she wouldn't even open them.

But they weren't. There were no return addresses, and they were addressed to her. How could this possibly all be for her? Her first thought was that Emile had sent all this. And maybe that was true. Maybe it was hockey equipment after all. He could have bought it on this trip and had it shipped to her. But he would have told her to expect it.

She stood motionless. *Why don't you just open it?* a little voice whispered. *Because I've got a cold feeling in my stomach*, she answered, *that tells me that once I open one of these boxes, everything is going to change.*

She ripped into the first one. It contained her luggage—empty. The second one—purses and shoes, all carefully and professionally packed. Her hanging clothes were in four wardrobe boxes. By the time she found her bullet journals and wrapping paper, she was crying—not because she was happy to have reclaimed her lost belongings, but for what she knew it had to cost her. At first, she'd told herself that for whatever his reasons, Cameron had sent it all back. She'd wanted to believe that, but the cold feeling in her stomach reached out and slapped her face in the form of reality. Cameron wouldn't have known where to send it.

Well. That was that.

She went into the living room, took out her phone, and dialed a number.

He answered right away. "Hello, baby girl."

"Daddy, can you come get me? Now?"

She knew his hesitation came not from indecision but surprise. "Of course. I'll be there in about seven hours."

"Text me when you get here. I'll come down."

He wouldn't like that. He'd want to come to the door and get her, but he didn't argue, didn't try to make the decision for her.

"If that's what you want."

"I do."

"Is there anything you want to tell me?"

"No. Not yet. I'd rather wait until I get home and tell it only once." Once would be hard enough.

"Then I'd better get on the road."

She sat completely still for a full five minutes, willing herself not to think, not to feel. Then she picked up her bullet journal and crossed out all the reasons that "it was a good idea to find out." She'd found out. What was it she'd thought? That if it didn't work out, she could walk away. She brushed away her tears. Who knew it would be this soon?

She pulled one of her suitcases from the box and rambled around in the other boxes until she found enough clothes to last her for a while. Emile could ship the rest of it to her. Or not. She'd already let it go. It didn't matter. Next, she emptied her wallet of all the money there except for the $84.38 she'd come with. She left the excess on the kitchen counter along with the keys to the Land Rover and the credit card Emile had given her for household expenses.

Then she sat down to wait. When puck drop time came, she didn't turn on the television. She just sat. And waited. When the text came from her daddy, she answered it. Then she deleted her texts and call history and placed the phone beside the credit card, keys, and money.

Finally, she picked up her suitcase and went out the door—the door she had come to watch with happy anticipation at the thought of Emile walking through it.

CHAPTER TWENTY-FIVE

This could not be happening! It could not!

Emile ran from room to room, calling Amy's name—but she wasn't there. The Land Rover was there. Her boxes were there. That nasty blood orange yogurt she loved was there.

But no Amy. He'd call. She'd answer. She wouldn't be that cruel—she wasn't cruel at all. She was the best, kindest person he'd ever known.

Ah, the phone was ringing. And ringing. And ringing. But wait. It wasn't ringing in the phone next to his ear.

He took the phone from his ear and walked toward the sound. Her phone was there on the counter, with his keys, credit card, and some cash.

Merde. She really was gone. He'd check her texts and call history. That might give him some clue where she was, who she was with. *Baise-moi*. She'd deleted it all.

Maybe she'd be back. After, all she'd left her boxes, though she'd opened them. They were supposed to be celebrating now—the win over San Jose, that he'd gotten her things back, and that they were *considering*.

But it seemed she'd considered and found him wanting. Well, that was fine. She didn't have to want him, but he needed to know she was safe. There was no way she would have gone to her family in south Georgia. She had been adamant about that and never wavered. And since she didn't have a car or any money to speak of, that meant she was in Nashville.

He was off the next two days, and he would find her if it took every second of those two days.

• • •

The homecoming had been just as hard as Amy had known it would be. When she and her father had arrived home right after daybreak Tuesday morning, she'd gone to her childhood bed and slept ten hours. When she got up midafternoon, they were all waiting for her at the big round kitchen table—parents, grandparents, brother, both dogs, and the cat.

On the drive over, her father had respected her wish to not discuss what had happened, but she knew the wait must be killing him—killing them all.

So she'd told the whole story, leaving out nothing except her sexual antics with Emile. Her mother cried, her brother got out of his chair twice with the intent of going to California and killing Cameron, her father asked again and again why she had not come to him, and her grandfather asked if hockey players were paid as much as football and baseball players.

Finally, Mimi spoke, "So, what now?"

"I've come home to work in the family business if you'll have me."

Grandpa laughed a friendly little laugh. "Picking or pie baking?"

"I guess that would be up to you," Amy said. "I might be more suited to pie baking."

"You should have said picking. Picking season is over, but pie baking never stops," Grandpa said. True. They would have canned enough peaches to last until next season.

"I did nothing for too long." She met her father's eyes. "Everybody should work."

"Your peach pies always were better than mine," her mother said.

They all hugged her, told her they loved her, and welcomed her home.

No one said, "I told you so."

But Mimi did pull her aside. "I'm not clear on something, Amy. Tell me again what this Emile did that was so bad?"

"He made Cameron send my belongings back."

"I see. I'm glad you cleared that up."

Amy knew sarcasm when she heard it, especially Mimi's brand. But she didn't have the energy to explain—or the heart for it.

CHAPTER TWENTY-SIX

Emile went to early skate Saturday morning only because he had no choice. It was game day, and this was his job. Four days Amy had been gone, and Emile still had not told anyone connected with the team. But what would he have told them? "My personal assistant left?" That hardly sounded like a disaster, but it was—a huge one.

He wearily sat down in his stall, though he didn't reach for his stick. There was plenty of time to prepare it. Despite not wanting to be here, he'd arrived even earlier than usual. Why not? He hadn't been able to sleep.

Too bad he wasn't an accountant or a shoe salesman. He'd call in sick. If he called in sick to Coach, they'd just send Bombay, the team doctor, to get him going again.

"Eat this."

Emile jumped. Packi. How did he appear out of thin air without making noise? "Do you sneak up on everybody, or is it just me?"

"I couldn't sneak up on you if you didn't allow it. You should be more aware of your surroundings."

He'd been plenty aware in the last four days, and he had been surrounded by a lot of nothing.

"Here's your food." Packi held out two protein bars, a can of pears, and a carton of yogurt. "Water's in your stall."

Emile took the food. "How did you know I needed breakfast?" Packi hadn't brought him food since that day when Emile had refused it because Amy had made his breakfast.

Packi sat in Swifty's stall, placed an ankle on one knee, and locked his hands around the other one. "Power of deduction. You've come in here the last two days, refusing to look me in the eye or string more than two words together. Today, you're here even earlier than usual, looking like a minor league player who just got pushed off the last chance bus. Last weekend, I saw you talking to Snow. I figured that's something Amy didn't want you to do, but since you did it anyway, she wouldn't be so open to spoiling you rotten with omelettes and organic fruit all cut up and ready to go." How did he know Amy had cut up his fruit? And if he had to take this up, why did he have to wait until game day? "*If* she's even still here." Packi's questioning eyes bored into him.

Might as well go ahead and admit it now. He would in the end anyway. He tore open one of the bars and took a bite. "She's gone."

Packi nodded. "Uh huh. Gone where?"

Emile shook his head. "I don't know. I've looked everywhere. That's all I've done for four days when I wasn't here."

"Apparently not everywhere. If you'd looked everywhere, you would have found her."

What an ass. Emile decided not to point that out. "Amy had become friendly with my sister, but Gabriella has not seen her." She'd had plenty to say, too. There had been a lot of talk about "letting her get away from *us*." What was this *us*? He was the one who'd lost her. "I called all the hospitals and went to every homeless shelter in Nashville."

Packi registered a rare, true expression of surprise. "Why would you think she would go to a homeless shelter?"

Emile downed the rest of the bar and shrugged. "Something she said once … or maybe it was me. No matter. She wasn't there. I went to the shop that sells the little books and pens that she likes. I talked to Merry Sweet, who works there and also works at Bridgestone. You know her?"

Packi shook his head, indicating neither a *yes* nor a *no, but get on with it.*

"Anyway, she had not been there. They hadn't seen her at the dry cleaners either, or that fancy market where she gets eggs that come from happy chickens and meat from animals that have never been medicated. The last people from Star View to see her were the couriers who delivered the boxes of her belongings."

"Boxes of belongings?"

"Her things that Snow took. I asked him to send them back to her."

"It was that simple, was it? You *asked* him to send them back, and he happily complied? When are the two of you going fishing or out for a beer?"

He ignored that last part.

"*Oui.* It was simple. There was more to it than that, but I enjoyed outsmarting Snow, so it was simple."

"You enjoyed it. Uh huh. Are you enjoying the aftermath?"

"I had expected to."

Packi laughed and shook his head. "I'm sure you did. Son, I've been there."

"Been where? I do not understand. You mean you have come home to find Mrs. Packi lost?"

"Not that exactly, but we've all been where you are—in love and totally screwed."

In love? Was that what he was? He thought they were only "considering."

"Not the same. Mrs. Packi is not gone."

"She might have been, maybe on more than one occasion when I was young and stupid if I hadn't stepped up and fixed things. But I had a better excuse than you. I was only nineteen when I got married."

"So, it is not hopeless?"

"Truthfully, I don't know. But it is for sure if you don't try."

"What would you do?"

"I'd go to her with a made-up mind about exactly what I wanted, and I'd make a grand gesture."

"I thought I had already made a grand gesture when I got her things back from Snow."

"No. That was a grand display of idiocy."

All that sounded good. He was pretty sure he knew what he wanted. No, not pretty sure, definitely sure. And nobody did grand better than he did. Just look at his car. But there was only one problem.

"I still don't know where she is."

Packi rose. "Have you looked in south Georgia?"

"She wouldn't go there."

"You sure about that?"

Of course he was sure! Hadn't she said so often enough? But he'd been sure that she would shower him with praise and love for recovering her belongings, too.

"I suppose it's possible."

"My wife says that according to Mr. Robert Frost, home is where when you go there, they have to take you in. Or something like that."

"Hmph. I'd like to talk to this Mr. Frost. He knows nothing of home. Home is where they *want* to take you in." Just as Johanna and Paul had wanted him and Gabriella, just as they would want them even today if it were needed.

Which meant Amy's home was with him.

"You might be right about that. But you'd better get to work. The Senators are coming for you. You're getting low on stick tape. I'll get you some."

When Emile looked up from his canned pears, Packi was gone. How did he do that?

• • •

For the first time in the four days since she'd been back, Amy was alone in the big, rambling farmhouse. It had been a busy Saturday. Fresh peaches were a distant memory, but there was still plenty to be done with all the fruit Mimi, Mama, and the summer help had canned and frozen. Today, Amy had made twenty-eight pies with homemade crust and twenty loaves of peach bread.

Amy's family had gone to the chili supper and Fall Festival at the church, but she'd begged off. She'd showered and was now making a grilled cheese sandwich that she intended to eat while she binge-watched *Outlander*. Maybe she'd have two sandwiches. That would still be less than she would have eaten if she'd gone to that chili supper the way her mother had wanted her to, but there was no way that was happening. Not tonight.

Word was already beginning to get out that she was back, but she wasn't anywhere close to ready for a social debut. The day was coming soon enough that she'd have to work the front counter, dipping ice cream and ringing up pies, cider, and preserves. But so far, her family had taken pity on her and let her confine her labor behind the closed doors of The Peach Stand's commercial kitchen. Her emotions were all over the place, though, oddly, her emotional state had little to do with Cameron. A worse thing made a bad thing seem small, and Emile's betrayal was a much worse thing. But the hard work helped, ensuring that that she fell asleep easily at night and left little time for thinking.

She'd canned gallons of peach salsa and jam, fried at least two hundred peach hand pies, and made dozens of oven-ready cobblers that would be packed in dry ice and shipped overnight.

A little involuntary smile crossed her face. Would Emile have ordered oven-ready cobblers if he'd known about them? Probably not. He was pretty good about staying away from sweets during the season. Besides, waiting for something to bake in the oven wouldn't suit him. He was more about instant gratification.

Except in bed. He'd always been willing to take his time there.

Damn. These were exactly the kinds of thoughts she had been combating with rolling pie dough and sterilizing canning jars. Maybe she needed to go down the hill and make some muffins. They always sold well on Sundays. But she couldn't bake her thoughts away forever. She took her sandwiches to the den and turned on the 70-inch flat-screen television where they always watched football. If she was going to spend the evening with Jamie Fraser, might as well go big.

She settled in and clicked on ESPN—the station that had been on when it was last turned off. Naturally, here the last week in October, a college football game came on the screen. Ordinarily, she would have probably watched it no matter who was playing, but she was in no mood to think about sports of any kind or athletes of any age.

She reached for the remote to bring up the TV streaming app, when the crawling banner at the bottom of the screen slapped her in the face: NHL: CAPITALS VS. BRUINS 8 PM ET. SENATORS VS. SOUND 7:20 PM ET. BLUES VS. BLACKHAWKS … Amy didn't catch the time on that last one, but who cared? Who cared about any of it?

7:20 p.m., huh? She was in Eastern Time. It was 7:08 p.m.

She shouldn't watch, shouldn't even consider it. If she saw him, she might go running back to Nashville and throw herself into his arms and say, "Make all my decisions, take over my life, you don't have to listen to me at all. Just let me be with you. Boss me around all you want."

On the other hand, she couldn't go running back to Nashville— literally. That is unless she ran—literally. She had no car and no money except her $84.38. So what would it hurt to just look at him? And how pitiful was that? The wanting to look at him on

TV? But that's how she seemed to deal with her anger—by being pitiful and deflated. Sometimes she had cut through all that to even remember she was still mad—mad at his arrogant, domineering ways. And now she was mad at herself for wanting to watch him on TV and mad at him for being on TV and tempting her.

And how rational was that? Not at all, but the more the anger coursed through her, the less she cared about rationality and the less deflated she felt. How dare he make her want him, make her think they could have a future, that they were having some whirlwind fairy tale that was going to end in soul-mate-happily-ever-after. She wasn't deflated anymore! No. She was mad like a warrior, fire engine red mad. Making her think they had a chance was just part of his bossy, interfering, French-speaking self. Oh, *oui*, it was.

But she knew all that, so what would it hurt to turn on the little dictator's hockey game? Fire engine red mad felt good! The last time she was this mad was … was the night she'd been so mad at Cameron that she'd had sex with Emile so Cameron wouldn't be the last man who had touched her.

The big, red fire engine shrunk to a toy—a toy not even made of metal. It was plastic.

Some warrior she'd turned out to be.

She was deflated again because she knew that, no matter what, there wasn't a man alive she would have sex with now. She didn't want to wipe Emile's touch away.

And therein was the difference, and it was that difference that crushed her heart.

Pitiful—there was no other word for it. She couldn't be with Emile. Everything that mad Amy thought about that was true.

But she could look at him on TV if she wanted. No one would even know. Her family was eating chili, bobbing for apples, and playing cake walk.

So, to hell with Jamie Fraser.

She pressed the guide button on the remote. They probably didn't have the NHL Network or Center Ice, but her father had at least as many TV channels as he had peach trees. Emile was bound to be on one of them.

She scrolled quickly. Now that she had decided, might as well get on with it. Ah. There it was. If she had been fast enough, she'd be able to see him without his helmet during the national anthem.

And she was in time. The team was coming through the big silver musical note, as lights flashed and music played. Glaz, Thor, Swifty—of course, the announcers called them by their real names, but this is how Amy thought of them, because that's what Emile called them.

"And in goal," the announcer said, "number thirty—Emile Giroux!" And no one after that mattered. He skated out with his stick over his head. And then—dammit—the camera panned to someone else. But she knew he was skating round the goal, roughing up the ice, tapping the posts, kissing the crossbar.

Lucky crossbar. She'd thought that before, but it had been funny then. It wasn't funny now.

At last, national anthem time. Maybe it wouldn't be someone famous. If it wasn't someone famous, they might show the players more. But no. Luke Bryan. She'd be lucky if she got a tiny glimpse. And that *was* all she got. His hair was a mess, and he rocked back and forth on his skates. And that was all. Back to Luke Bryan. Then a pan to the starting skaters. And it was over.

"And that was Luke Bryan, ladies and gentlemen." The camera showed him exiting the ice. Emile from the rear would have been a better shot. "He's not the only star in the house here at Bridgestone Arena tonight as the Nashville Sound get ready to take on the Ottawa Senators." The camera panned the audience. "We have Keith Urban and Nicole Kidman. Jackson Beauford, here with his brother, Tennessee Titan Gabe Beauford."

"And speaking of the Titans," the other announcer said, "here in town with the San Francisco 49ers, who take on the Titans tomorrow, is Reynolds Fallon."

What? Amy sat forward as the camera panned.

"Looks like he's here with his family in bench side seats."

Amy's jaw dropped until her mouth was as wide as the tunnel from the locker room. There big as day were Cameron and three other people—presumably the wife and billionaire parents.

Well, hell. That couldn't be good.

CHAPTER TWENTY-SEVEN

Emile hadn't performed this poorly since he'd been a mite and played with the chicken pox. If Andre could see him, he would beat him for sure and lock him out of the house.

The score was 3-4, Ottawa's favor with 2:20 to go in the third period—but all was not lost. Far from it. Senator rookie Able Killen, a big rawboned boy out of Idaho, had made the mistake of high sticking Thor. For once, Thor had kept his cool. So, off to the sin box with Able, and the Sound was on a power play.

If they could tie it up—and they could—overtime was a clean slate, a new beginning. If they could just get that point, they would win this. Nobody was better than the Sound in overtime.

Emile didn't get much action on that power play. He didn't expect to. A couple of times, the Senators got control of the puck and Emile skated out of the net and shot it back down the ice, but his teammates pretty much kept in goal range.

Though they shot time after time after time, Heinrich Muller blocked every single one. A fine piece of play. Win or lose, Emile would tell him. Five seconds left with five on four. Emile beat out the seconds on the ice with his stick to let his teammates know there was still time.

And then there wasn't.

Twenty seconds left in the game. Emile poised to skate to the bench even before he got the signal from Coach Colton. He took his place on the bench and accepted the water bottle and towel Packi handed him. Pulling the goalie was what was done in such circumstances. This would give the Sound six skaters against five and the goalie. With any luck ...

But there was no luck. Ottawa scored an empty net goal with eight seconds to go. Emile skated back to his net. At 3-5, it was done. Even Emile, who never gave up, knew that.

And then it really was over. The clock and the buzzer said so.

The Sound skated out, circled up around their captain, and banged their sticks on the ice as they always did. No one would blame Emile. Win as a team, lose as a team, but the only thing worse than a locker room after a loss was his bed without Amy.

Baise-moi, merde, and all the rest of it.

Hands clapped his shoulders. Eighty-two regular season games. There was no such thing as undefeated season. In other sports yes, but it had never been done in the NHL. But that first loss was always bitter, because you always thought, it *could* happen. And maybe it will be *this* year and *my* team.

Swifty skated up beside him. "What you say we go get clean and go get some women?"

Emile shook his head. He'd finally told his friend today that Amy was not to be found. "What do you say we go get clean and go get a beer?"

"Man, you've got it bad."

Emile paused at the tunnel entry to take off his helmet. "Go ahead. I'll catch up." Someone handed him a towel, and he mopped his face as he went.

Then he felt a hand on his shoulder from behind—and it was not the comforting hand of brotherhood and shared loss. It was a hand meant to stop him.

Slowly, he turned and looked over his shoulder.

Snow! How did he even get in the tunnel? Ah, someone had given him a VIP pass.

"It was good to see you fuck up," Snow said.

"You annoy me, Snow. I thought you were in Milan annoying Italians until All Saints Day—Tuesday, is it?"

"I thought that, too. Unfortunately, when I didn't fly back as expected after my *meeting* with you, my wife flew home—and she wasn't happy. So the honeymoon was over. I have you to thank for that, among other things. So, we're here in Nashville with her parents and her brother. Not what I had in mind."

People milled all around them, oblivious to the storm brewing. Emile could have stopped the storm, could have walked away like he'd done a hundred times. But he was in no mood.

"Having everything stolen from her was not what Amy had in mind, either. You did not have to come when I summoned you. You made your choice." But it was time to walk away, mood or not. Emile turned toward the locker room. "Go back to your wife. Go get some hot wings or something. I recommend blue cheese. It's *trés* good."

"I'm not through with you!"

Emile might have kept walking. A VIP pass would only take a person so far, and the locker room was beyond that boundary. But he was curious about what else Snow would have to say.

"Voleck fired me. But I guess you know that."

Interesting. "Hmm. No, I did not know. But good for him. I like that boy. He is young and has made some mistakes. It is good to see him showing good sense."

Snow closed the distance between their faces. "He was my only hockey player, and you were the cause of my losing him. He called me while I was in Milan. I told him I would return his call after the first of November. Then he saw me at the Staples Center with you and thought I had lied—that I was avoiding him."

Now Emile remembered the short exchange with Jan on the plane. "Did you speak with him that night? Seek him out at all? *Non?* Then you *were* avoiding him. Or maybe not. Maybe disregarding him, which is much worse."

"Giroux, this is all your fault, and I *will* find a way to make you pay."

Emile was tired of this and ready to walk away, but there was one last jab rattling around in his brain that was determined to make its way to his tongue and out of his mouth.

"Where's your Sound sweater, Snow? I guess you don't need it since your face is already purple. Or maybe you would have liked a Senators sweater tonight. Perhaps a woman will buy one for you before next time."

Emile might have seen it coming if he had not been turning to go.

Snow bellowed like an infuriated caveman—and landed a fist on Emile's jaw.

Stand still, he commanded himself as he tasted blood. *Stand still and take it, and it will be over sooner.*

The second blow landed on his nose, and the blood gushed like a red waterfall.

Don't react. Stand tough. While it was true that Snow was running to fat and balding, he had played in the NFL, however briefly. His punches had some power behind them.

"It's *your* fault!" Snow bellowed again. "You *made* me come back from Milan. You made me ruin my honeymoon, made me ruin things with my only NHL client!"

It's your fault.

Just like Andre.

If you had played better, I wouldn't have had to lock you out of the house and the neighbors wouldn't have called me out and humiliated me. Now I have to beat you for that, and that's your fault, too.

If you had tried harder, you would have won tonight and I wouldn't have made you walk home from the rink. Now your mother is mad at me.

Your fault, your fault, your fault.

Just like Andre.

The third blow landed on his eye. It began to swell immediately. Just like Andre—but *not* Andre.

It must have happened faster than it felt, because later, Emile clearly remembered making a conscious decision. He was going to do what he had never done with Andre, what he'd never done on the ice, even when a full-force brawl was in session.

He was going to defend himself before someone intervened—and he had time. Maybe it was because this was a hockey crowd and they were used to fighting, or maybe it was because everyone around them was stunned, but no one interfered.

So defend himself he did, along with Amy, his mother, sister, and every child who'd ever suffered at the hands of a savage monster.

And he—Emile Giroux, the Excellent Wolf, the French Kiss—was *not* a savage. Or a monster.

He was a man who'd had enough.

The enraged bellow that rang out of Emile's lungs made Snow's sound like the mewling of a sick kitten.

He threw off his gloves and fell on Snow like a high-powered Weed Eater in a vat of cotton candy.

Snow did not land another punch.

CHAPTER TWENTY-EIGHT

Sunday morning, Amy was still reeling.

After the Sound's loss to the Senators last night, she had almost switched the television off. Her family had been due back any minute, and she hadn't wanted to be caught watching Emile. But then the after-game interviews had started—first the Ottawa goalie and next Nicolai Glazov—but before Glaz could even open his mouth to respond to the question he'd been asked, the camera swung around and another announcer said, "Whoa, Kelton! There's something going on over here!"

And, indeed, there was. Emile stood motionless with blood pouring down his face. "It's Emile Giroux! And who is that he's fighting with? A fan?"

"Not sure, Gino," the other reporter said. "Not a Sound fan, for certain."

But Amy could have told them. Cameron landed another blow to Emile's face.

Then Emile wasn't motionless anymore. His big goalie gloves went flying, and Emile dropped to the ground as quickly as he'd ever dropped to the ice, only this time Cameron was beneath him.

It didn't last long—but long enough for Amy to say aloud, "Kick his ass, Emile! He's got it coming!" Then there were people pulling Emile off Cameron and carrying him away, blood flying, fists flailing, mouth angrily moving, no doubt cursing in French. At least she didn't have to worry about his injuries. Nobody that mad could be hurt very bad.

Amy completely lost track of what the announcers were saying, but that didn't matter. They knew less than she did.

Security guards seemed to have Cameron in hand. It was probably too much to hope for that he would land in jail.

The announcers had calmed down some now, and the camera was back on a part amused, part perplexed looking Glaz.

"Any idea what that was about, Glaz?"

"No idea, Kelton."

"Unless an arena burns to the ground before midnight, I would bet we've just witnessed what will be the top story in hockey tomorrow."

Glaz laughed. "Is a better thing, then, for the Sound—better than the loss on home ice."

Amy was scrambling eggs and frying bacon for her family when her brother came in the kitchen dressed for church with his jacket over his arm.

"I guess you aren't going." Terrance eyed Amy's shorts and T-shirt as he poured a cup of coffee.

"Tomorrow's Halloween. We've promised the high school three dozen pies for the carnival. I'm going to get on it." A couple of college students would have already opened The Peach Stand to sell coffee, early morning muffins, scones, and Sunday dinner desserts. After church, business would pick up, and Mama, Mimi, and possibly Terrance and Daddy, depending on when the Falcons played, would show up. Grandpa steered clear of The Peach Stand, insisting he was a peach farmer, not a peddler.

"Can't blame you." Terrance leaned on the counter sipped his coffee. "Did you know your boyfriends have gone viral? Do you think it's over you?"

Just when things couldn't get better. Amy took up the bacon and put it on a paper towel-lined platter. "I don't have any boyfriends. I have a former boyfriend, who robbed me blind and married someone else, and someone who might have been my boyfriend, but isn't and never will be." *Never* was a terrible word.

"Don't you want to know what caused them to go viral?"

"I know. I saw it live."

"I see. So you watched the game?"

"I did. I've been carbing Emile up for a couple of weeks now. I wanted to see if it was paying off."

"Apparently not in the net, not last night. But they are saying he got the best of Snow."

"So they know who Cameron is now. Are they saying anything else?" Amy stirred the eggs.

"No. Nobody seems to be talking. They're speculating on whether Giroux will be suspended for brawling with a fan."

"*Suspended!*" Amy slammed her spatula down. "That's not fair! He didn't start it. And Cameron's not a fan."

"Hey." Terrance held up a hand. "I never liked the sanctimonious SOB." There was noise on the stairs. "Here they come."

Amy's heart sped up. "Do you think they know? Since they're not hockey fans?"

"Possibly. I know, and I'm not a hockey fan."

She did not want to face this right now.

He held his hand out for the spatula. "Go. I'll take credit for cooking breakfast."

She ran out the back door, jumped in the golf cart, and sped toward The Peach Stand.

• • •

The filling was made and ready for the pans. The pastry for seventy-two crusts for thirty-six double-crust pies was mixed and chilled. Amy had just finished rolling and lining the fifteenth pie pan when Mimi came into the kitchen.

"You have company," she said. "Up at the house."

She'd been expecting this. There had been Fall Festival and a church service since Amy had hit town, and she hadn't gone to either. The time was just about right for her cousin Becky and friends Lulu or Cassandra to show up. They would have talked among themselves and decided to wait a few days to see if Amy would call them first. Then they would have started calling, only to discover she wasn't picking up her phone. Or maybe Emile had been answering. For all she knew, the four them had planned a BFF beach trip. He'd speak French and pass out wine. They'd laugh. He'd take his shirt off.

What was wrong with her? It wasn't even beach season.

"I have pies to make," Amy said. "Is it Lulu? Or all three of them?" Amy didn't have to explain. Mimi knew well who she meant by "all three."

"None of them. A woman in a rental car. Margaret, I think she said."

Amy didn't know any Margaret, except Margaret Teesdale, who would be more likely to be visiting Mama than her. Besides, Mimi knew her.

Mimi reached for an apron. "Go on. I'll work on these pies. I gave her some iced tea and put her in the parlor."

Might as well find out. Amy shed her own apron, went outside, and got in the golf cart. Surely it wouldn't be a reporter, come to ask her about Cameron and Emile—though it was possible. Amy hadn't heard anything new about that, even if Emile had been suspended. It was hard to know things without electronics.

She went in the back door and stopped in the kitchen to splash water on her face. She was still drying it with a paper towel when she went in the parlor door. People who came without calling first got what they got.

The young woman sitting in the middle of the couch was pretty—chestnut hair, slim, with pretty skin. She didn't see Amy at first because she was intently studying her white-knuckled hands in her lap.

"Hello," Amy said.

The woman's head jerked up. She looked like a scared rabbit. Her eyes were clear amber, but there were dark circles under them. It was only when she rose and held out her hand that Amy noticed the barest suggestion of a baby bump.

"Marley Fallon." Amy had only seen that one picture that one time. She'd never been tempted to go back and look at it again. Marley's handshake was firm, and she looked straight into Amy's eyes.

"Please sit." Amy sat in the wing chair nearest the couch. When Marley sat again, she sat on the end nearest Amy. "So, not Marley Snow?"

She looked at her hands again. "Well, no. I didn't take his name."

"Some don't," Amy said.

Marley looked at her again. "Would you have? Changed your name if you'd married him? He wasn't happy when I didn't."

"You can be sure of it. I let Cameron do all my thinking for me."

Marley didn't respond, but to be fair, there was no response that wouldn't have been insulting.

"You've come a long way, especially since you couldn't be sure I would be here." The question was *why* was she here? And how much did she know?

"I was fairly confident I'd find you here. Where else but to her family does someone whose been robbed of everything go?

To Emile. She can go to Emile. He'll take in anybody.

But at least that answered one of the questions. Marley knew— if not all, plenty.

Marley nodded. "I am so, so sorry. I wanted to tell you I never knew, never even suspected."

"How is it that you know now?" Would Emile never leave well enough alone?

"Long story. The upshot is, our honeymoon was cut short when Emile Giroux summoned Cameron to L.A. for a meeting. Cameron assumed Giroux was going to sign him, but he demanded that Cameron send your personal possessions back." She closed her eyes and shuddered. "I can still scarcely believe … Anyway, I ended up returning home—though understand, I was still in the dark. Then Cameron's Sound client fired him. By now, Cameron's nerves were stretched pretty tight. He didn't want to come to Nashville, but since we were back anyway, I wanted to come and see my brother play football. So he came. Then Pickens Davenport—the Sound owner, he's a friend of my father's—offered us bench side seats for the Sound game. I didn't care, but Reynolds and Dad wanted to go. So we all went. And then, after the game—"

Amy could stand it no more. She wanted this woman to get to the point—whatever that was—and leave. She had pies to make.

"There was a fight between Cameron and Emile," Amy said.

"Yes, and all this came out."

Amy's gut clenched. "Publicly?"

"Oh, no. No. But I know now, as does my family."

"And how do you know? Did Emile tell you?"

Whether he did or did not do the main thing she'd asked him not to—tell Marley and her family what Cameron did—wouldn't make things better or worse, but she had to know.

Marley looked surprised. "No. It was Cameron. He came a little unglued and ended up confessing it all."

"Emile didn't say anything?"

"No, as a matter of fact, my father tried to discuss it with him, to find out if Cameron had done even more. Emile refused to discuss you or anything about the situation. And believe me when I say my father can be plenty persuasive."

Amy nodded. That was something, she supposed. Too little, too late, but maybe Emile had learned something for the next time someone asked him to leave something alone.

"Anyway." Marley reached into her purse. "I have this for you." She handed Amy an envelope. "There's a cashier's check inside for what Cameron took from you. I think you'll find it fair."

Curious to know if Cameron had come completely clean about just how much he'd stolen, Amy looked at the check and gasped. "There's almost eight million dollars here. That's more than I had."

Marley shook her head. "I had our accountant and attorney fly in last night, and Cameron turned the books over to them. For all Cameron's shortcomings, he'd made some good investments. And that check also includes the cost of your car and interest from the day he left until this."

"I can't take this." She held out the envelope toward Amy. "I can't take your money—or your parents'. I did this to myself. You heard what I said when I saw the amount. I didn't even know how much I had."

"No," Marley said. "Cameron did it. I won't pretend that you shouldn't have been smarter about it—and don't tell me you're not smart. Dumb people don't sell a business for five million dollars at twenty-six years old." She folded her hands in her lap again. "Anyway, it's not my money. Or my family's. This was in Cameron's accounts. I made him turn it over."

A little shiver of possibility went through Amy. If what Marley was claiming was true, she really was going to get her money back.

"How did you get Cameron to do that? Come to think of it, how did you get him to turn the information to over to the accountant?"

Marley's smile was triumphant, sad, and a little mean around the edges. "I told him if he'd do this—rectify what he did to you as much as possible—we'd start over and move on, that we'd have our baby and raise him."

Amy nodded. She wouldn't want Cameron after learning all this, but more power to Marley. "Then I wish you luck with your marriage."

Marley laughed. "You don't think I'm really going forward with that, do you? If my lawyer hasn't presented him with the divorce papers yet, it will happen before I get back to Nashville."

"So, you lied to him."

Marley stood up and pulled keys from her purse. "With all that's happened, for all he did to you—and me—are you really going to judge me for that?"

"No."

"I'd better get to the airport if I want to get back in time to see my brother fire him. He's going to do that right after his game."

"Wow. Fallons don't play."

Marley shook her head. "No. Fallons don't play."

Amy stood. "Thank you. I guess you're missing your brother's game. You don't want to miss your plane."

"I can't. It's a plane that waits for me." At the door, Marley hesitated. "Another question. How long did you know?"

"From the day you got married. I saw the tweet."

"Oh, yes. The tweet. Why didn't you go public? Or at least tell me?"

"I didn't go public, in part, because I was humiliated and I wasn't ready for my family to know. I didn't tell you or your family, because I thought you ought to have a chance to make something of your marriage, to have a father for your baby."

Marley considered that for a moment. "Make a marriage with a man I didn't know. Amy, I appreciate that you meant well, but should you have made that decision for me?"

Amy was too startled to answer—at least when Marley was still in earshot.

It was only after Marley waved as she got into her rental car that Amy whispered, "I was trying to do something nice for you."

CHAPTER TWENTY-NINE

Amy sat on her bed and looked at the check. She hadn't told her family that she was rich again. After Marley had left, she'd just taken the check to her room and gone back to her pie making. After all, people wanting pie didn't care. They just wanted pie.

Still, this changed things.

She could get a phone, laptop, and a tablet. She could spend her $84.38.

And a car. She would ask Terrance to take her to a dealership first thing in the morning. She wouldn't even haggle. She could probably call Mr. Dayton, who owned the Volvo dealership, and ask him to meet her tonight. She'd known him all his life. Terrance had taken his daughter to the prom, and he was in Rotary with Daddy.

A Fallon sure wouldn't wait around all night to buy a Volvo. Maybe she'd start acting rich, flying in accountants and not having to show up at a particular time at the airport. She wasn't as rich as they were—not by a lot—but rich enough.

Of course, she didn't have a phone to call Mr. Dayton. But even if she borrowed someone else's in the house or went down the hill to use The Peach Stand's landline, she could imagine what Mr. Dayton would say.

"Amy, does your daddy know you're calling me with the Falcons playing?" Mr. Dayton always thought his friends' adult children were about ten years younger than they were. "Where do you need to go so bad that you can't wait until morning?" Besides, no one here was going to take her anywhere while the Falcons were on.

Face it, getting a Volvo just didn't mean that much to everyone.

But most important, this money gave her options.

She would put away most of it to open her new organizing business when she could legally do that. It would be nice not to have to start out the way she had the first time, with only a phone, a second hand computer, and a file box in the back seat of her car—though she could have done it.

Meanwhile, she wouldn't have to take any job she could get to support herself. This money would give her the opportunity to volunteer her time to do something meaningful. Maybe something for the homeless or abused children. Those were things that she had always deemed worthy in her head, but they had never hit her heart as they had lately. Those things could make for a good day's work.

But, ever practical, Amy knew none of that could even begin to take shape before she'd gone to the bank, the Volvo dealership, and the Apple store. There was research to be done and decisions to be made before she could even know whom to reach out to. She'd need a brand new bullet journal for all that. Maybe while she was making her plans and getting it on paper, she'd stay here and bake peach pies. One thing for sure: she would never again sit around idle living someone else's life while she was waiting to start her own.

Everybody works. Those people down there in the den watching football knew it.

Maybe she'd go downstairs and join them for the game. Terrance had made tacos, and Mimi had made those little baked ham and cheese sandwiches with the mustard, butter, and poppy seed sauce.

Or maybe she'd stay up here and watch the Sound play the Hurricanes. She never had found out if Emile had been suspended.

Not for the first time since Marley had left, her parting words came back to haunt Amy. *I appreciate that you meant well, but should you have made that decision for me?*

There was a light tap on the door.

"Yes?"

Mimi opened the door. "You're popular today."

"What do you mean?"

"You have another visitor. He's waiting in the same place as the woman. He didn't want any iced tea."

He?

Amy went to the window and looked out. There it was—the county fair ride car.

"You don't seem surprised that he's here."

Amy shook her head. "I don't know if I am or not. With all that has happened lately, I don't know if I'd be surprised if I went down to find the devil swinging from the dining room chandelier."

Mimi chuckled. "Is he the devil?"

"No. No. He's not the devil—just sometimes misguided. Though he does his own misguiding."

"The misguided can be redirected."

"I don't know if I have the energy for that."

"Do you have the energy not to?"

"I don't know what you mean," Amy said.

"Learning not to love takes a lot more energy than loving."

"What makes you think I'm in love?"

Mimi took her head. "A heart that's never had love in it can't be broken. And you seem pretty brokenhearted to me. I don't know for sure why your heart is broken, but it's not over Cameron Snow, the loss of your money, or that you don't have Apple Pie Order anymore. You've been sad about those things, but they haven't broken your heart."

"Maybe it was just about lost possibilities." After all, they had been going to *consider.*

"Then maybe you'd better go down there and see if there's any possibility in the parlor."

"Maybe I should." Or not, but there was no getting around it. He'd driven seven hours. Or possibly less. The county fair ride car was fast. "All right." She patted her hair and headed toward the door.

"Amy?" Mimi said. "Don't you want to freshen up? Maybe take a shower? You smell like peaches."

She looked at herself in the mirror. For sure, she'd looked better. There were peach stains on her shirt. Thirty-six Halloween carnival pies would do that to a person.

"There are worse ways to smell. I come from peaches."

Mimi nodded. "And never forget the peaches are always here for you."

"I forgot that for a little while. I won't again."

When Amy entered the parlor, Emile stood up. "I like your house. It is a home." His face was bruised, his lip split, and his left eye was swollen almost shut.

"Looks like you've had a little scuffle." She sat in the wing chair.

He let himself down on the couch. "Yes. But not in the game. It was later—"

She considered letting him tell the story. It might have been entertaining. But she put a hand up. "I know what happened, Emile. I saw the game. And the aftermath."

"*Oui?*" He smiled. His swollen lip did nothing to detract from the beauty of that mouth. "You watched anyway?"

"Ever arrogant, aren't you? Yes. I watched. Are you suspended? Is that why you aren't at Bridgestone Area right now?"

He shrugged and moved his head back and forth like he did when he meant, could be yes, could be no. "*Non.* Not suspended— though there were those who thought it should be so. Mostly those who do not understand hockey. Still, I am hurt." He gestured to his face. "It's time for Case to play a game. So it was decided I would not go to the arena. There will be some other controversy tonight—perhaps from football. But for tonight and me—how do you say it? Out of the eye, out of the brain."

"Out of sight, out of mind."

"Yes. I was glad. I was able to come to south Georgia today instead of tomorrow. I would have been here before, but I didn't think you'd come here. I looked everywhere. Then when I thought you must be here, I couldn't work out how to find you. Googling *peaches* and *south Georgia* made me think I would have to go to many peach farms. Then I remembered your phone. The contacts were there. I found the number of your family business—The Peach Stand. After that, it was easy."

She did not point out if he had added her last name with *peaches* and *south Georgia* in the Google search that would have been easy, as well.

"So, why are you here, Emile?"

"Because you are not out of sight, out of mind. I have come to take you back."

She shook her head. "It's not that simple."

"*Non*. I didn't think it would be. And it may not be possible. But I must tell you, though I didn't see it at first, I should not have called Cameron Snow. You told me what you wanted, and I did what I *thought* you wanted. That was not for me to decide. I hope you can believe me."

"You treated me like a child. I have to be my own person and make my own decisions. I'm never going to say that was all right."

"I wanted to be your hero."

If she had not put her hand to her heart, it might have melted out of her chest. "Can you be a different kind of hero? The kind who respects a person's right to make her own decisions? Because, Emile, I let Cameron take over my life. That's on me, but I can't do it again."

"Yes." He said it quickly and matter-of-factly—a little too much so.

She wanted to believe him, wanted to so much. And a part of her did—or maybe it was more like she believed a part of him believed it—his head. She wasn't sure it went all the way to his heart.

His face clouded over. "I hope I can be that kind of hero. Open Hearts and Arms doesn't want me for a hero anymore."

"What?" Despite it all, Amy was incensed on his behalf. "How dare they? That means so much to you."

"*Non*. It's okay." He put a hand up. "They are right. You can't have someone speak out against abuse who had a brawl on national television. They did what they had to do. But I am not a monster. Or a savage."

"I never thought you were. And it makes me angry with that organization if they made you feel that way."

"*Non*. It was something I think I feared, but I don't anymore. I had a nice talk with Open Hearts and Arms. They have facilities in some cities where children can go to be safe. I think I would like to see that done in Nashville. Better than magazine ads and television commercials, don't you think?"

"Much better." Amy swallowed her tears. In another time and another place, she might have told him right then she would go with him. He was a good man, but he'd been a good man all along and he'd still overruled her wishes.

"And now." He reached for a large shopping bag at his feet. "Someone wise told me that to try to fix things with you, I must first figure out what I want. Then I must make a grand gesture. I tried to make him tell me what this grand gesture should be. He said I had to figure that out myself, or it wouldn't be grand."

"He does sound wise."

"He is. If I listen to him, maybe someday I will be wise, too?" And God help her, he smiled that smile.

"Stranger things have happened."

He opened the bag. "About the wants. The reason I said it might not be possible for you to go with me is we might not want the same. I wanted to ask what you wanted and say that's what I wanted, too, but Packi said that was the talk of a lunatic." He pulled out the little purple bullet journal that she'd bought to keep up with his schedule and waved it in the air. "I found this. It was about me. So I thought I could write in it. Was that okay?"

"Of course." She could hardly wait for this.

He opened the book and held it up. "I tried to make my pages like yours, but you are better at it."

Sure enough, he'd written at the top: "Things Emile Wants," with a list of bullet points after. In the margins he'd drawn rough pictures of wolves, hockey pucks, houses, trophies, hearts, dogs, and the number 30. And was that supposed to be a baby? Her breath caught in her throat. It was clear this was a model for how he wanted their lives to be—together, some time in the future. It was easy to imagine and play along. It didn't mean it was happening.

"All right. First, the things that I always knew I wanted that I have gotten: to play hockey, win trophies, be the excellent wolf."

He was so serious, so sincere, but she had to laugh.

He looked pleased. "So, it's good so far?"

"Very good. Though I'm glad you don't have on that list that you want to be an artist."

"*Non.* Just an artist of the net. I do that. I want a house." He gestured around him. "A house such as this, a home with a fence and a garage for the Bugatti. The helmet must be protected."

How had he known how much she wanted a house? Or had he? "You wouldn't miss Star View Towers?"

"*Non.* That was never more than a stopping-off place. Not a good place for dogs and children. They sent a memo to say if you allow children to trick or treat, tell them and they will put a paper pumpkin on the door. And only children who live in the building are allowed. I want a home where the pumpkin is not paper and all children may trick or treat. I like Halloween. I want children to share it with." He held up the book and pointed to the baby he'd drawn. "Well, a baby at first. Then see what happens."

She nodded. Everything she'd ever wanted.

"Now, for part of the grand gesture." He pulled a large parcel out of the bag. "For you, for the home."

She unwrapped first the brown paper and then the tissue. "It's my quilt! It's Stir Crazy!" The one she'd walked away from in Piece by Piece.

"This makes you happy?"

She wouldn't have thought so. She would have thought she would associate that quilt with a bad day and with homes and dreams that were never going to come true. But when she'd seen the quilt, she'd known it was hers. And it was.

"Very happy." Now she could look for the all the hidden spoons, even if she never spooned under it as Noel had suggested.

His face went serious. "I thought it was very possible that we would want the same things with the house, and the dog, and the baby. Fence for the dog. But you must be warned of something."

"What is it?" Surely he wasn't going to threaten her.

"I want to play hockey. I have to play hockey as long as my body and skills hold out."

This wasn't news. "You're doing that."

He nodded. "But it could mean leaving the house and the fence behind. We would take the baby. And the dog. The Sound could be sold to Massachusetts. Or I could be traded and have to move on a day's notice. With hockey, there is no assurance of how long you will be in a place."

She'd moved for Cameron without a question, though that was no recommendation. Still, this was all hypothetical. "Are there houses and fences in Massachusetts?" she asked slowly.

He smiled. "I have heard that's true. This is the hockey grand gesture." He pulled a jersey out of the bag and held it up. "For you. I would not want you to cut it up. See?" He pointed to a dark stain. "Blood—like the sweaters Noel and Sharon wear."

Amy's stomach lurched, and not in a good way. But maybe this—the blood—was just all part of it.

"The blood came from my fight with Snow—when I beat him up," he said proudly.

"I got that. Thank you." She took the jersey and folded the stain to the inside.

"The next part might be hard for you," he said. "You remember how we had agreed to *consider*? Before I almost ruined things—at least I hope it was almost."

"And you are asking me to consider. It's safe to say, I will consider."

He vehemently shook his head. "*Non*. No considering. It must be *being*."

Must. The word tore through her like sandpaper on silk. *Must* was not a good word, not under these circumstances.

Emile went on. "I do not want you to consider, to wait and see. No waiting. No just living together with only promises of considering and good sex. I want you to be my wife. I want it now. I want promises of forever. I want to make you promises of forever. I want to begin our lives together, with the house, the baby, the dog. I want you to sit in the WAG suite in my bloody sweater now and also later when you are so pregnant that you are glad it is a goalie sweater."

It all sounded so heartfelt, so romantic, that she was surprised she didn't fall at his feet and weep *yes* in every language she knew, which come to think of it, was two.

But she couldn't. *Must*. He'd said *must*. And *want*. And stated vehemently how it had to be. He would never leave her to make own decisions. And she could never live that way again—even if he meant well.

She took a deep breath and prepared to say the words that would break her heart—and maybe his.

"But!" He held up a finger and gave her a radiant smile. "That is what I *want*." He held up the bullet journal. "See? It says 'Things Emile Wants.' I can write anything I please on this page. But these are the 'Things Emile Demands.'" And he turned the page. Except for the heading at the top, the page was empty.

If it works on paper, it will work in implementation.

He came to kneel before her and took her hands. "I stated what I would like. But, Amy, I demand nothing. Consider if you like. Think of what I want and of what you want. I'm right here, waiting for you to make your own decisions about how you live your life."

She put her hand over his heart. "You really do understand, don't you? You understand here."

"*Oui.*" His eyes wore all the truth that had ever been in any universe. "Amy, I will *never* disregard your decisions again. That is a promise I make."

Must didn't matter anymore. Neither did that they had only been together for a brief time. Nothing mattered except the truth and the love in his eyes.

"Then, yes. No considering. No waiting to see. Just yes." Then she stopped and slowly translated in her mind the next words she would speak. "*Je serai votre femme.*"

"Amy! You have been learning French?" The look on his face was all she'd hoped for.

"A little. Did I get it right?"

"So, so right—that is, if you meant to say you would be my wife."

"I've never meant anything more."

And then he gifted her with the most beautiful smile she had yet to see on that beautiful mouth. "And soon? As soon as you can get together the fluffy dress and the cake? It must be a fluffy dress."

That was a *must* she could live with. "Yes. Soon." And she would have the money now to pay for the fluffiest dress in fluffy land. She'd tell him that soon, but in this moment, it didn't matter.

"*Dieu merci!*" He kissed one of her palms and then the other. "*Je t'aime*, Amy."

"And I love you."

"Now." He reached for the bag again. "We come to the last part of the grand gesture. I wasn't sure we would reach this part."

Amy wasn't surprised when he pulled a ring box from the bag.

"Close your eyes." He slipped the ring on her finger. "Now open."

The weight on her hand should have prepared her for what she encountered when she first caught sight of the ring she would wear for the rest of her life.

But, then, even a federal government emergency preparedness agency couldn't have done anything to abate the shock from the sight that greeted her.

The ring left her gasping for breath, and not just from the weight. It covered her finger all the way to the knuckle and wrapped around the sides. Clearly Emile had taken his taste in car embellishment when he'd gone shopping for rings. She'd seen chandeliers with less going on.

"Pretty, *oui?*" He was so pleased with himself.

"I've never seen anything like it." Perhaps there was a place for batteries so it could be used as a hazard light in case of car trouble. But a smile warmed her from inside out. Such would be life with this man.

He paused, admiring the giant ring on her hand. "It's real," he said. Maybe he wanted to make sure she knew he hadn't gotten it at Pottery Barn.

"And so are we."

When they sealed their commitment with a kiss, it wasn't a French kiss, or much more than a peck. But that was all right. His mouth would be healed soon, and they had forever.

ABOUT THE AUTHOR

Alicia Hunter Pace is the pseudonym for the writing team, Jean Hovey and Stephanie Jones. They are *USA Today* best-selling authors who live in North Alabama and share a love of old houses, football, hockey, and writing stories with a happily ever after.

Find Alicia Hunter Pace at:
Their website *www.aliciahunterpace.com*
On Facebook at *www.facebook.com/pages/*
Alicia-Hunter-Pace/176839952372867
On Twitter @AliciaHPace

Subscribe to their newsletter at:
http://aliciahunterpace.us3.listmanage.com/subscribe?u=8dee
88167294a57b8b340f8e7&id=2054b7cbe8

Check out *USA Today* bestselling author Alicia Hunter Pace's entire collection:

CROSSROADS series:

Misbehaving in Merritt

Misunderstood in Merritt

"I absolutely love Alicia Hunter Pace's books. They have such a quirky sweetness, and the characters always ring true and make me cry!" —Linda Howard

Mistletoed in Merritt

BEAUFORD BEND series:

Forgiving Jackson

"This story is about much more than boy meets girl. Crisp dialogue …[and] supportive secondary characters add to the solid story line." —Library Journal

"…[an] engaging story of healing and discovery." —Heroes and Heartbreakers

Nickolai's Noel

"Whether you like sports-themed romance, small town settings, family and tradition, or compelling characters, there's something for just about everyone…" — The Romance Reviews

Reforming Gabe

"Pace's writing is so real that you experience it. There was one argument in the novel when I could actually hear the characters yelling at one another." —4 stars, Pure Jonel

"A story that will both lighten your heart and pull on it at the same time, this one is well worth your time." — Eat, Sleep, Read Reviews

"This novel was a great as addition to the Beauford Bend series or on its own. Pace definitely has a winner with this one." — Pure Jonel

Redeeming Rafe

"Pace combines romance and chemistry with family and turbulent pasts in a manner that had me glued to the pages. She weaves a tale that is so much bigger than simply her main characters." —5 stars, Pure Jonel

Heath's Hope

"For a short story to warm you on a cold night, take a trip to Beauford Bend. Plus, there's a cool bonus at the end of this book. Don't miss it!" —LAS Reviewer

Healing Beau

"I found myself rooting for this couple every step of the way … Pace created something magical." —Pure Jonel

LOVE GONE SOUTH series:

Sweet Gone South

Scrimmage Gone South

"For a sweet and fun romance that will make you laugh and enjoy from beginning to end, *Scrimmage Gone South* by Alicia Hunter Pace is a great choice." —Harlequin Junkie

Simple Gone South

"…a heartwarming, sweet and entertaining read that will keep you laughing and sometimes even have you shed a tear or two." —Harlequin Junkie

Secrets Gone South

"What a story! Pace has nailed writing emotions into her stories … She definitely had me jumping for joy and bawling like a baby more than once … This was a thoroughly enjoyable read that I couldn't put down." —Pure Jonel